KEN PISANI

AMP'D

ST. MARTIN'S PRESS ✿ NEW YORK

AMP'D. Copyright © 2016 by Ken Pisani. All rights reserved. Printed in the United States of America. For information, address St. Martin's Press, 175 Fifth Avenue, New York, N.Y. 10010.

www.stmartins.com

The Library of Congress Cataloging-in-Publication Data is available upon request.

ISBN 978-1-250-08520-7 (hardcover)
ISBN 978-1-250-08521-4 (e-book)

Our books may be purchased in bulk for promotional, educational, or business use. Please contact your local bookseller or the Macmillan Corporate and Premium Sales Department at 1-800-221-7945, extension 5442, or by e-mail at MacmillanSpecialMarkets@macmillan.com.

First Edition: May 2016

10 9 8 7 6 5 4 3 2 1

For Amanda, my best thing

MOMENTS

If this were a book you'd know that the guy you meet on page 1, shattered and mutilated and staring into the abyss, would by the end of the story transcend his terrible circumstances to become a better man. But this isn't a book, this is just me talking . . . and I'm not the guy who beats the odds and overcomes adversity; I'm the guy who wakes up in the hospital to find out his arm has been amputated and says, *Fuck me.*

This is that moment, I realized as the doctor confirmed my sudden asymmetry, *the second moment that follows the first.* The first moment was the one that changed everything, when the SUV plowed into the midsized car I'd bought without driver's-side air bags. This second moment is the one when men stronger than I resolve to overcome this giant random hurdle, to rise above its indiscriminate awfulness. If I've ever been sure of anything it's that I wasn't strong enough in the second moment to overcome the first. And then I couldn't hear the doctor anymore, his words lost to a deafening tinnitus. (This would recur.)

In the weeks of rehabilitation that followed I was reminded to *Look at the bright side,* which did little to dim the glare of my own anger. I also had to endure *You're lucky to be alive,* that smallest of consolations, and *It could have been so much worse,* intended, I imagined, to provoke giddy joy that I wasn't left a human torso by the accident. And being right-handed I was supposed to take comfort in "only" losing my left arm, the one I've seen other drivers dangle with impunity outside car doors as if their vehicles were too small to contain such poor judgment. Yes, I suppose I should have been grateful that it wasn't my right arm, the one I use to sign my name and click my mouse and throw the ball to my dog, back when I had one (before the divorce), and reach across the car seat to clutch my wife's leg, back when I had one (a wife). But it's hard to feel grateful when you're rendered a quarter less than you once were in the limb department, and physical therapy hurts so fucking much.

When my mind wandered during rehab I tried to remember the accident, which still only comes in flashes—probably false memories, including an imagined traffic alert cautioning other drivers to detour around my inconvenient, mangled self, heard on my car radio as EMTs pulled me from the wreckage with *the jaws of (my now ruined) life.*

And then I'm sent home—not the home I had managed to toggle together after my marriage collapsed (an apartment slightly less crappy than the one I'd imagined would be mine should my marriage ever collapse) but to the home of my boyhood in eastern Illinois where my father, also recently divorced, offered to let me stay until I "got back on my feet," a tauntingly inaccurate metaphor.

THINGS YOU CAN'T DO WITH ONE ARM

Clap

Floss

Juggle

Climb a ladder

Button a shirt

Tie shoelaces

Wear mittens

Open a jar

Shuck corn

Butter toast

Toss a salad

Cut a steak

Rope cattle

Count money

Fold laundry

Put a shirt on a hanger

Bench press

Drive a stick

Pet two dogs

Cover your ears

Use a bow and arrow

Monkey bars!

Push a wheelbarrow

Pump a fireplace bellows

Build a snow fort

Make meatballs

Open one of those
   grocery produce bags

Scratch that spot just
   in the wrong side of the
   middle of your back

Play an instrument*

*Yes, there are instruments you can play with one hand—minor ones like bugle and harmonica and tam-tam. But even an instrument as useless as the triangle requires one hand to hold it while the other strikes it. And anyway, you're not making the philharmonic with one arm. It would disturb subscribers. (And before anyone brings up the drummer from Def Leppard: sure, Thunder God gets to keep his job with the band after his accident, but he sure doesn't *start* playing drums after losing an arm. That would be stupid.)

PARIS

I used to like telling people I grew up in Paris. Which was true, only it was Paris, Illinois. Eventually I figured out that this hilarious "joke" was on me: setting up a false, fascinating childhood only to deliver the punch line that it was in reality painfully mundane is as self-defeating as showing up at your divorce hearing visibly drunk. As time went on I grew content with being inherently uninteresting until now, as a one-armed man, I have a permanent, unavoidable topic of conversation.

Except with Dad, who refuses to mention it.

After driving three hundred miles to pick me up at the Illinois Treatment Center Hospital, even as I struggled, one-armed, to dress and pack (long since realizing that everything would be a one-armed struggle from now on), Dad never once mentioned the accident, acknowledged my struggling, or admitted my missing arm. Nor did he do so when he had visited twice before, once at the hospital immediately following the accident and again about a month into rehab at ITCH. Not when I couldn't cut my food or shrieked at a sudden stabbing pain, or stared blankly at the place my arm used to be. He didn't mention *why* we might have agreed, just a couple of days ago, that I should move back home for a while; and for six hours in the car and now, having arrived in Paris, he still hasn't mentioned it. Nor will he, I believe, up to and including the day he dies.

"Aaron . . ." Dad has found it necessary to begin most of his sentences addressing me by name, three times—the first, lost like a rock down a well; the second, heard but failing to register, as if the name belonged to someone else; the third, a memory jolt of who I used to be. "We're here," he announces as unnecessarily as a masked gunman declaring *This is a stickup!* This is after all the house I grew up in, and eventually escaped from, and I recognize it: from the crooked carport that threatened imminent collapse upon our every departure and return and somehow remains erect, to the peeling shutters framing the upstairs window from which I dropped into Mom's zinnias, slipping into the night to commit random acts of juvenile delinquency.

The gravel crunches as Dad slows to a stop, turns off the car, and leaps from the vehicle like a stuntman on fire, unable to stand the heat of sitting adjacent to my stump for another second. He pulls my bag from the trunk with one hand and slams it shut with the other, proving this stooped, faded father is twice the man his son is. I follow as he trudges up the walkway, pants clinging to bony hips as if desperate not to fall. I recall all the thousands of times I followed this man into this house, thousands of moments jump-cut together and ending with this one that finds us both diminished. Dad pauses a moment, his hair darting in all directions like a flock of feeding geese suddenly startled, and then swings the door open without a key.

"You still don't lock the door? You were away overnight."

"What are they gonna steal, my Victrola?"

"Don't be cute, Dad. You own lots of valuable things. Or they could just be meth-addled psychopaths, lying in wait to bludgeon us to death with your toaster."

"Toaster oven," Dad corrects me, stepping through the doorway ready to face an even more formidable weapon than I'd imagined.

Inside, the house is just as I remember it, a funny thing to notice; certainly it would be more remarkable if it had somehow become completely unfamiliar—say, clean and orderly and not smelling of cigars. Mom and Dad lived like the Collyer brothers, saving things not because they thought they might someday want them but because it was easier to shove them into a dark corner rather than arrange for their removal . . . or, in the case of stacks and stacks of magazines, that they'd "get to" them someday, despite the fact that *Money* magazines from the nineties weren't likely to be worth getting to. It only got worse after Mom left. You might think one Collyer brother couldn't do the work of two, but Dad would prove you wrong.

I trail Dad past rows of family photos on walls paneled with knotty pine and then upstairs, as if he were a bellhop and I needed help finding my room, which I don't . . . until he continues past my room and tugs the rope unfolding the attic stairs, and I realize, *I do*. I stare back at the doorway to my room and suddenly know exactly what lies within. Unlike other children's rooms turned into home offices, sewing rooms, or preserved as childhood shrines after their departure to adulthood, my old bedroom is packed floor to ceiling with the flotsam of decades lived and a marriage gone bad. I twist the doorknob and the door swings inward about six inches before thunking against a landfill of old furniture, boxes, magazines, books and records, clothes, luggage, blankets, artwork, drapes, broken televisions, and other no-longer-transmitting electronics—discards that one at a time didn't seem to matter much until they piled up on one another like years; all stacked and filling every inch of the twelve-by-fourteen-by-eight-foot expanse that was once the domain of a boy and later prison to a teen, until his release to attend college in a city far away. Only now to return, recidivism imposed by injury. And forced up to the attic, the difficulty of which offers further evidence of a father's denial.

"It seemed preferable to the basement. No windows down there, and it kind of stinks. Can you make it okay?" he asks about the attic stairs, and I seize the opportunity to force him to acknowledge my missing limb.

"Why, what could possibly slow me down?" Dad shrugs, staring at my throat, inches from my eyes but miles away. I feel a flush of shame for pressing him. "I'll be okay."

"You go first. In case of the lunatics who broke in."

"*Walked* in," I correct him, but really, I know he's sending me up first so he can break my fall with his already broken body if I slip.

The first thing you learn about missing an arm is not the obvious—all the things you can't do without it. It's the havoc it plays on your balance, like a glass suddenly removed from a passing waiter's crowded tray that causes the rest to tumble to the floor. The simple act of standing up is difficult, and one lone arm swinging freely is a pendulum trying to tip you over. (And just try walking without swinging your arms.) Gripping the railing to pull myself upward, I can at least enjoy a momentary steadiness against the permanent imbalance of the one-armed.

When my head breaches the surface I'm surprised by what I find: it's actually quite livable, considering the haste with which it must have been thrown together. First of all, it's cleaner than any other room in the house, and freshly painted, although apparently the only paint handy was garden-shed green. Mine will be the dreams of a man sleeping inside a martini olive. Dad's unfurled a plush little area rug over the wooden boards that give ever so slightly under every creaking step, and he's somehow managed to get a fold-out couch up here. (I imagine ropes and pulleys and exasperated deliverymen suffering under Dad's shouted direction from the ground, perhaps having to replace a broken window afterward.) He's also hung a vintage black-light poster belonging to my older sister, Jackie, serializing in six panels the melting face of a drugged cartoon character and proclaiming, "Stoned Agin." Finally, he's taken all the books I remember strewn in precarious stacks about the house and organized them in a short bookshelf that runs the length of the attic, adding one disturbing touch: my old sports trophies from school and summer camp.

"We did the best we could."

"'We'?"

"Your mother helped. And her boyfriend. He's a fireman." Good God, Mom's dating a fireman. As if he could read my thoughts, Dad continues, "She saw him on one of those charity calendars, *Hot and Hunky*, or some such thing. Went after him like a foxhound. He never really stood a chance."

"How old—"

"He's a lot younger. But your mother is a decade younger than me, so if you ask her, it's all the same. But I wouldn't advise asking her."

"Do they live—"

"Let's have an early dinner, I'm pretty beat from the drive." Dad trundles back to the attic stairs and submerges with the authority of a U-boat commander, safe again beneath the surface where the onrushing torrent of emotions swirls around him but cannot touch him, secure in his dry, airtight vessel.

I'm left alone in the attic, where the junkyard of a life is supposed to accumulate. Instead, I'm the remnant of a broken thing, stored here for spare parts should they prove useful at a later date before leaving the rest of me out by the curb. I'm nearly forty, divorced, woefully out of shape, clinically depressed, on "sabbatical" from my job as a high school teacher, alone, living in the attic of my father's house, one-armed. That last label, "one-armed," now punctuates every description that will ever define me, an exclamation point to all that preceded—a litany of life's disappointments—adding a final, sad coda to the person I once was.

Suddenly, I need to lie down.

In my dreams I imagine my missing arm looking down on me from the afterlife of dismembered limbs—legs lost to cancer, feet to crushing accidents, toes to frostbite, fingers, hands, and yes, arms. The arm watches and knows, *He's fucked. This is not a guy who faces down hardship and emerges a better, fuller person. Those things that don't kill him do not make him stronger; they just further diminish him over time, until he disappears.*

EXCEPTIONALS

Randy Pausch was a professor of computer science at Carnegie Mellon University in Pittsburgh who learned in September of 2006 that he had terminal pancreatic cancer. A year later, he gave a talk at CMU entitled "The Last Lecture: Really Achieving Your Childhood Dreams," an inspirational monologue of life lessons in the face of certain death. It went viral on YouTube, getting eighteen million views and counting. (But, I'll point out, fewer than hundreds of music videos, a thigh massage instructional, something called "Charlie Bit My Finger," and the on-air meltdown of a beauty pageant contestant.) Pausch's lecture was turned into a bestselling book, and he became an inspiration to anyone struggling with a terminal illness, and an exemplar of human bravery.

But the rest of us are not like Randy Pausch. That's why we call him and others like him *exceptional*, because they are the *exception;* the rest of us are not brave or strong or fearless—we are not fighters against all odds, preferring the odds to be with us rather than against. We don't welcome the challenge of adversity but run from it, and the only struggle we offer when it catches us is to weep and flail and cry out for it not to be so.

We are not Warren Macdonald, a double-leg amputee who managed to summit Kilimanjaro in 2003, or Aron Ralston, whose self-inflicted loss of his lower arm saved him from certain death and freed him to pursue life as a one-handed adventurer. We are not Sir Douglas Bader, who lost both legs in a 1931 plane crash only to lead an RAF squadron during World War II; or Basque Naval midshipman Blas de Lezo y Olavarrieta who, in the early eighteenth century, lost his left leg from a cannon shot, his left eye in defense of Toulon, and his right arm in the siege of Barcelona, yet subsequently captured eleven enemy British ships.

We are not Franklin Roosevelt, who overcame crippling polio to become president, or Stephen Hawking, whose mind would not be shackled by the amyotrophic lateral sclerosis that claimed his body. We are not Helen Keller, or Randy Fucking Pausch. We aren't even Cher, with dyslexia.

The rest of us, when our bodies are broken, break along with it. And these heroic exceptions with their incredible ability to rise above the most awful circumstances imaginable just make us look bad.

MORNING

Mornings are the worst. The disorientation of unfamiliar surroundings since the hospital—then ITCH, and now the attic—is compounded by hours of sleep during which the pain meds wear off, and the stinging realization, before I even open my eyes, that my arm is *gone*. Mornings are made worse by the dream interrupted in which, regardless of whether I am being chased by dogs, losing teeth, flying, drowning, or having sex with a woman I never met, I am always whole.

I start the day with a V^2 boost (Vicodin and Valium), and Dad and I are in the car on the way to breakfast before the wooziness overtakes me. I'm not thrilled to be up and out in the world, especially a world as small as this one. It's still the place where I grew up; the only unfamiliar thing here is me, the temporary blemish of an angry pimple.

The din on the radio recedes behind the shimmering tinnitus that recurs at irregular intervals like visits from the neighbor's cat. But then a woman's voice cuts through the ringing—it's sweet, sultry, smart, and belongs to the station's science reporter. Her name is Sunny Lee and her show, ninety-second interstitials of fun science fact, is called *The Sunny Side*:

Think your shiny new car's GPS is sophisticated? Well, it's got nothing on this tiny traveler: the ant! Foraging ants travel distances up to seven hundred feet from their nests—which may not seem like much to you and me, but that's one giant leap for ant-kind. So how do they find their way back to the colony? The same way a mom finds her teenage boy's gym clothes: scent trails! Ants leave a distinctive odor allowing them to find their way back, even in the dark.

But what if the ant in question is, say, all stuffed up with a head cold? Ants are also visually inclined, and some navigate using a combination of physical landmarks and the position of the sun, while others can detect Earth's magnetic field. And some even measure distance with an internal pedometer that actually counts their steps! Amazing! And all this time you thought they were just . . . clairvoy-ANT. This is Sunny Lee, for The Sunny Side.

Over the coming days and weeks Sunny Lee will tell me things I never knew, about the speed of falling raindrops, the peripheral vision of hammerhead sharks, the torque of a spun pizza. By the time we pull up to the Four Corners Diner, I'm in love with her.

Although located at an unusual intersection of *five* corners, the Four Corners seems to have been named in deliberate denial of the unusual in favor of the mundane. Sometime after my departure from Paris, this became Dad's ritualistic breakfast place. For someone who expresses incredulity at the concept of "eating out" ("Why would I pay someone to cook me a steak? I can cook my own steak. And seven dollars for a beer—you can buy the whole six-pack for that."), Dad has embraced breakfast here with an enthusiasm usually reserved for a child hearing the jingling approach of an ice-cream truck. I could go ahead and point out that eggs cost about a dime apiece or that for the price of three or four cups of coffee he could buy himself an entire one-pound can, but he would disregard both like my missing limb. What Dad enjoyed about breakfast out was the camaraderie, the sheer comfort of the familiar.

All of which flee upon our arrival like birds.

Heads turn and conversation stops. Dad's oldest friend, Fred Weber, is frozen, a forkful of omelet poised to enter his mouth. Behind the counter Michelle's attention is wrenched from the act of refilling a coffee mug, but it doesn't matter because, I swear, the coffee itself has stopped pouring midstream. Even the kitchen roaches have petrified midscurry. The only movement in the room belongs to hastily averted eyes, as anything and everything—the food on the plates, the speckles in the Formica tabletops, the lint on George Jones's sleeve, the faded painting on the wall (a boat in a Venice canal, which had adorned the wall unnoticed for decades until this moment)—suddenly demand attention.

Dad slides into a booth and gestures for me to sit across from him and then disappears behind his newspaper. It would be very still and quiet here were it not for the ringing in my ears. By the time breakfast comes (me: mushroom egg-white omelet; Dad: Lumberjack Special, despite no previous lumberjacking experience), things have resumed some degree of normalcy. Michelle sprays the room with toothy smiles, and Mr. Weber, in full attorney mode, orates at a decibel made necessary by his failing hearing, as coffee flows and roaches scurry once more. Dad circulates among his neighbors and occasionally recalls me to them—"You remember Aaron"—and I nod from the table, waving with my good hand lest I appear double-amputeed.

"You look good," Michelle flirts, as she once did with the

handsome teenager I used to be, and I wish I could muster a flattering lie in return.

"He lost weight!" Mr. Weber shouts from his table, and as the room is now forced to ponder what an arm might weigh, silence reigns once more and George Jones returns his attention to the problematic lint on his sleeve.

Michelle presents a rhetorical diversion—"More coffee?"—the space between offer and delivery too narrow for refusal. This is my third cup, and anyone here longer than I've been has surely suffered their fifth or sixth. It's astounding our sleepy little hamlet isn't rife with insomnia.

Dad slips back into the booth across from me. "How was that omelet?"

"Well, you know you can't make one without breaking a few eggs."

"Why does it cost more for egg whites? You're getting less; they take out the yolks."

(That's more like it, Dad.)

"I wonder what they do with the yolks," he ponders.

"I think they just pour them over the Lumberjack Special."

Dad pokes at the nub of a sausage link on his plate as if trying to provoke a reaction. "Have you thought about what you're going to do?"

"I'm going to finish my breakfast. Then, there will be lunch."

"I mean when you're feeling fit again."

"I'm not sure 'fit' is what I'll be feeling, but whatever it is, I'll only be feeling it with one hand."

"You planning on going back to that fancy high school?" he asks as the sausage squirms away from his fork.

Any return to the life I knew seems so improbable, especially my previous position teaching social studies to the profoundly disinterested. Shaking off the discomfort of commanding a room's attention had taken my entire first semester as a teacher, and I'm loath to return to face the scrutiny of teenaged eyes riveted to the place where my arm used to be. Or to manage its awkward opposite—the averted eyes and frozen smiles of fellow teachers cornered in the break room (not to mention the one-armed wrangling of coffee and stale doughnuts).

"It's not fancy," I deflect Dad's notion. "We have the same challenges any high school faces in trying to prepare kids for a future in a hazardous world. We're like NASA, training astronauts for a mission to Mars that we know can only end badly."

And here we are, in our own future of sorts: this moment where all the events and circumstances of our lives have led, here at the Four Corners where Dad asks me what my plans are to find local work and my ears begin to ring some more. I excuse myself and head to the bathroom, momentarily pulled to one side by the heaviness of my arm and the equilibrium-fucking combination of V^2. Eyes veer from my path and avoid my clumsy trail, and as the bathroom door snaps shut behind me I imagine the rush from the diner to escape the awkwardness of my return. I make it to the toilet before throwing up breakfast, consoled at least that my drug dosage has already been absorbed into my bloodstream and cannot be so easily expelled.

I stare at my own face in the mirror, still boyishly handsome enough for Michelle, with haunted eyes that tell me not to go back out there to face Dad and his hopes for my future, or the other diners and their discomfort, or Michelle's bottomless pot of heart-palpitating cheeriness. And then the bathroom window offers the solution to all my problems.

JOBS YOU CAN'T HOLD WITH ONE ARM

Baseball player

Umpire

Croupier

Police officer

Fireman

Bartender

Roofer

Surgeon

Skycap

Bellhop

Boxer

Cowboy

Goalie

Crane operator

Alligator wrangler

Orchestra conductor

Courtroom stenographer

Airport landing signal
    officer

EMT

Astronaut

Plate spinner

And of course,
    Paperhanger

Sure, someone will feel compelled to point out a guy who, against all odds, held one of these jobs, maybe still does. Like Jim Abbott, born without his lower right arm, who somehow managed to pitch for the Yankees, Angels, White Sox, and Mariners (all American League teams, so he wouldn't have to bat). As if that invalidates the point. Exception does not disprove the rule, and the rule is, guys with one arm don't have these jobs. And if you needed any of these jobs done and a guy with one arm showed up, you'd demand a guy with both. (I know I would.)

SCHOOLED

I'd escaped through the Four Corners bathroom window before, back during a time when I still believed I didn't have to do things I didn't want to do, and what I didn't want to do then was finish an awkward lunch date with my teenaged chum Joel and two girls whose names I can't remember. Not only was Joel stuck paying the check, but he had to suffer the stereo diatribe of the girls on a long, shameful walk home. It took an inordinate time for me to properly assess my escape as an unforgivably cruel act.

This time the struggle with one less limb was greater and my good arm is dotted with splinters from the rotted window frame, my karma having traveled a quarter century to get here. Drifting down the narrow boulevard of our town's best attempt at a "Main Street," my options for hiding out are few: too early for the bar, the Loading Zone being closed; daunted by the two hands required for page thumbing at the bookstore; and loitering in the bank is likely to call the undue attention I'm trying to avoid.

A beautiful woman at the bus stop scans her phone, and I want to approach and talk to her or pull up in my car and offer her a ride, only to head to the lake instead where we'll laugh and enjoy each other's company and maybe even have sex, in the car or by the lake, it won't matter. Instead I can't help but wonder if I'll do any of those things again—meet a beautiful woman, drive a car, swim in a lake, laugh in the company of another, or have sex, in a car or by the lake or any place on Earth. It would take a very special woman to overlook my shortcoming—perhaps a blind one, but even then the charade would be difficult to keep up for long, and would probably end with screams.

My best option for losing myself seems to be the used vinyl store, Broken Records, which offers to recommend it "open for business" status and rows of record albums that flip easily with one hand. The proprietor is older than I might have imagined if I'd bothered imagining him at all—less Jack Black in *High Fidelity* than Jack Palance in *City Slickers*.

"Just gonna look around a little," I announce before he can ask, "Can I help you?" and I'm forced to respond, "I could use a hand."

I start flipping through the *A*s and figure by the time I make my stoned way past ZZ Top, that should kill the best part of the day. "Show Tunes" should take care of the rest. I barely make it to ABBA when he insists on engaging me.

"You went to Paris Middle School."

"I did," I admit, before jabbing back at his age. "Were we in the same class?"

"I taught math. Or in your case, tried to."

It's Mr. Madnick, my eighth-grade math teacher. I needled him for nine months, September through June, like a gassy, unwanted pregnancy, birthed and then handed over for adoption to the oblivion of summer, never to be seen again until now. *Of all the record stores in all the towns in all the worlds*, he must be thinking, *he walks into mine.*

"Math was an abstract concept I couldn't grasp," I explain. "And with fewer fingers to count on, I've only gotten worse at both math and grasping. Also, air guitar."

"It had nothing to do with concepts. You didn't want to do the work."

"Maybe I just needed it in simpler terms: 'Aaron leaves town, heading west, at fifty-five miles an hour. When he intersects twenty-five years later with an SUV, traveling east, how many limbs will be subtracted from Aaron?'"

"That's recent, then? Surely you can't be whining about something that happened a long time ago."

I slam the stack of *A*s upright and stare at him.

"Respect the vinyl," he says, instantly rendering records as uncool as textbooks. "So, Aaron. What do you do now?"

"I'm a teacher," I say, and I can't help laughing, but it's no match for his.

"God, you want to talk abstract concepts? I love that the universe does shit like that!" He steps down from behind the counter, and his transformation to actual human is complete enough to make me feel guilty about the terrorist snark that only a fourteen-year-old boy is capable of wreaking upon a teacher.

"And my eighth-grade math teacher retired and opened a cool record store."

"Actually, I had sex with one of my students and got fired. Did a little time! You'd be surprised how really bad shit can turn out good for you."

"Right. People keep telling me that."

"Oh. Your arm," he realizes. "No, I wasn't thinking that. That's completely fucked. I can't think of one good thing that might come from that."

I'm not sure if he's serious or if this is some residual teacher mind trick meant to inspire me to prove him wrong, but even my currently stoned self isn't buying it.

"So, do you own a phonograph, or are you just browsing?"

"My father still has the stackable components that were so popular in the late eighties." It makes me wish that of all the things Dad has squirreled away, he'd have kept the younger, whole version of me.

"Just one of many things wrong with the eighties. Ease over virtue. A good stereo system is comprised of the best pieces. That might mean a Fisher tuner, Marantz amplifier, JBL speakers, Technics turntable. And of course the cartridge, and even the stylus matters. But that's too much trouble, so you buy the single-manufacturer stackable set in the prefab unit with the Plexiglas window to display your mediocrity."

"Or, I just play my iPod through my clock radio dock."

"It's a slow, downward spiral," he laughs. "No way to treat our best memories." He pulls The Allman Brothers from their place among the *A*s and gazes at it as if it were a mirror reflecting his younger face. "Our favorite versions of ourselves are tied to music. 'Whipping Post.' 'Ramble On.' 'Layla.'"

"'It's a Long Way to Tipperary.'"

"I get it, I'm old! All right, in your case"—he assesses me—"some nineties grunge crap? Hootie? Or are you more of a residual eighties guy?"

"At least you didn't say 'Achy Breaky Heart.'"

"Music can be transporting . . ." He slides to the *B*s and riffles through the albums, a flip-deck animation of music eras from Basie to Butthole Surfers. "But they lose that power through familiarity. Now, when I hear Bowie sing 'Changes,' it's impossible to go back to the time I first heard it, because it's been painted over by all the times I've heard it since. It has no temporal resonance anymore. But 'Eight Line Poem'? 'Quicksand'? I've heard them infrequently enough over the years that I've got half a chance of *tasting* a moment from 1971."

He crosses to the facing stack of *M*s, practiced fingers dancing across record jacket edges, and randomly pulls Morrissey's *Viva Hate*. He looks at it and me, assessing, believing he got it right.

"I could play 'Everyday Is Like Sunday' or 'Suedehead,' and you'd dig hearing it again." He walks it over to the turntable. "But can it make you feel fifteen all over again? Nope. But this . . ."

(The initial thud and scratchiness of the needle is nearly enough to take me back.)

"Half a chance."

He guesses right: I probably haven't heard "Little Man, What Now?" since the year it was released, and with its opening drumbeat I can summon up everything about it and who I once was. Thirteen, I guess, with the billion great and infinitesimal shifts ahead that make a life but an adolescent's sense of permanence— that I'd always be some version of *this*: likeable enough to have a crop of friends but still falling short of "popular," good-looking enough to attract girls who only made me feel clumsy around them. Essentially, this brain, these thoughts . . . this *me* that would always love comic books and Nintendo and toaster pizza, housed in a fuller, elongated body better suited to adulthood. And with two arms.

I can't help but think about my three years of middle school, and the three years of high school that followed, years that felt like a lifetime. So why have the last three years been a blur? And why does it feel like the next three might already have happened before I can finish this thought?

What became of you, indeed.

A scant 1:49 later, memory gives way to currency: I'm stoned and tired from standing so long, both hungry and nauseous, the ringing in my ears has returned, and the place where my arm used to be hurts. In the millions of grooves on the thousands of records neatly stacked in hundreds of rows, there may be dozens of songs similarly capable of triggering more sense-memory . . . but none that could possibly make me better.

I say good-bye to Mr. Madnick and thank him for not flunking me those years ago. Teetering outside, I see Fred Weber waiting outside the Four Corners with Dad, concern etched on his face, and I realize I now have another unforgivably cruel window escape to atone for.

DAD

Dad was a time traveler.

Because we lived near the boundary between time zones, Dad went back and forth *in time* every day on his way to work. He had to get up at 5:00 A.M. to leave the house by 6:00 for the one-hour drive to work that, because it crossed from central time (here in Edgar County) into eastern time (there in Terre Haute), hurled him an hour into the future. He arrived at work at 8:00 so he could leave early enough to be home at 4:00 P.M.—*exactly the same time he had left work*—when Jackie and I returned from school. All this in the futuristic-sounding Lincoln Mark IV, in silver "moondust" metallic paint with matching silver leather interior and silver-grained vinyl roof, a V8 engine capable of escape velocity, and opera windows through which the present hurtled into the past.

It seemed to me at the time that all that time jumping took its toll on Dad. To my young eyes he appeared older than most of my friends' fathers, who didn't have to battle the time continuum twice daily. In a decade of excess seemingly engineered for subsequent embarrassment, they sported Florida-shaped sideburns and wide lapels while Dad preferred three-piece suits and an astronaut's haircut generously flecked with white. Mom seemed to appreciate neither the grounding of Dad's common

25

sense nor the boldness of his time traveling. (It wasn't always apparent what Mom wanted, and it remains unclear today.)

Before he was a time traveler Dad was an athlete, a cross-country skier who had even made the U.S. biathlon team. To the untrained eye, biathlon might seem a pointless mix of cross-country skiing and target shooting. In fact, the sport is not without purpose, the challenge being to test an athlete's ability to go from heart-pumping activity to the completely restful state needed to hit a target. The lesson Dad took from this seemed to be to live his life the opposite way—modulating everything away from the poles toward the center: neither heart-pounding exhilaration nor peaceful focus would be his purview. Wherever possible, Dad avoided transcendent highs as much as debilitating lows, preferring instead to live in that dull middle where nothing was terrible, nor would it ever be great. He shunned conflict, which might have resolved some things but instead avoided shouting; he stopped reaching for big, uplifting moments rather than risk failure and disappointment, or even the letdown of the quiet moments that lurk between the triumphant ones.

But back in 1964, before he had chosen the wide stripe of the middle, Dad traveled as a member of the U.S. biathlon team to the Olympics in Innsbruck, Austria, where he finished forty-seventh. (Even the best American biathlete has never finished higher than eighth at the Olympics. Apparently we're built, like a muscle car, for power and speed, not emotional complexity.) Whenever I'd asked about Innsbruck Dad never talked about his own experience but about his roommate, Tommy Baker, the highest-scoring American, who finished sixteenth. According to Dad, Tommy also fucked a Russian figure skater, an East German luger, and all three women's downhill medalists from Austria. Those are perhaps odd details to share with a child, but the larger lesson didn't escape me that Tommy excelled at both physical endurance and hitting his targets.

And while Tommy joined the Alaskan National Ski Patrol and became a bush pilot for Alaskan Mountain Air, Dad chose instead the path of least resistance and low reward closer to home. I remember even as a teenager being aware of the limitations of Dad's emotional genes, and while not wishing Tommy Baker was my father—I adored Dad, and suspect Tommy was not the first one home at 4:00 P.M. to greet his children every day—I did occasionally wish Tommy Baker had secretly slept with Mom and gotten her pregnant with a dashing, reckless version of me.

The ride home from the breakfast I failed to keep down is made in complete silence, a reminder of how effective at shaming me mute Dad could be over scolding Dad or especially shouting Dad, which tended to make me laugh and therefore threatened to unleash red-faced super-angry Dad. We coast past "Crawlywood," hilariously named by preteen boys in mocking homage to distant Hollywood. Its furtive acreage dense with trees and underbrush provided a welcome sanctuary for boys to set off fireworks, smoke stolen cigarettes, or set recreational fires (all flammable acts perhaps better performed at a place without "wood" in its name).

Rolling through the neighborhood I'm struck by how irregular everything is: no two houses alike, fenced and open, treed and bare, front yards or dirt driveways, winding roads that twist and curve arbitrarily, some dead-ending and picking up half a mile away, and dotted with the occasional clothesline dangling wash flapping under the sun. Paris, Illinois, is the opposite of the planned community where I once made a home outside of Chicago—built on a grid and every house the same from the outside (some flipped in the minor variety of a mirror image)—an entirely *un*planned community.

The haphazard growth that took place here makes more sense

to me now. It's hubris to think one could plan anything, much less the needs of a community, against an unknowable future with infinite possible outcomes. Ours is a universe in chaos, not order; if there are patterns to be found in nature, they are patterns only of repeated anarchy.

Upon arriving home I declare my intention to lie down, and if Dad considers this, as the doctors at ITCH have cautioned, a warning sign of depression he betrays no alarm; if he finds it merely annoying, as he did when my teenage self spent an inordinate amount of time in a slumbered tangle of sheets, he keeps it arrested behind the blankness of his expression. If his intention is to wait until I fall asleep and then creep into the attic and kill me with his marksman's rifle before turning it on himself, that too is completely unknowable, although entirely understandable in the face of looming days, weeks, months of this. Me. This me.

PHANTOMS

A pain in the neck can be a real . . . well, pain in the neck! This is Sunny Lee with The Sunny Side.

Since prehistoric times, man has suffered two kinds of pain: acute and chronic. Acute pain is triggered by a harmful external event, like when you touch a hot surface, or are gored by a mastodon. Pain receptors chemically send an impulse from the nerves of the affected area into the spinal cord, and all the way up to your brain—all within fractions of a second! It's like the world's fastest messenger telling you to pull away from the hot surface or run like heck from that prehistoric pachyderm! So, pain is actually a good *thing—if you didn't feel it, you couldn't do what was necessary to make it stop.*

Chronic pain is different, in that those pain signals remain active in the nervous system for months—or even years. Yikes! And there's nothing your brain can tell your body to do about it—no hot surface to pull away from or mastodon to flee. There's nothing "cute" about acute pain—imagine a goring that lasts for years! That might make you a little cranky . . . and a real pain *to be around. I'm Sunny Lee, for* The Sunny Side.

I awaken in the darkness knowing that Sunny Lee understands my pain. (Another reason to love her.) I sit up rubbing my shoulder, slow to remember where I am. My left arm burns with tiny hot jolts of electricity. Except I don't have a left arm.

As cruel jokes go, "phantom pain" is brilliantly engineered, proof that the same God that hurls heavy metal at you without warning also enjoys a good practical joke. The only possible upside of *not* having an arm is that it's the one part of you that cannot be hurt; yet one's nerves, blind to the havoc outside the body, continue to seek out the extremity via signal sending and when those signals don't get where they're going—smacking instead into a fleshy cauterized stump—the nerves respond with the hot jolt of a live wire, a cosmic hand buzzer.

On a small table in front of me on a breakfast tray is Dad's signature dish, tuna casserole. It's his signature because besides scrambling eggs and burning meat over an outdoor grill, it's the only real dish he's got. Its real asset—that it can be served hot or cold—is evident here, as it is well past lukewarm and dropping. Dad's also left a bottle of beer, which means either he doesn't know how much Vicodin I'm taking or has forgotten everything he ever knew about raising teens who once mixed pills and alcohol like partners at a square dance. I pluck two caplets from the small stash tucked into the tiny key pocket of my jeans, washing back 1,500 milligrams of Vicodin with a long, grateful swallow of beer, and then I shovel greedy forkfuls of tuna casserole into my mouth until it's gone.

The introduction of beer into my system reminds me that there's no toilet here in the attic, and now I remember having to descend to one of the upstairs bathrooms in the middle of last night (another in a series of tiny annoyances that threaten to nibble away at me like flesh-eating bacteria). In my sleepy, sedated state, it had taken me a while to notice a live alligator staring at me from the bathtub. I recall entertaining the strong likelihood that this wasn't an alligator at all but the result of too many painkillers, until it opened its mouth wide and hissed at me. Curious now though scarcely more clearheaded, I scramble to the bottom of the folding attic stairs where I can see into the bathroom, the gator's tail twitching above the tub, periscope-like.

A dim memory stirs from a decade past of Mom telling me she'd bought Dad a tiny alligator for an anniversary present. (I can't find it on any of the lists of traditional anniversary gifts, not even wedged somewhere between *wood* and *bone china*, but apparently, Mom thought it was appropriate to commemorate their years together with a reptile.) They called him Muhammad Ali Gator (Ali for short), and while it seems impossible this four-foot lizard could be him, I go for confirmation to Dad, sprawled on the living room couch pulled close enough to the television to bathe him in its glow.

"There's an alligator in your bathtub."

"I thought you knew."

"If I did, I'd forgotten."

"Now you know how I feel about everything."

"Is that legal? Keeping a full-sized alligator, I mean."

Dad shrugs. "It's my house."

"The fact that you bought a house doesn't necessarily make it okay to own an alligator, keep a bear, harbor a fugitive, or imprison a Girl Scout in your basement," I argue. "If it did, real estate ads would be a lot more entertaining."

When I plop on the couch next to Dad, he leans away from me as if we were in a roller coaster that just made a sharp turn. I'm still feeling mentally logy and don't know how long I've slept. The dim gray hue outside makes it hard to determine if it's dusk or just before dawn.

"What time is it?"

"I don't know. Used to be you could tell by what's on TV. Guys yammering on a couch, it was after 11:30. Older guys praying and asking for money, even later. Now goddamn *SportsCenter* is on so many times, it could be midnight or seven in the morning."

"The cable box says it's 6:22."

"What makes you think I can make out the little floating numbers on the cable box?"

(Dad's right: the numbers float.)

"It's tonight," Dad clarifies, adding, "Sleep as much as you need. Your body will tell you when you've had enough."

We sit in silence for a while and watch highlights of baseball players doing incredible things: hitting a ball over a wall, spearing a line drive and turning a double play—all things, I can't help but notice *that require two hands.* Even the pitcher, after firing a fastball, has to get his glove hand up to snag a ball hit right back at him, and a runner stealing second uses both hands to gather up the base. The final indignity is the umpire calling a play at the plate by signaling "safe," both arms spread wide like a fat airplane.

As if realizing again what I'm thinking, Dad changes the channel and soon we're watching cable news, six pundits shouting at each other in a six-pointed attack, a Hebrew star *shuriken* of bluster flung into the neck of reason. My head, and non-arm, begin to throb in unison.

"Brokaw never yelled," Dad grunts. "Neither did Koppel. Or Rather, for that matter, but you wouldn't expect a guy in a sweater vest to get all that excited. And six of them? Why do we need six people talking at once? Look at that: I got a big-screen TV—why do I have to watch six faces in little windows? They look like baseball cards. Only of guys nobody wants and you couldn't trade. Like opening up a pack and seeing six Marv Throneberrys looking back at you."

Even when Dad was right, I'd forgotten how hard it was to listen to him complain.

"And what's all the writing on the screen? Thing in the corner, title in the other corner, type running across the bottom like a ticker tape."

That rifle-blast murder-suicide I pondered earlier remains a possibility, although not in the order I was thinking. It occurs to me that the best way to survive our forced proximity is if there's less of it. "I think I'll go upstairs and read a little."

"Good," Dad nods sharply. *For God's sake, go back to the attic so I can forget you're here and stop pretending this isn't agony for both of us.*

As I proceed up the attic stairs I can hear Dad change the channel back to *SportsCenter*, the anchors describing another breathless play as the crowd cheers. I pull up the steps, the sharp *thunk* silencing the celebration of physical perfection below.

RESISTANCE

Crouching low under the slanted attic ceiling, I shuffle over to the low, squat bookshelf, on top of which the sports trophies of my youth mock me: seventeen testaments to the athletic achievement of an able-bodied youth with four fully functioning limbs. These are mostly second- and third-place awards, only one true winner (for swimming), evidence that I was a good-not-great athlete. And, looking closely at the representative figures atop the trophies, I understand why: too many disciplines, impossible to master them all. The small, tarnished figures frozen midaction tell the story of a boy whose desire to experience many different things precluded greatness in any one; sprints and long distance, swimming, diving, basketball, lacrosse, even a tiny silver boy hurling a javelin. (What in the world ever compelled me to throw a javelin?) I snap his arm off, and one by one I snap the left arm off each of them, leaving them in a tiny pile of seventeen discarded limbs that mirror the medical waste heap in some hospital after a busy day of amputations, bundled and bound for off-site biohazard incineration.

I slide a book from the shelf—something easy to skim in my semi-stupor, a thin volume from a Time Life series from the early eighties on World War II, this one called *Resistance*. I seem to recall we had a bunch of these, if not the whole series, with one-word titles like *Besieged* and *Aftermath, Juggernaut* and *Blitz-krieg*. Bought by Mom to help me muddle through grade-school history, they arrived by mail every few weeks until history was replaced by social studies and Mom tried to cancel the series. (I also remember Mom shouting into the phone at the perpetra-tors of this serialized negative option to *Stop sending these god-damn books—we're not paying you another goddamn dollar!*)

The book consists mostly of photos and captions and, much as I did in the fifth grade, I skip completely any pages filled with dense copy. It strikes me that all these people in the photos are now certainly dead, even the ones who were not dead when these were taken (there are several lurid photos of executed Resistance fighters, German soldiers, and villagers discovered to be traitors). I'm especially taken by a chapter on "Subversive Gadgetry," a mind-blowing photo essay of *fuck you* ingenuity: tiny homemade radios hidden in matchboxes, shortwave transceivers disguised as birdhouses; safety razors that hid printed messages, pens that carried poison, hollow shoe heels for smuggling. False bottoms, secret compartments, hollowed-out books to hide guns, explo-sives, bombs. I'm amazed at what people are capable of in the face of the worst circumstances imaginable—

Wait a minute.

I get down on a knee and take a closer look at the books on the shelf: an endless line of titles extolling hope, triumph, the virtue of struggle, and the struggle of the virtuous, including *Between a Rock and a Hard Place* and *Soul Surfer,* both autobiog-raphies by newly armless authors, and numerous self-help titles, including *Turning Obstacles into Opportunities: The Jujitsu of Positive Thinking, Adversity Is Not Your Adversary,* and *Beggars CAN Be Choosers!* I don't need to see *Overcoming Amputation for Dummies* to figure out what's going on here. I pluck two books at random and skim twin stories about heralded arms and the people who once bore them:

Dan Donnelly was a bare-knuckled prize fighter from Dublin who became one of Ireland's most celebrated sportsmen when he defeated English prizefighter George Cooper after eleven rounds in 1815. Donnelly died at the age of thirty-two, his corpse stolen days after his funeral and the remains later traced to the home of a Dublin surgeon who agreed to return them on the condition that he could amputate and keep Donnelly's right arm, the one that had claimed so many victories. In 1953, the owner of the Hideout public house in Kilcullen put the mummified arm on display in the pub, where it remains.

As **General Stonewall Jackson** *and his staff were returning to camp on May 2, 1863, they were mistaken for a Union cavalry force and fired upon. Hit by two bullets, Jackson's left arm had to be amputated and was buried at the Ellwood house in Orange County near the field hospital. In 1921 during a U.S. Marine training exercise, Marine Commander General Smedly Butler, skeptical that Stonewall Jackson's arm was buried nearby, took a squad of Marines to dig up the spot—where he found the arm in a wooden box. He replaced the box with a metal one and reburied it under a granite marker, which says simply: "Stonewall Jackson's arm—Buried May 3, 1863."*

I know instantly that this clumsy propaganda is Mom's doing. Annoyed, I slap the book shut and stand suddenly straight up, conking my head, hard, on the sloping attic ceiling. Worse, it's the left side of my head and my stump instinctively leaps to rub it, squirming futilely; I drop the book from my right hand and struggle without success to reach the aching part of my skull. (And I swear, I hear sirens.)

And that's how Dad finds me—hunched over under the low ceiling like Gollum, swearing, my arm craned around and behind my head as if trying to apply a half nelson to my own self—when he peeks up to tell me Mom's here.

MOM

The fire engine pulls away and a mustachioed firefighter a decade younger than Mom waves at her from his perch on the back, while the driver toots three quick blasts from the horn. Mom waves back and turns to find me in the doorway, her narrow face framed in a chin-length bob unfamiliar to me. (She'd always worn her hair long.) Immediately, her eyes drop to the place my arm should be and she says, "That doesn't look so bad."

Unlike Dad, Mom is no withholding stoic. But neither is she capable of hysteria. Since leaving Dad (the reasons remain a little vague), she's become something of a Zen master of her own life, living in a yurt and quietly accepting every condition and circumstance of the universe around her, even when that universe chooses to snap off the arm of her only son.

"But that's exactly what it is," I disagree. "So. Bad."

She pulls me into her embrace, and as I clutch her with my good arm and my face hits her shoulder I begin to cry, uncontrollably, tears flowing and body shaking. I make no sound, as if that one concession makes this any less humiliating.

My father grabs his jacket and heads for the door. "I'm going to put some gas in the car."

"There, there," Mom reassures me, and I feel oddly comforted by the meaningless redundancy.

———

When I was a small boy, Mom was a chain-smoking pool shark. She'd spend hours at the table in our basement, cigarette dangling from the corner of her mouth, practicing cut shots, corner hooks, caroms, and kill shots—practical shots the way they might happen in a legal game. (Trick shots were "bullshit," she assured me.) She preferred the linear simplicity of nine ball, striking balls in ascending numbers over the more random solids and stripes of eight ball. Mom liked things linear if not orderly; I'm pretty sure she named me "Aaron" to afford me the lifelong advantage of being first in any alphabetically ordered lineup that didn't include aardvarks.

I'd empty Mom's ashtrays and rack all the solid balls in a diamond-shaped cluster, organization she'd undo in a hurry, stubbing out a succession of butts and scattering balls with a thunderclap break that reverberated through the house. Leaning over the table, she bore some resemblance to a praying mantis, all skinny limbs stretched at odd angles from the end of her backless heel to the tips of her fingers, dusty with chalk. Elbow swinging behind her, she'd lean low and I'd stand close to her, surreptitiously inhaling her smoke as if her cigarette were mine. I missed them when she stopped suddenly one day, after we'd taken down an old basement painting of a racehorse and it revealed a clean rectangle against walls gray with smoke. It was as cautionary as a spot on an x-ray, and Mom stubbed out her last cigarette. (Unable to find a replacement painting of similar dimensions we returned the racehorse to its place, where it still runs today.)

Mom was penurious in her love, releasing it in small and infrequent doses like a shipwreck victim might ration just enough water to survive. But as she circled the table, eyes never leaving the felt battlefield, I'd linger close enough for a soft pat on the top of my head as she passed, a brief caress of my hair I can still call up from memory. Then she'd lean down and repeat the cycle—smoke, swing, stroke, slam, crash, drop, circle, pat on the head.

I remember feeling sorry for the billiard balls, nestled safely together under the protection of the triangle until it was lifted, left to face the concussive force of the cue ball. As the security of their huddle was shattered, some fell instantly into darkness while others were left to drift and roll, perhaps pondering their fates as they were stalked and dispatched by the cue ball like victims in an Agatha Christie novel. Sometimes their own numbered brethren were complicit in their downfall, set in motion by the cue ball and crashing them into dark pockets of oblivion. But even the cue ball had no will of its own; it was just a thug doing the bidding of the cue stick, and the cue stick didn't give a shit about anything.

Mom and I sit in the yard as night falls, outdoor lights attracting a horde of flying insects and casting their giant, fluttering shadows. She crosses one pant-suited leg over the other, a backless shoe dangling, waiting to drop. We sip lemonade made from lemons fallen from the Jaffes' tree on our side of the fence. I remember as a kid Dad telling us, *If it falls on our side of the fence, it's ours,* and always hoping something more valuable than lemons might someday land in our yard, like luggage full of diamonds from a passing plane, or sixteen-year-old Pam Jaffe tumbling naked out of her window into Mom's zinnias.

"Have you thought about a prosthetic?" Mom sips her drink coolly.

"They're expensive. And cumbersome. I don't have my elbow or lower muscles to really work one of the good ones. Pain in the ass to put on and take off, and they'll rub the skin raw. Last thing I need is an infection."

"You'll see some money from insurance," Mom says, dismissing multiple arguments by addressing only one of them, a lion tamer cowing the lead lion so the others fall in line. "They can do amazing things these days."

"*We can rebuild him, better than he was before. Better, stronger, faster.*"

"Honey, you can wallow all you want. I'm immune."

"Was I wallowing? I thought I was flaunting my bionic wit."

"You're not the first one in this family to have these kinds of problems. Your father had a pacemaker put in last spring. Actually, a cardio-defibrillator. For arrhythmia."

"How come no one bothered to tell me that?"

She shrugs. "It's no big deal."

"Really, *no big deal.* Come lie on the table and let me stab you in the chest and jam a bunch of electronics under your skin and run wires into your heart."

"It's a very common procedure."

"Then I *am* the first one in the family to have this kind of problem. Because this"—I wave my nub at her—"is sort of a big deal."

"This is why I worry about you, honey. When things are bad, you pour accelerant on them." Mom quietly sips her drink. "These would be better with vodka."

I'm embarrassed to tell her mine *has* vodka, a splash snuck from Dad's liquor cabinet when she wasn't looking. As I returned the bottle I noticed the $5.98 price tag, and the name, Fleischmann's, a brand I wouldn't want to drink unadorned by Mr. Jaffe's lemons and gobs of sugar.

"I know it's hard," she says. "Talk to me. Tell me anything."

"It's surprising how difficult it is to pick your nose."

Mom refuses to be rattled. "Is that what you want to talk about, nose picking? Fine, let's do that, then."

She gets up and heads inside, and I follow, the slamming of the screen door behind me that once announced the comings and goings of her children now just another angry noise I make.

"I'm serious," I insist as she leans under the liquor cabinet that was once theirs and produces the Fleischmann's. "It's one of those things you don't think about."

"No, I don't." She pours an impressive amount of barely distilled vodka in both her virgin glass and my already sullied one.

"Try it," I challenge her. "Try picking your nose with your opposite hand."

"You think I won't?"

And of course she does, sticking her left pinky in her right nostril.

"Everything's backward, right?" I coax her. "It's like trying to tie your shoes in a mirror."

"Yes, I see where it's hard," she snorts. "Everything is just a little off."

"It's worse with your index finger," I go in hard with mine. "Everything just feels flimsy, like you could pull your nose off."

That's how Dad finds us on his return, both picking our noses in his kitchen, his bottle of Fleischmann's a guilty accomplice.

"Right," he finally says. "There never was anything to do in this town."

"Aaron was just showing me how hard things are with one arm."

Without a word, Dad pulls a coffee cup from the sink and pours the last of the Fleischmann's into it in an act of muscle memory.

"Another dead soldier," I declare as he drains the bottle.

"Not yet," he reminds me.

Dad had fostered a theory of relative emptiness, that every so-called empty bottle still had eleven drops left. He'd proven it serially over hundreds of beer, wine, and liquor bottles at dinnertime across the decades, his wide-eyed children awestruck over this tiny miracle. Sometimes we'd erupt with glee that the drops had ceased at ten, and he'd say nothing, just hold it there and wait for that eleventh drop that was always forthcoming; when challenged that there might in fact be *more* than eleven drops, Dad would hold the bottle in place for minutes and not another drop emerged. Children like to believe their parents are capable of miraculous things, however small.

"I thought we'd go get some Chinese," Dad announces, holding the empty bottle over his mug.

One.

"A restaurant?" Mom gasps playfully. "I'm in."

Two.

"What about your boyfriend?" I ask with the maturity of a taunting schoolboy.

Three.

"He'll eat at the firehouse with the guys," Mom smooths the shirtsleeve over my nub. "And don't try to provoke me. If you want to talk about my 'boyfriend,' let's."

Four. Five.

"Let's not."

Six.

"I'm fine with that too."

Seven.

"Your *Zen* is getting a little annoying. The universe is not a complacent place."

Eight. Nine.

"It's whatever you perceive it to be."

Ten.

"I want it to be a universe of armless beings, where the one-armed man is king."

Eleven.

"'Want' and 'perceive' are different things, honey." She pats my head the way she used to around the pool table, giving me goose bumps.

Dad continues to hold the upturned bottle in place a long

beat, awaiting the drop that never comes, before setting it down. He sips, hiding a satisfied smile behind the lip of his mug, and I'm oddly reassured that Dad is still capable of small miracles.

FORTUNE

Dad signs the check at Dim Sum & Then Some, pocketing the restaurant's pen—extracting his personal rebate against the extravagance of dining out. (Over the years, he'd collected thousands of pens, bundled in rubber bands all over the house.) Mom scoops up her fortune cookie, and I reach and miss mine completely, the interaction of three Tsingtaos and two Vicodin doing their job with the efficiency of the men who built the railroads. While dubious of a fortune cookie's ability to prognosticate—after all, none had ever warned me of a one-armed future—I nonetheless crave some tiny bit of hope to look forward to. Instead, I get:

Good luck is the result of good planning

"See, this isn't even a fortune, it's . . . some kind of homily." I bite into a chunk of cookie. "And a statement of dubious fact. Was my bad luck bad planning? Did I turn left instead of right, leave later instead of earlier? Is bad planning what put me in the path of a speeding SUV?"

"Just because one thing is true doesn't mean the opposite is," Dad says, coming as close as he has to acknowledging my "bad

47

luck." "*A small dog may bite* doesn't necessarily mean a big dog won't."

"Wouldn't 'big cat' be the opposite of 'small dog'?"

Mom reads hers, proclaiming:

> A member of your family will soon do
> something to make you proud

"The burden's on Jackie. I'm a little spent."

"Well, in fact, your sister's coming to visit."

"What?"

"When you say *What?*, does that mean you didn't hear me, or you're so thrilled with the news that you want me to say it twice?"

"She doesn't have to do that."

"According to this fortune, she does." Mom pops half a fortune cookie in her mouth for punctuation.

Dad examines his fortune. "What the hell is this?"

"Let me see . . ." Mom takes it from him and reads:

> chī (chee)—eat

"It's Chinese, the word for 'eat.' *Chee.* See, fortune on one side, Chinese phrases on the other."

I turn over my own fortune to read:

> kuaàilè (kway-UR)—happy

"*Kway-UR.* 'Happy.'"

"Anyway, yes, your sister's coming. She wants to help."

"How, exactly, can she help?"

"Just try to be nice."

"I'll try to be *kway-UR.*" I snatch Mom's fortune and flip it.

"What are you doing now?"

"Learning Chinese."

yīngéer (yin-UH)—baby

"See? I just learned a sentence: *Kway-UR yin-UH chee. Happy baby eat.* Or, it could be *Eat happy baby.* Yes, that's better! The next time I see a happy Chinese baby, I can tell his parents to eat him. Hey, if I have every meal here for the next ten years, I'll have a Chinese vocabulary of . . . nearly eleven thousand words. I could get a job at our embassy in Beijing or a tech company outsourcing child labor."

Dad's already got his jacket on and is halfway to the door before I finish. When the waiter comes to pick up the check, I tell him, "That man has your pen."

I make my way down the attic stairs the next morning, each descent a little better, although the possibility of falling and snapping one of my three remaining useful limbs is never far from my mind. I'm not surprised to find Mom and Dad having breakfast in the kitchen.

In the middle of the night I'd been awakened by a series of grunts and noises, the sounds of a struggle downstairs—a home invasion, maybe, and of course the assailants would have no way of knowing there was a one-armed man in the attic. While deciding whether to rush downstairs to be killed in the same bloodbath that was likely claiming my father, I recognized the sounds as less combative than collaborative and realized, *My parents are having sex.* It couldn't have been more disturbing if I were ten years old and walked in on them, and failed to comprehend why Daddy was thrusting himself into Mommy.

Mom pats Dad's hand at the breakfast table, a sweet habitual gesture that makes me wonder how Dad lost out to a firefighter, even one who represents February on a calendar wearing nothing but his helmet and a fake Abe Lincoln beard.

"I didn't know you stayed over." I slump into a seat at the table.

"Yes, I 'stayed over,'" Mom grins over her coffee cup. "I 'stay over' with your father from time to time. You should find yourself a nice girl to 'stay over' once in a while."

"Okay, we can drop the awkward euphemism."

"Sex was never the problem between your father and I."

Dad stares deeply into his bowl of cereal as if hoping *it* might eat *him*.

"What does your fireman think of that?"

"They prefer 'firefighter,'" Mom corrects me gently. "And we have an understanding."

"Dad, you're okay with this?"

"What the hell do I care? We're not together anymore. Except when we are."

"And when we are, there is no fireman."

"They prefer 'firefighter,'" I remind her.

Mom *stabs* a stack of sausage patties clean through with her fork, alerting me with a five-alarm glare that her buttons are still pushable, although I might wish not to do so.

"I'm going to feed Ali," she says on her way out of the kitchen.

Dad slides the box of cereal in front of me. "Have some breakfast. We're out of Fleishmann's."

I pour a bowl and we eat in near silence, except for the cooing and soft splashing from the bathtub at the top of the stairs.

"Mom says you had a pacemaker put in?"

"She did? Well, yes. No big deal," Dad manages through a mouthful of bran flakes.

"She said that too."

"What about you? Did you sleep okay?"

"Mostly," I say, not really recalling how I slept at all.

"Sedation isn't sleep," he swallows. "It's induced paralysis and memory loss. It's not a restful state. 'Coming to' isn't the same as waking up."

"Who says I was sedated?"

"Who are you kidding? I knew when you were stoned in high school. Glassy eyes, stupid grin. You thought you were an amusing fellow. Like last night, and you weren't."

"I'm sorry. I was just playing."

"You were being a stoned jerk. What are you taking—OxyContin? Vicodin? God help us, some pharmaceutical cocktail you made up on your own?"

"You want me to be brave and suck it up?" I square up at the table and slap my right hand on the surface. "Right now, I can feel *both* hands in front of me on the table. Only the one on the left is all hot needles."

I pick up a knife and stab at my missing hand, the blade sticking in the table's surface. Dad stares at it.

"I was going to suggest medical marijuana," he says softly. "Instead of that chemical crap. Weber uses it. Awful arthritis, pain, can't sleep."

"You want me to smoke pot?"

"It would be preferable to whatever boozy combination of pills you're taking."

"Sorry about the table," I whisper.

"Pretty sure your old doctor's still in town. I can take you for a prescription."

"Dr. Mittman's a pediatrician."

Dad shrugs, a silent *so what?* as Mom returns from feeding their alligator. Without comment, she plucks the blade from the table with the practiced flair of a circus knife thrower, setting it in the sink.

PATIENTS

I'm easily the tallest patient in Dr. Mittman's waiting room and Dad the oldest parent by decades, extremes that in other cultures might elicit awe or respect but here in a pediatrician's office simply render us more freakish than usual to kids and parents alike. Thumbing one-handed through an issue of *Sports Illustrated Kids*, I have to admit I'm curious whether LeBron James could in fact outrun an ostrich, while Dad just found the wishbone in the greenhouse in his issue of *Highlights*. I have no doubt he'd have made more amazing discoveries, but we're invited inside.

Dr. Mittman was probably in his thirties when I last saw him, and here he is in his sixties, and I can't help but wonder what his life has been like in between, as he must be speculating what might have happened to my arm. So like any good pediatrician, he asks Dad.

"Car accident," Dad replies, willing to admit to a third person what he hasn't yet acknowledged to me. "Awful. Bones too damaged, arteries crushed, couldn't save it."

Dr. Mittman checks the pulse in my good hand. "How's the pain?"

"Bad, I think. He's taking Vicodin."

"I'm right here," I declare, and the doctor sticks a thermometer under my tongue.

"How long has he been on it? You have to be careful with that stuff. Just reclassified as a Schedule II drug because of its addictive properties."

"We were hoping to switch him to medical marijuana. I've heard good things."

"Can be," Dr. Mittman muses, tugging down on the bags under my eyes. "But also tricky, especially figuring the dosages." He removes the thermometer and checks it. "No temperature. That's good. We need to watch for signs of infection. Is he sleeping?"

Before I can answer he probes the inside of my mouth with a tongue depressor. "Aahh . . ."

"Aahhhhh . . ."

"Sleeps a lot, but at different times of the day."

"That's sometimes an indication that he's not getting a full night's sleep." He checks for swollen glands in my neck. "Medical marijuana might help there too."

He finishes and hands me a lollipop.

"He can't be all doped up, though," Dad cautions. "He needs to be alert when he goes back to school." Before Dr. Mittman can ask, *What grade is he in?*, Dad explains, "He's a teacher."

I stick the lollipop in my mouth and swing my feet while Dr. Mittman explains the virtues of medical marijuana to Dad, how it's available in many different strains, each genetically engineered for the individual purpose of alleviating pain, anxiety, nausea, sleeplessness, and other conditions; there are even varieties that maintain alertness. On our way back through the waiting room, I resist the urge to high-five the other kids as I pass them with my pot prescription tucked into my shirt pocket.

Dad drives me to The Hemp Collective (THC), conveniently located near the five corners where the Four Corners sits, so he can go have coffee with his pals while I step inside this wondrous emporium of reality-altering substances. The shabby, caged anteroom I have to pass through for security belies the wonder that awaits within.

Display cases and rows of shelves hold dozens of large glass jars fit for housing brains (one of them is even labeled "Abby Normal"), containing instead an array of pungent, colorful knots of marijuana buds. Along a far wall is another case set up like a miniature greenhouse where tiny pot plants just begin to sprout under LED grow lights; on the opposite wall is a case containing various "means by which to take the medication," as described by the bearded bud tender, meaning pipes, bongs, and vaporizers. Behind the counter, employees dutifully roll joints while others carefully weigh and sort fat buds of pot. They're knowledgeable, eager, and polite, with a pharmacist's efficiency and sommelier's panache. I'm quickly brought up to speed on the sweet science of medical marijuana:

- There are two varieties of cannabis, *sativa* and *indica* (as well as hybrids of both):
  - *Cannabis sativa* affects the brain and central nervous system, and is helpful in alleviating anxiety, depression, and chronic pain;
  - *Cannabis indica* primarily affects the body and muscular system, and is best used for acute pain, sedation, nausea, and as a muscle relaxant.
- There are scores of different strains of medical marijuana, with names like Kush Hour, Marley's Ghost, Brainspotting, and the apparently fearless-of-litigation Skywalker.
- You can smoke it straight, cool it in water, or vaporize it.
- It's available in edible form, from cookies to soft drinks, organic powder you can drink like cocoa to cheesy-delicious cannabis goldfish; there is marijuana butter you can spread on a sandwich, THC tincture you can pepper a steak with, infused olive oil for your salad.
- You can even apply it like lip gloss, or rub it on a sore neck in lotion form.

• Stores offer free gifts for first visits, will *beat any advertised price*, have a "Happy Hour" (M–F 2–4P 10% Off), and *Wheel of Fortune* spin-giveaways with every "donation" (since they can't legally give away a controlled substance).

• There is all manner of cannabis merchandise and apparel to be purchased, for personal use or as gifts, from T-shirts, hoodies, and hats to mugs, mouse pads, and license-plate holders. (I can only imagine that the latter might invite closer inspection, and how a traffic cop might react to a pulled-over motorist wearing a cannabis hat and hoodie and drinking from a cannabis mug.)

On the drive home, I clutch the hemp bag containing my new bong, glass pipe, portable vaporizer, butane torch, rolled joints, and an assortment of fat golden buds to my chest like a boy who just got everything he wanted for Christmas.

"Promise you're not going to make me regret this."

"You can't regret the things you do, only the things you *don't* do," I enlighten Dad, immediately regretting that I didn't phrase it like Yoda.

"Semantics," Dad grumbles. "You can flip any decision into a negative—*I regret having children* could just as easily be *I regret not remaining childless.*"

"I got this for you," I say, slipping a trucker's cap bearing a giant pot leaf insignia onto his head. "Wait—you regret having children?"

"Only. Right. Now."

THINGS YOU CAN'T DO STONED WITH ONE ARM

Roll a joint

Hold a bong and light it

Clean seeds on an album
  cover

Hang more black-light
  posters

Remove a large pan of
  brownies from the oven

Eat frozen ice cream

Make a peanut butter
  sandwich

Open a can of tuna

Uncork a bottle of
  wine

Shotgun a beer

Pass a sobriety test by
  touching your nose with
  both hands

Masturbate while holding
  a magazine

Hold an alligator's jaws
  shut*

*I'm not sure why I attempted this, but it nearly cost me my good hand. The dim mental state and lack of coordination that accompany the condition of being stoned renders impossible already difficult multitasking. Not to mention decision making. On the plus side, you don't care as much.

JACKIE

With nothing but time on my hand, I spend much of the next several days smoking different strains of medical marijuana and evaluating each one's efficacy against the scientific standard of Jackie's retro black-light poster, with its six gradually melting "Stoned Agin" faces. The "body high" of the *indica* generally keeps me in the general range of face #2, just beginning to wilt . . . while the *sativa*—which generates more of a "head high"—takes me further. Currently, I'm significantly less stoned than the face in the final panel but dangerously close to face #5, beginning to pool. The goal I've set myself is to hover consistently between face #3 or #4—*really* stoned, but short of face #6, with eyes melted into a puddle staring up at a head caved in on itself. (I'm able to quickly surpass the pleasant buzz of face #1 like a man hopping an inconvenient puddle.)

I also find myself staring like a cat fascinated by its own reflection in the mirror, struck by heady insights like *I only have one arm but technically two armpits,* and that if I have a heart attack I will not feel the symptoms in my left arm, like Pa Kent did in *Superman: The Movie.*

It seems absurd to think I might be capable of holding some kind of job in this perpetually buzzy state. Even were I capable of some kind of menial, one-handed work, the probability of falling into some kind of grinding factory machinery seems inordinately high; as for returning to my former teaching job, with my train of thought so easily derailed, making it all the way through a lesson seems improbable. As if to prove this deficiency of focus Dad honks impatiently from outside, reminding me that he's waiting while I came up here to get . . . who the hell knows? Something lost to memory that must go ungotten.

I stagger out to the car and we drive in a silence that makes the ringing in my ears even more pronounced, so I turn on the radio and wait to hear the voice of Sunny Lee tell me something I never knew or even thought of, about the physics of soup or the anatomy of trees or the secret life of a camel. Or, in this case, cat guts:

Every teenage boy wants to be a guitar god . . . but do you have the guts for it? This is Sunny Lee, with The Sunny Side.

Stringed instruments are famously made from something called "catgut"—that actually has nothing to do with cats! But before you get too comfortable, animal lovers, catgut traditionally comes from . . . other animal guts—usually sheep or goat intestines, but also cattle, hogs, horses, or mules. The intestines are cleaned of fat and steeped in water, and then again in lye, before being drawn out and twisted into strings, dried, and polished to a specific diameter. Talk about "plucky"! Who knew intestines could be so resilient? Maybe that's how the phrase "He's got guts" came to be a euphemism for toughness.

Anyway, most modern musical instruments produced today use strings made from synthetic materials, like steel or polymer, although gut strings remain the preferred choice for many classical and baroque players. Somehow, knowing that is going to make my next classical concert a little . . . harder to stomach.

I imagine being the young "guitar god" of whom Sunny spoke, thrashing steel strings with my right hand and deftly skimming frets with my left in an act of seduction no woman could resist, willing to abandon a life of groupies in favor of fidelity with Sunny Lee, whom I love more deeply every time I hear her voice.

Completely lost in amorous, two-handed fantasy, I'm unaware of whatever it was Dad just said, now punctuated with a familiar sigh and then more silence—the customary expression of disappointment by dads everywhere. It's seventy-five miles to Decatur Airport, and the malleability of time as experienced under a combination of drugs has me feeling every long minute of the scheduled three-hour round trip.

Against Dad's wishes I've continued to experiment with Vicodin, noticing that taking an odd number seems to have a negative effect: two is perfect, and I can handle four, but three or even one make me nauseous. In keeping to an even-numbered dosage, I observe that taking four Vicodin gives me the ability to concentrate on one thing at the center of my field of vision to the exclusion of all others, like looking through a pinhole, everything but the center rendered a fuzzy blur I like to think of as "bluzzy." I find this useful when I want to focus on a single thing only, like a beautiful woman walking down the street, or when I wish things around me to disappear, like now.

Jackie has arrived, all the way from California, bursting into tears at the sight of me and drawing everyone's attention as if I had just slapped her with my good arm.

I pull Jackie close to me with my arm and whisper, "There, there."

"Wh-where, where?" she sniffs back, and we both start to laugh, and that only makes her cry harder.

Behind her I watch a barista pull coffee and a skycap tug bags off his dolly while a TSA agent pats down a traveler with both hands, realizing those are three more jobs I can't do. Dad stands far away from us, so distant from the emotional fray that I don't need four Vicodin to reduce him to a pinpoint.

"Daddy!" Jackie runs to take hold of him with both arms and starts to cry all over again.

"What are you crying for?" I shout over to them. "He has two arms."

"I must be jet-lagged," Jackie sighs as we drift outside to the car.

"Hey, bro." Her husband Steve's abbreviated greeting carries no camaraderie. "Lend a hand with the bags?"

I turn to face him. "What?"

"Kidding!" He spews foamy laughter. "Hey, you want us to ignore it? Wouldn't it be worse if we pretended it didn't happen?"

"All I can say is aim for somewhere in the middle."

Back when Jackie had emigrated from Paris to Los Angeles, I worried that she was going to wind up married to some rich entertainment industry asshole. Instead, she picked a completely different kind of asshole, one without the redeeming quality of monetary success. Steve is long, lean, and dumb, as if some god-like being took an average-size man and stretched him, only in doing so pinched the head too hard resulting in minor brain damage. Measured against Jackie's type-A personality, he falls deeper in the alphabet, perhaps not as far as Z but no higher than U-V—as a frequency, beyond notice. It's impossible to know what drew these two together—the magnetism of opposites, the complementary gaps that fit into each other with jigsaw puzzle perfection, lingering childhood issues that continue to hammer the self-esteem of one while blinding the other to his true dumb self. If love is a mystery, these two are like digging up Stonehenge to find the Sphinx on Easter Island.

Steve sits behind Dad in the car and refuses to slide over so that Jackie could sit there and she and I might make diagonal eye contact as we pepper the long drive home with uneasy, intermittent conversation. As Jackie trudges around the car to climb in the other side, I get the impression that Steve's usual position on cooperation is to withhold it. We stop to pay the parking attendant, who I can't help but notice faces traffic while we face opposite, his left side against Dad's as he accepts the money, left-handed.

Toll is paid and barrier lifted and Dad slams the car into drive and leaps for the street at a speed that thrusts all of us back into our seats. This is no Lincoln Mark IV, but Dad seems determined that the four of us should spend as little time as possible trapped together for the journey back home.

Twenty minutes later my buzz is wearing off, making it harder to disappear into bluzzy oblivion, so I break the previous nineteen minutes of silence.

"So, how are things in sunny California?" God, I sound like someone's uncle.

"Busy!" Jackie practically shrieks, startled back to her usual heightened state of anxious urgency. "It never stops. I don't have a second for myself."

Jackie is a marketing director at a Jenga-like vertically integrated international conglomerate that sells toothpaste, soap, deodorant, shampoo, diapers, detergent, razor blades—products the civilized world has come to consider indispensable, although in the carnage of a postapocalyptic dystopia we'd manage without any of them (although you might be willing to trade all of them for a good roll of toilet paper). I imagine in the course of her day she multitasks like a cartoon octopus running a day care center for fish babies.

"I have my hand full too," I reply, and Dad applies greater pressure to the accelerator.

Steve stops poking at his cell phone long enough to ask, "Can we stop?"

"I'd like to keep moving," Dad says, fearing the inertia of a body at rest.

"Gotta drain the monster," Steve insists, so Dad pulls into the next rest stop we see and remains behind the wheel with the patience of an INDYCAR driver waiting for his pit crew to finish.

Tucked under my good arm, Jackie leans with me against the car while Dad occasionally revs the engine.

"Really? 'Drain the monster'?"

"Don't start," she warns me. "I've heard it ten thousand times, and each one is like nails on a blackboard."

"You know we don't use blackboards anymore, right? Although I admit 'Nails on a dry-erase board' doesn't have the same lilt to it."

"Do you think you'll go back to your school?"

"Hard to say," I say without difficulty, knowing I will not. Not that I'm ready to bravely face an uncertain future; just self-aware enough to know that, thus halved, any attempt at who I used to be is doomed to the humiliation of a baseball player on Old-Timers' Day swinging for the fences.

"Have you thought about what else you might do?"

"Just in the past half hour I've ruled out barista, skycap, TSA agent, toll-booth attendant, and personal chauffeur."

Steve exits with a satisfied look and a twelve-pack of beer, and before he can get back in the car Jackie jumps into his place in the seat behind Dad, a little too pleased by this minor victory. We're back on the road at rocket speed to make up for the lost time of the pit stop, and Steve pops the top off a beer bottle with the bottle opener he carries on his key ring like a badge of stupid.

"Hey! An open bottle in a car is illegal," Dad announces.

"So's driving eighty in a sixty-five," Steve counters, and as if to remedy the problem Dad pushes the needle to eighty-five, and three beers later, we're home.

Except for the occasional holidays we both tried to avoid when we could, Jackie and I have never lived at home together even temporarily as adults. When I was fifteen she left for college; by the time she'd graduated and returned home, I was already gone, and on my return from college Jackie had already moved to California. Two thousand miles and twenty-five years is a lot of distance. Our relationship as people remains arrested as teenagers, trapped like a bug in amber.

Which is another reason why Steve is such a disappointment. In high school, Jackie ran through a series of cool boyfriends who feigned tolerance of me, thinking it would appeal to the primitive nurturing instinct they'd been led by hygiene class to expect in the inscrutable female of the species. A senior she dated would even high-five me if we passed in the hallways, and not even the greeting "Little Man" could diminish that skin-slapping transference of cool.

"Is my room just the way I left it?" Jackie asks as we enter the unlocked front door.

"Only if you left it looking like a storage shed," I warn her. "You're both staying in Dad's room. He moved to the den."

Jackie drifts through the hallway, absently scanning the photos on the wall like an amnesia patient trying to remember what any of this might have to do with her.

"Gotta drain the monster," Steve says again as if for the first time. "Bathroom?"

"Right at the top of the stairs," I smile.

Steve clomps upstairs just behind Dad dutifully playing bellhop. I can count to five before . . .

"Jesus fucking Christ on a stick!"

Jackie rushes back from the hallway. "Did you tell him about Ali?"

"Forgot," I grin.

"One arm or two, you're still a jerk." She races upstairs as Steve tumbles out backward, pants around his ankles.

"*Kway-UR* to have you home."

Jackie and Steve are "exhausted" from their journey and need to lie down, despite the fact that it's technically only two in the afternoon to their West Coast–set internal clocks. Minutes later as Dad and I settle in front of the television, the unmistakable sounds of clumsy lovemaking rain upon us from overhead and I can't help but think: this is not a man who can't keep his hands off his wife; this is a man who takes pleasure from the discomfort he knows he's generating with each plunge into the daughter of the man in whose bed he's doing the plunging.

"We're out of Fleischmann's," Dad announces, grabs his coat and is gone.

When they emerge hours later, Steve catches my eye in the upstairs bathroom, a proud smirk, raised eyebrow, and knowing nod wrestling for control of his face, as if banging my sister in my father's bed is the bond-forging event our relationship has been missing until now. His expression changes suddenly when he realizes what I'm doing—feeding leftover chicken drumettes to Dad's alligator—and he continues down the stairs.

Jackie enters and crouches next to me, gently stroking Ali and avoiding my eyes as strenuously as Steve sought to offend them.

"Hot wings?" she scoffs.

"Drumettes," I correct her. "Washed off the hot sauce. They should just taste like chicken . . . so should Ali, come to think of it."

"God, it stinks in here!"

"Shh! He can hear you . . ."

"I can't believe how big he got!"

"That is four feet of placid alligator," I marvel. "But you don't have to tell Steve about the 'placid' part. His healthy fear of the alligator is the only thing that makes me think he's not so dumb."

"You don't have to like Steve—"

"Okay, then, the pressure's off."

"But you don't have to hate him, either."

Even with her eyes averted I can see them welling with tears, and I feel worse for someone other than myself for the first time since the accident. "I'll aim for somewhere in the middle."

She turns her face toward me and smiles, "That would be great. We're in a little bit of a rough patch. He's having a hard time at work."

Steve is a meter reader for PG&E, a job that, here in the twenty-first century, seems as unnecessary as milkman, lamplighter, or sextant operator. Respecting their "rough patch," I should be kind enough not to point that out, but I do.

"He drives around counting energy usage. Imagine your cell phone provider sending someone to your house to look at your phone every month to see how many minutes you used before they could bill you. As a job, that's pretty useless." Whatever tears might have welled seconds ago freeze in her now-icy glare. Wisely, I soften my stance. "I'm just saying I know how it feels to be useless."

Her glare wilts, no match for my status as object of pity, an awesome power I should probably use for good, not evil, but know I'm going to milk like a dairy farmer.

"Steve wants to stay in and nap," she cheers me up. "I thought it would be fun for you, me, and Dad to eat out."

"It'll be fun for two of us. Hey, do you want to get stoned and stare at your black-light poster before dinner?"

Half a joint of Grandmaster Stash later, Dad has to pull us away from the poster in the attic, and we titter all the way to Dim

Sum & Then Some, where Jackie and I order too much food and somehow manage to finish all of it. Dad pays the check and pockets the pen and we head out into the night, Jackie once again slipping under my good arm and clinging tightly to me, and she doesn't let go until we're home.

LAGGED

With Jackie passed out, I make my way to the kitchen. Dad is also asleep in the glow of the television, awash in unwatched sports highlights. I pull open the freezer door and spy Caramel Swirl Crunch, instantly certain in the excellence of any flavor that both swirls and crunches. I plunk it on the counter and fish around the drawer for the proper tool to excavate the swirly crunchy goodness from within, settling on the spork half of a set of giant salad tongs. I sit the container inside a drawer and then close it, wedging the ice cream tight enough to attempt pulling the lid off when Steve totters in.

"Can't sleep. All kinds of fucked up from the time diff. Here, give me that."

He gently takes the carton of ice cream from me, places it in the microwave, and sets the timer for twenty-two seconds, which I assume is another labor saver (his finger can punch the number "two" twice without having to make its way all the way down to the "zero" twenty seconds would require). As the already swirled dessert spins some more Steve watches quietly, his energy claimed by jet lag, and it occurs to me that he'd be a better person to be around if only he could fly every day. The microwave beeps and we soon face each other across the kitchen counter with mugs of ice cream between us.

"If you wanna sell some of that med mar, let me know."

(Ah, there he is.)

"You want to try some?" I offer with all the sincerity of a five-year-old who's been told to share his toys with the dim boy next door.

"I don't smoke that shit. Makes me stupid."

As luck would have it, my tongue is too frozen under a swirly gob to reply.

"Might help you sleep," I finally offer. "They engineer it now so precisely—the place I go to has twenty-two different strains. I have stuff that makes you calm and other blends that keep you alert. They even make one that has no psychoactive effect—it doesn't get you stoned. I don't have that one."

"Like nonalcoholic beer. What a waste of fucking time."

"Decaf."

"Women who don't fuck."

"All right, all done here," I take my half-empty mug to the sink.

"Anything still open?"

"Like what?"

"Bar?"

"Hard to know. Last time I pulled an all-nighter here, I was twenty-two."

"Well, let's go see what's what."

"I don't even know what that means."

"Yeah, you do. You just have to stop being such a smart-ass."

"My ass is no smarter than yours."

"Then let's go ass up into the world, and see what's what."

Our unassuming midwestern village offers exactly one option for late-night drinking, the Loading Zone, where said drinking is done with remarkable efficiency. It smells of beer and sawdust and the booths are almost dark enough to disguise the seats clotted with tiny buds of burst upholstery. This isn't a place for the sophistication of a martini or the frivolity of blender drinks; it's a beer-and-a-shot kind of place, and the shots are nameless, neither Jack nor Jägermeister. Even ordering a Sam Adams instead of a Bud earns me a look of disdain from the bartender; I consider asking him, *Then why the hell do you serve it?* but the answer might be as simple as *To weed out the ass wipes* while he beats me with a cue stick, so I don't.

This is a practiced lot of late-night drinkers, hunched over glasses like guard dogs and pasty faced from a preferred avoidance of daylight: out-of-work townies drinking their emergency funds, blue-collar guys who'll be piloting forklifts in a few hours, criminals meeting after a heist to divvy up the loot while planning how to bump each other off. And Fred Weber.

"Can't sleep worth a damn," Mr. Weber confides when we slide into the booth on either side of him.

"I thought you were taking medical marijuana."

"Does the goddamn pot barista tell everyone my business?"

"Sorry! My dad. You're right; he shouldn't have told me, and I shouldn't have brought it up."

"Forget it," he waves me off. "I've been your father's lawyer for thirty-seven years; if we have any secrets, it's only because we've forgotten what the hell they are."

The guy at the next table coughs up a thumb-sized wad of phlegm and spews it into his empty beer glass. Now that he has our attention and we have his, he stares for a very long time at the place where my arm used to be, as if trying to process the information—is it gone, or merely tucked behind me, or some other optical illusion, or yet another alcoholic hallucination? It's why I don't like leaving the house, aside from breakfast at the Four Corners and the occasional trip to Dim Sum, both places where they've grown accustomed to me. But I'm especially uncomfortable here, where even two arms might provide inadequate defense against the unpredictable, and the mere act of causing someone to question his own eyes could be enough to incite confrontation. Or in this case, cause the man to rise from his table and wobble to sit at the bar.

"Anyway," Mr. Weber continues, "I had to stop. It helped me sleep, but it also made me stupid."

"What did I say?" Steve beams at this affirmation as if he were a quantum physicist who just had his theory of infinite universes confirmed by multiple versions of himself.

"Have you tried Sleepapalooza?" I produce a pair of marijuana cakes packaged like Ring Dings from my drug purse, something I don't need to carry but for the fact that I enjoy the company of its tacit illicitness made legal by prescription.

"Ate so many I put on eight pounds." Mr. Weber fishes in his own small leather bag, and Dreamboat, Happy Nap, and Sandmancipation spill out on the table, peaceful marijuana-induced sleep packaged with the shorthand of hoary clichés: cartoon character in a nightcap, sawing wood in a thought balloon, sheep jumping a fence, and lots of Zs. "Two of these make me dizzy. I can't remember which two. Last thing I need is to fall and break a hip. They should put you down right then, right there, like a racehorse. It'd have more dignity than what inevitably follows."

It all proves too much for Steve, who escapes to the bar.

"In the Merchant Marine, if you gave me a single star in the sky and a horizon, I could navigate ten thousand miles of empty ocean. Now I can't even get to the bathroom before I piss myself."

Mr. Weber stares at my non-arm, perhaps aware that if his diminishment happened over time—an accumulation of small disappointments that built up like hair in a drain—mine did not. He pats me on the shoulder, and it feels good—he's the first person to touch it in a completely normal act, as if it didn't matter.

"I sometimes wonder what it would be like to lose my left leg. I'd be like two-thirds of a person vertically," I note, mentally conjuring the image.

I can see I've made Mr. Weber uncomfortable and am actually grateful for the distraction of Steve's return as he shoves his way back to the table with three shots of something brown.

"This is what grandmothers do, get together and compare meds. Put that shit away, do a shot, and watch the titties on TV."

The titties on TV belong to the competitors in a decades-old wet T-shirt contest on a grainy VHS tape playing over the bar. If anyone gave it any thought at all, they'd realize the current state of those breasts are as worn and stretched as the plastic polyethylene tape on which they've been immortalized for future generations. But the Loading Zone is not a thoughtful place, and no one seems to mind.

"Words to live by," Mr. Weber swallows his shot, and before long, we're all drunk as pirates.

I wake up in the morning on someone's couch, and since Mr. Weber is staring down at me, I assume it's his.

"Well, that was pretty dumb," he says, and by the look of the bloody gauze on my nub, I'm forced to agree.

It's hard to tell what time it is by the diffuse light coming through the frosted windows of Fred Weber's bathroom, but I can hear Sunny Lee on his radio telling how to make a battery out of a watermelon—

And you think a car battery is tough to lug around . . . !

—so I know it's just before nine in the morning. Steve is asleep in Mr. Weber's bathtub, and I can't help but think that if we were home I'd be looking over his gator-chewed remains without remorse. Mr. Weber gently removes the gauze pad from my arm and I'm face-to-face with a scabby, cartoonish sea serpent. Even by the low standards of tattoos, this one is exceedingly moronic. And it writhes like a dying monster when Mr. Weber pours peroxide on it, although the shrieks are mine.

"Jackie's gonna kill me," Steve stirs and moans behind me. "She said if I got another tattoo, she'd cut it off."

"I guess I did mine the other way around."

Steve peels back the gauze pad on his calf and is immediately pleased, somehow impressed by the cartoon cherub-devil holding a pitchfork and urinating on his calf muscle. "Hey, pretty cool!"

"What made you think this was a good idea?"

"Whoa, don't blame me. Weber passed out in the backseat and you wouldn't let me wake him up. I couldn't just drive around—I was hammered!"

"So you found the only all-night tattoo parlor in town."

"You were up for it."

"I probably would have been 'up for' running with the bulls at Pamplona or being fired from a catapult."

"Yeah, well, we didn't do any of that," he says as he stands and urinates, loud and long, into the toilet. "Aahhhh . . . a good piss is better than sex. All that work and you shoot your load in, what, seconds?" He explains. "This right here is a minute of ecstasy."

Mr. Weber leans over and pours peroxide on Steve's penis, and he shrieks louder than I did.

"Ow! What the fuck?"

"That's for the prostitute."

"I wasn't with a prostitute!"

"Well, you could have been. I was asleep in the car." Mr. Weber puts away the peroxide and grins at me. "Thanks for letting me sleep. Feel pretty good today! I'll call your dad and let him know his boys are okay."

Trumping the tattoo, risk of infection, possible alcohol poisoning, venereal disease we might have contracted from the prostitute we weren't with, or the narrowly averted death in a fiery car wreck we managed to avoid, the idea that Dad might think of Steve and me as "his boys" is by far the worst prospect of my morning. And then the tinnitus kicks in, blessedly reducing Steve's further protests to the background.

CAROMS

If there had been any concern over our "missing" status overnight—fear for our well-being, bargaining for our safe return—it's gone, vanished like a magician's assistant in an empty box. In its place are split levels of fury (shrieks from upstairs as Jackie shreds Steve behind a closed door inadequate to its task) and Zen (Mom's thunderclap break indicates she's working out her feelings in the basement). In between, Dad sulks in silent fatherly disappointment in front of *SportsCenter*.

I head downstairs to find the more familiar Mom of my youth, leaning over the table, still all skinny limbs and angles, fingers dusty with chalk but absent the yellow traces of those long-ago cigarettes. She slams the one ball into the nine ball and it caroms into the corner pocket nearest her and just like that, it's game over. I gather all the solid balls in the triangle in an easy one-handed sweep, pluck the nine ball from the pocket and add it; forcing them into a diamond is harder—even the two tiny hands of a small boy are preferable to one adult hand—but Mom waits patiently, quietly chalking her stick. I lift the rack and Mom leans in and with barely a look scatters the balls, sending the nine ball into the side pocket. Game over.

"One of us is just as good as ever," I poke, struggling with the triangle to gather all the balls again.

"Don't do that," she says. "It's bullshit, and I won't have it."

"I'm sorry to be such a disappointment."

"You don't mean that. What you're sorry about is the discomfort you think we're all feeling, but then you go ahead and point out you're not as good as you used to be. It's bullshit, and you should stop. But that's up to you. It's not going to become my problem."

"So this"—I wave my bandaged nub—"isn't disappointing?"

"Only to someone who's foolish enough to allow themselves to be disappointed by others. Yes, like your father. And your sister, who hasn't figured out that it's impossible to change another person's behavior. We can't . . . but I can control how it affects me, so I make sure it doesn't. Now, are you going to rack those or not?"

No one calls bullshit like Mom. It's completely without judgment, like an attorney summarizing inarguable statements of fact in her closing argument and leaving the opposing counsel to squirm, knowing he has nothing to counter with but transparent glibness.

"Look what you just did," I grin, scooping the balls into a perfect diamond. "You turned me from a guy just standing here to one who racked your balls. That makes you wrong about not being able to change someone's behavior."

"If only there was a future in bullshit, Aaron," she says, "you'd be unstoppable."

She leans in and breaks, sinking the two and the eight. She circles the table, surveying her next shot and as she passes, I lean in, yearning for a pat on the head that's not forthcoming.

"Children are inherently disappointing. As parents, we watch you disappear and be replaced all the time. That squishy pink baby who gurgled and smiled at me, her eyes trying to focus?"

She lines up the one ball and the distant seven against the rail, and drops them both into the far corner.

"Gone," she continues without judgment, "replaced by a preschooler with a lisp, and then a ten-year-old with ballerina aspirations. And both of those vanished into a teenager who alternated between aloof in front of her friends and clingy when they weren't around."

She eyes the five-six-nine balls in a cluster and slams the three into them, dropping the five and leaving the nine dangling over a corner pocket like a damsel in distress.

"I've watched every version of you and your sister disappear into adulthood, and however wonderful as human beings you might continue to become, all those other versions of you are as gone as a dead child. I won't see them anymore."

I ponder the dead children Jackie and I used to be, but all Mom sees is the vulnerability of the nine ball hanging on a precipice. But the three ball, which needs to be struck first, hides behind the six. Mom has to play a deep carom off the far rail to make it work, a difficult shot even at the height of her game.

"I watched you become a man with one less arm . . . and today he's gone, replaced by a man with a tattoo where that arm used to be. More bullshit. And there's some version of you in the offing that's bound to disappoint anyone who lets him. But it's not going to be me."

Instead of targeting the far rail she raises her cue stick vertically, taking careful aim straight down on the cue ball. She strikes it, squeezing it with a whirling backspin that draws it around the others and back to the three ball, kissing it into the nine, which drops into the pocket.

"I thought trick shots were bullshit."

"It seemed appropriate," Mom replies, laying her cue stick across the table and giving me a gentle pat on my head as she passes on her way upstairs.

RAMIFICATIONS

Things remain tense over dinner, the silence so thick you could stab it with a fork—which, as is apparent from her demeanor, is exactly what Jackie would like to do to her husband. For his part, Steve is surprisingly docile, a dog who knows he did something bad even if he cannot understand why, only that at the first sign of trouble there's a rolled-up newspaper waiting for him. Or a fork.

"They say proportionately, dinosaurs had the smallest brains of any creature," Mom speaks up. "Imagine that. Those majestic beasts, lumbering around the jungle, enormous in stature and the most powerful beings on Earth, but barely able to think. Colossal in size and ignorance."

Steve sighs deeply and I swear, Jackie's fork is poised to deliver a deathblow.

"Let's call it what it is," Dad offers by way of clarification. "Stupid."

"He could get gangrene, and there's nothing left to cut off!"

"Nobody's getting gangrene," I declare to Jackie with the supreme confidence of a man about to succumb to gangrene.

"It's just nature, is all I'm saying," Mom continues. "When the big, stupid *Tyrannosaurus rex*—or *two* of them—knock over a thicket of trees, or eat the helpless baby dinosaur, you don't get mad at them. That's what they do! They're not acting with malice or anger, or even forethought. It's simply the act of a dumb, unthinking creature. So when we expect them to behave differently, we're disappointed. And that makes us unhappy."

Jackie *stabs* at her food.

"Or angry. The key to not being those things is to manage expectations and to accept the natural limitations of things. Pass the potatoes."

"*How could you let him get that?*" Jackie finally shouts at Steve.

"Whoa! I'm not the boss of him."

"*And who does that?*" Jackie shrieks. "Who would tattoo a . . . a . . . a stump?"

"Are you saying people with stumps don't have the same rights as non-stumpy people?" I object. "That doesn't seem fair."

"Shut up! Isn't it illegal to give a drunk person a tattoo?"

"You can't tell me to shut up and keep asking questions."

"Be nice to your brother, he's been through a lot," Mom mediates. "Also, he's stupid."

"Thanks, Mom."

"Have some more broccoli. It's a superfood, good for your tiny brain."

I accept the bowl and immediately pass it to Steve.

"I wish I could shed some light on this, but I remember nothing after leaving the bar," I strain to recall. "Actually, I don't remember leaving the bar either."

"Great!" Jackie enthuses. "We can add alcohol blackouts to your litany of recent problems."

"Or you can stop keeping score. No one asked you to come here."

What follows isn't the good kind of silence—a quiet, peaceful respite—but the kind that immediately precedes explosive confrontation or foreshadows lifelong estrangement. As if sensing this, Dad attempts to redirect Jackie's fire to a different target.

"Who drove last night?" he asks no one in particular. "Weber?"

"I did," Steve boasts.

Jackie's head swivels, an angry tank turret. "Really."

"Whoa, I wasn't near as fucked up as those two. I remember everything."

"Bring me up to speed," I urge him. "There's not enough liquor under Dad's sink to make me want a tattoo. What the hell happened?"

"You weren't going to, but then the tattoo artist started talking about tribal tattoos and manhood rituals and how some cultures use them to mark life changes, and some other shit. And then you both creamed your jeans over this Sunny Lee chick."

"*We did?*"

"Jesus God," Dad exhales.

"Who's Sunny Lee?" Mom perks up, genuinely interested.

"*What?*" Jackie shrieks. "I went to school with her. What does she have to do with anything?"

"You went to school with Sunny Lee?" I'm stunned.

"The tattoo artist was a big fan of this *Sunny Side Up*, or whatever the fuck it is," Steve remembers perfectly. "You were like a couple of girls sharing lipstick. Then we all did shots, and he got to work. You went first."

"It's called *The Sunny Side*."

"Whatever," Steve says, bored now.

"She's on the radio," Dad explains to Jackie. "Weird facts, science, history, that kind of thing."

"I'm in love with her," I announce.

"Do you even know her?"

"No! But she's your friend; you can introduce me."

"I haven't seen her in twenty years! She barely knows me!"

"You're in love with her but you never met her?" Mom finds this unusual.

"I love everything about her. Her voice, her dry humor. And she's smart. Is she cute? I think I'd like to marry her."

"If she's so smart, she's probably not into guys who drunkenly tattoo sea serpents on their stumps," Mom suggests.

"Really, 'guys,' plural? Like there's more than one of me."

"It does seem pretty unlikely," Dad muses.

"Mom!" Jackie shouts, desperate. "Do something!"

"This is exactly what I'm talking about, sweetie. You're letting the dinosaurs make you crazy."

My sister knows Sunny Lee *my sister knows Sunny Lee* MY SISTER KNOWS SUNNY LEE! Fuck, my nub hurts.

I'm smoking Somnambublast and plugged into podcasts of *The Sunny Side* archives—about Viking sunstones, mummy prosthetics, molecules that make music, and cocoons made of mucus—so I don't hear Steve as he clomps up the attic stairs. But when I see him, lugging blanket and pillow, it's not hard to figure out he's been banished.

"The basement might be more comfortable. We can lay a mattress on top of the pool table."

"I slept in a bathtub last night; you think the floor's gonna bother me?"

"Bathtub! We have one of those. Why didn't I think of that?"

"Give me some of that," he says, groping for my pipe. "If I'm gonna be accused of being stupid, I might as well be stupid."

He takes a long toke before I tell him, "That won't make you sleep. It's designed for alertness and may cause anxiety."

"Thanks for the fucking warning!"

"You didn't even ask. I could have been smoking angel dust laced with a laxative for all you knew."

"Anything else I should know?"

"If you find blood in your stool, call your doctor immediately."

I go back on earbuds and the botanically engineered alertness kicks in, heightening my appreciation of Sunny—the silkiness of her voice, the deep timbre that perfectly expresses intelligence and wry humor, the wonder of discovery:

Look! Up in the sky! It's a bird, it's a plane, it's a . . . grasshopper? Because the physiological constraints of muscle power are limited per kilogram of muscle, a grasshopper should not be able to hop nearly as far as he can—which is roughly the insect equivalent of leaping tall buildings! Researchers at the University of Cambridge discovered that Orthoptera caelifera overcome this limitation with an elastic apodeme, or tendon, anchored to the leg muscle. The use of elastic storage allows as much as seven times that of equivalent muscle—which is like a human throwing an arrow by hand instead of using a bow . . . and even Robin Hood couldn't make that work!

I can visualize it all perfectly: the super-enlarged image of the grasshopper under observation, its explosive slow-motion leap, the white-coated researchers in their white Cambridge lab . . . Sunny in a recording studio, headset on, lips wet from the bottle of water she sips to lubricate her voice, content smile from her little joke at the end. The audio engineer—as much in love with her as I am—gives her a thumbs-up, and she smiles warmly back, dark almond eyes sparkling with intelligence as she removes her headset and tosses her thick black hair, taking a final sip before recycling the bottle.

I want to run to wherever she is and take her in my arm.

Instead, I'm in my father's attic with Steve, who's videotaping me on his cell phone.

"What are you doing?"

"Cool room . . . taping it . . . maybe we can get you on one of those home-makeover shows."

"If it's so cool, why would I want to make it over?"

"No, you'd be the 'After.'"

"But there's no tape of 'Before.' Isn't that how these things work? Wouldn't they want to come in *before* and do the back-story: here's a one-armed guy who has to move back home with his father . . . let's see if we can make him a place where he won't want to hang himself or if he does, he matches the drapes?"

This seems to sink in but it's hard to tell with Steve. If there's any alertness behind his glass-dot eyes, it's difficult to discern.

He suddenly thrusts his phone at me. "Tape this." He pulls up his pant leg and shows off his newest tattoo, explaining that what he likes about it is the contrast of good and evil, that "Hot Stuff, the Little Devil," does good deeds to irritate real demons.

"Then why is he pissing on your leg?"

He shrugs. "Because it's easier to draw than a good deed?"

"You could have had him rescuing a cat out of a tree with his pitchfork."

I've always disliked the idea of tattoos—and now I have one—not because of any prudish Victorian looking-down-my-nose-through-a-monocle snobbery but because it demonstrates a lack of imagination, an inability to envision a future where one might not want, say, Hot Stuff pissing on one's leg. But Steve was a guy who barely thought even a moment ahead, about conse-quences or even simply a chain of events that might follow, as if in putting food in his mouth he was unaware that he might next chew and then swallow it.

Before I can object, Steve starts to expose and narrate the rest of his body parts, telling the fascinating tale behind each of his seven tattoos—where he got them, what they are, and what they mean:

- *Left Bicep:* Snake with a dagger through it. His first tattoo, and it's hard to argue with tradition.
- *Ankle:* war04, a calligraphic tribute to his dead friend Warren who drowned in 2004 (drunk, I'm guessing).
- *Inside Left Bicep:* An eagle eating a snake, which he got in Mexico and only later learned was the Mexican flag.

- *Shoulder Blade:* Stars and a crescent moon, matching tattoos he got with his then girlfriend but now feels is "a little wussy."
- *Right Bicep:* Barbed wire. No doubt to compensate for the above after the breakup.
- *Left Pectoral:* An eerily accurate portrait of Jackie, which was his last tattoo until now, and only the most obvious reason Jackie made him promise to stop.

Equally telling is what's missing: no religious iconography, historical figures, philosophers, or philosophy; no pretension of Chinese characters, which I'm pretty sure never mean what the tattoo artist says they mean but universally represent poor judgment; surprisingly, no hula girls, bathing beauties, topless mermaids, or Cherry Poptart; and thankfully, nothing on the small of his back. I'm so fascinated by all of it—what's there and what isn't, and my sister staring back at me from Steve's chest—that I don't even question when he takes the phone from me and says, "Now you."

As he records me on his phone I wiggle my nub and make up an insane story about a legendary sea serpent, Bob, who swam the seas when the earth was young and hated all humanity for throwing their excrement overboard from their creaky wooden vessels. Bob smashed Viking sailing ships and dragged their warriors to the briny depths where he played with their remains like Barbie dolls, until one day when a ship's cook named Evets, dim from an axe blow to the head as a lad, plunged a hot griddle into the beast's brain through Bob's eye, killing him, and then went back into the kitchen as if nothing had happened and made breakfast for everyone aboard the *Raging Scallop*.

"Wiggle it some more," Steve directs, and I do. He looks down at his phone. "Huh. Battery's dead."

"Just as well," I say, put my shirt back on, plug my earbuds in, and go back to *The Sunny Side*. I flick on the black light and Steve sets down his phone, drawn to the luminous poster like a child with the brain of a moth.

THINGS YOU COULD DO WITH A COOL BIONIC ARM

Punch through walls

Bend steel bars

Tear the door off a
    bank vault

Lift a car overhead

Stop a runaway
    locomotive

Catch a bullet

Crush diamonds into coal

Arm wrestle the
    Hulk

Launch projectiles

Fire a grappling hook

Shoot a laser

Hack a computer

Inject an immobilizing
    serum

Solder gun

Such an arm would probably be the ultimate weapon of a comic-book hero (no doubt dubbed "Armageddon"), and it should also be capable of small, intricate work, like threading circuits on a silicon chip, or etching a coded message on a grain of rice. But the tragic hero would trade it all for his own arm and hand that could feel things, like cold, or a woman's breast.

NICENESS

Overnight I dream about people I haven't seen in twenty years, as vivid now as then. All of us are missing an arm and it seems quite normal. We're in line at the school cafeteria and as we move through today's lunch offerings, a wrinkled woman in a hairnet slams one completely random full-sized human arm on each of our trays. Most of these are not a good match. Mine is a short, burly arm with the additional misfortune of being right-handed. My history teacher, Professor Boelts, is there to explain that it belonged to Admiral Lord Horatio Nelson of the British Royal Navy, and if I was displeased by it I need only look across the cafeteria to see Admiral Nelson sneering at my own mismatched appendage as he prepared to face Napoleon. Before we can properly trade arms, I wake up.

All that remains of Steve is a rumpled blanket and dirty socks, which I kick to the middle of the attic and then through the hole leading downstairs, implicit in the pile a sort of reverse welcome mat. I make my way downstairs to find the house is empty.

Outside, Dad sits in the yard in the same hunter-green metal chair I recall from my childhood, now wearing a patina of rust. Leashed to Dad's chair is Ali, basking in the sun. I hadn't realized Dad took him outside to our yard, and now I'm forced to wonder whether he walks him down the stairs like a poodle or carries him like a huge baby.

Somehow undaunted by the presence of a fearsome predator, a squirrel hops over and stands erect, and Dad tosses him a peanut. Spotting me in the sliding doorway, Dad blushes as if I just saw him give a dollar bill to a stripper.

"Where is everybody?"

"Steve took Jackie to the mall. I get the impression he hasn't done that since . . . probably ever."

Steve was just dumb enough to believe that he'd won the standoff with a random act of toadying, failing to understand that Jackie had merely holstered her argument to be drawn, blazing, at the slightest confrontation.

"She's smart enough to milk it. Until the next time."

I don't ask where Mom is, assuming the answer to be the disturbing coin toss between "firehouse" and "yurt." Instead I settle into a folding lawn chair next to Dad. There are seven chairs out here like snowflakes, no two alike. I take the peanuts from him and attempt to lure a squirrel closer but the squirrel, all spastic sudden motion, only stares at me, meaning I'm a less familiar outdoor figure than Ali. Dad plucks the peanut from me, leans down and holds it out, and the squirrel hops over and takes it directly from his hand.

"Wow. You two could be in a circus."

The squirrel twirls the nut, end over end, repeatedly, trying to find which identical bulge fits best between its teeth before he grips it there and hops away. Ali just blinks his strange sideways blink, eyelids sliding front to back.

"Your mother thinks we should talk."

"We are talking. Mission accomplished!"

"Remember that kid you used to play high school lacrosse with?"

"Artie Miller? We were best friends for, like, a whole summer. What a stud. Great athlete, girls loved him, funny kid."

"I remember he was very impressed with himself. A show-off. Liked attention. And a mean kid: you had a birthday party, we took you and a bunch of kids bowling, and he made fun of that kid from across the street, Joel."

"Everyone made fun of Joel."

"You didn't. That's my point. You worshipped this kid Artie, and I was scared to death you were going to try to be like him."

"Mom wanted you to talk to me about Artie?"

He watches the squirrel shred the shell to get at the peanut inside.

"I'm less concerned than your mother. All I ever wanted for you was to be nice. It was more important to me than you being popular, or good at sports, or having girls fall all over you."

"I wouldn't have minded a few girls falling all over me."

"You did okay. A handsome boy—your mother's genes there, thank God—girls liked you, even if you didn't notice. More important, you turned out nice. Taught kids, made friends, built a good life. I can't remember what you wanted to be when you grew up—"

"Pretty sure it was a guy with two arms."

Dad sighs. The squirrel watches us, equally exasperated.

"Weber got his first good night's sleep in a long time the other night."

"Because he got hammered."

"Because you wouldn't let Steve wake him up. Even if it meant that," he nods at my bandaged tattoo. Dad produces another nut, and the squirrel stands erect as a commuter packed into a crowded subway. "We're all worried about you. After what happened . . . you've been kind of a jerk." I admit, that hurts a little. But then he looks at me and smiles. "Somehow, the events of the other night have me less worried."

"Artie may be gone, but I have a sea serpent named Bob."

"Bad things don't only happen all at once. They also happen

slowly, over time. The career that sputtered, the health that deteriorated over the years . . . the love that just . . . dissipates." Both squirrel and I stare at Dad, speechless. "Feed the squirrel." He's suddenly said enough and places the peanut between my fingers. "Slowly . . ."

"All right, but if he bites me and I get gangrene, you explain it to Jackie."

The squirrel approaches cautiously, favoring Dad. It jumps up on the plastic lawn chair next to me, and I lean in slowly with the nut. It stretches its head out to reach, and I give it plenty of leeway—the safe distance of a long, three-nutted shell between us. The squirrel leans in, slowly gripping the shell between its teeth . . . it reaches up with its front paw to grasp it, and when its nails graze my finger, I instinctively jerk my whole arm back, but it has a grip on the nut with its teeth and the squirrel goes flying and the chair it was on tumbles, and I fall over backward. Ali lunges at me on the ground and Dad pulls him back by the leash, and we're all frozen in place for a moment. Then the squirrel collects himself, grabs the nut, and is gone up a tree while I'm still struggling to right myself. Suddenly Dad is laughing harder than I've seen him laugh since *Blazing Saddles*.

"You okay?" he finally gasps.

"This is why I avoid wildlife."

"I just pissed myself. I'm going inside to change. Get dressed. Let's see if we can't talk Michelle into bending the rules for a late breakfast."

And with that, he answers at least one of my questions, scooping up Ali in both arms and carrying him inside.

FISH

One fish, two fish, red fish . . . dead fish? The Illinois Center for Ichthyological Conservation—or as I like to call it, "Ick Ick!"—is studying the vanishing freshwater fish species of Illinois's rivers. Specifically, the blue paddle-snout sturgeon, a bottom-feeding sucker. I know, that sounds like an insult! But the real insult has been done by a combination of local dam projects and river pollution that has reduced Acipenser pseudoboscis to an endangered species.

The U.S. Fish and Wildlife Service budgets hundreds of millions of dollars annually to protect endangered fish species . . . but in order to save them, Ick Ick first has to count them, which is easier to do during mating season when they migrate to warmer, shallower waters to spawn under the watchful eye of local fish counters. Hey, fish, get a room! This is Sunny Lee, with The Sunny Side.

We pull up to the Four Corners just as *The Sunny Side* concludes and I snap off the radio so Sunny's silky voice will be the one that resonates in my head. Coffee and syrup flow at the Four Corners along with a stream of conversation between Dad and Mr. Weber, which I punctuate occasionally with an agreeable grunt. As stoned as I am it takes a while to figure out that they're talking about me, and I find myself in accidental agreement with their assessment that it's time I get some sort of job.

"A man needs to keep busy," Dad observes calmly.

"Idle hand does the devil's work." I shovel a glob of buttered belgian battered breakfast into my maw.

Don't they know how *busy* my life has become? I work harder in my first hour awake than these two do all day, starting with the shower: first, I have to take the shampoo bottle in my hand, open it with my teeth, and pour an unseen amount of goo on my head before setting the bottle upright and struggling to cap it. One hand has to struggle to reach the places the other hand used to wash. Despite having about 15 percent less skin surface to dry, toweling off with one hand is twice as slow.

"We understand returning to your teaching job might be uncomfortable."

"Especially when it comes time to bang a pair of erasers together." I stir my coffee with a strip of bacon.

Brushing my teeth starts with setting my toothbrush down on the sink counter and squeezing toothpaste onto it, which usually entails knocking the toothbrush sideways, so what I'm sticking in my mouth isn't just minty freshness but a clod of sink germs. (Flossing is out of the question.) Blow-drying my hair is impossible, so I keep it short and brush it carefully in the direction I hope it to dry in, which it mostly doesn't.

"We have some thoughts, but of course we'd like to hear yours," Mr. Weber coaxes me.

"That would make you telepaths." I drown a stomach full of waffles in coffee.

I have to dress sitting down so I don't lose my balance, rolling left and right on butt cheeks to pull on underwear and inching each foot into a sock. Jeans were a lot easier to zip up and button with the fingers of two hands working in concert; instead I'm reduced to sweatpants. Wriggling into a T-shirt is relatively easy, but button-down shirts are out of the question for now. Even sunglasses are hard: I hold one stem and tug the other out with my mouth, a poor substitute for another set of fingers. Needless to say, all my footwear is laceless.

In short, the burden of the one-armed keeps me plenty fucking busy.

"What do you want to do, Aaron?" Mr. Weber, without benefit of telepathy, asks.

"I thought I'd try my hand at NASCAR."

"You know what you have?" Mr. Weber is about to tell me.

"One less arm than average?"

"Inertia. You're at rest so you stay at rest. Because if you set yourself in motion, you're afraid your life would move in ways you can't control."

"How much control does anyone have, really? If we did, we'd all be astronauts or movie stars or billionaire industrialists. Not that I see myself being great at any of those . . ."

"Even the lowest plebe on a ship can do a job. Do you know that on whaling vessels there was a deckhand who was lowered overboard on a 'monkey line' into a dead whale's head to scoop out oil with a bucket?"

"'Whale Ship Monkey Boy' isn't a strong pitch, Mr. Weber."

They continue to discuss my limited local options, which in their estimation include telemarketing, customer service (also by phone), social work (really?), any clerical job in local government, and maybe even counselor to the newly disabled. ("He's not ready," Dad declares of this last one, and I can't disagree.)

I assess my job prospects differently: horror film extra, hollow-armed smuggler, some clerical job that requires only the repetitive use of a handstamp, cleaning the stripper pole between dancers, senator from Hawaii, and, because I have unique experience, crash-test dummy.

That's when Mr. Weber mentions that he's very plugged in to a federally funded local conservation effort to count fish.

"You're shitting me," Dad and I say in unison.

THINGS I KNOW ABOUT FISH AND CONSERVATION

COUNTERINTUITIVE

The counting of fish has been made necessary by the collapse of the local fish population, the cause of which is debatable: while some blame warmer oceans, overfishing, and pollution, others point to the proliferation of the dams that kill millions of fish as they attempt to swim upriver to spawn, only to bash themselves against a concrete barrier instead. As any hockey player could tell you, it's harder to score after repeated blows to the head, rendering future offspring unlikely.

Under the Endangered Species Act, the federal government is required not to allow any species to advance from "endangered" to "extinct" if it can help it. One obvious way to ensure the blue paddle snout's survival would be to tear down the obstacles to its natural migration, whose turbines shred any fish forced to pass through them like a coleslaw chopper. But because local farmers need the irrigation and business needs the cheap electricity (and politicians need the votes of both), the dams stand, as immovable as a fish-faced Rushmore.

Instead, the Army Corps of Engineers has created a multibillion-dollar industry whereupon each irrational act is countered by another more insane gambit—an infinite Möbius strip of ultimately pointless activity. They've spent half a billion dollars on a labyrinth of pipelines, sluices, and tunnels to divert populations of juvenile sturgeon and other fish species to be loaded onto barges and trucks—even at one time, airplanes—to travel safely downriver. Then they've spent millions building "fish ladders" that allow fish to struggle at heart-attack pace back up over the dam, and even utilized cannons to propel them one at a time at speeds upward of twenty-two miles per hour.

All of which fuck with the natural homing instinct essential to the survival of the species, programmed as they are to return in adulthood to the rivers they came from to spawn. It would be like meeting someone in a bar and excusing yourself to go to the bathroom, only to be kidnapped and whisked three hundred miles away and dumped in the ocean and left to find your way back. You'd arrive well past closing time after all the good fish eggs had been fertilized.

Another half a billion dollars was spent in an effort to increase the population by building fish hatcheries to produce large numbers of sturgeon that will eventually find their way back to the river—where they'll likely be killed by the dam. And since hatchery fish are fed by workers scattering food on the surface of their pools, while sturgeon are naturally bottom-feeders, baby sturgeon grow up expecting food to be on the surface so upon their release, they head not to the bottom but to the surface, where they are easy prey for the Caspian tern, a diving fish predator *not* indigenous to the region, having been trucked in to create a bird refuge (cost: $200 million)—by the same Army Corps of Engineers who, recognizing their error as they watched ten thousand tern scoop helpless endangered baby sturgeon from the river, attempted to remedy the mistake by relocating the tern (cost: $600 million), only to be stopped by the Audubon Society and a court order.

So, the federal government employs a system of eight different federal agencies as well as local government, private consultants, university fish scientists, biologists, bureaucrats, administrators, and workers at a cost of billions of dollars—not to save the fish *but to save the dam*. And to employ this particularly unemployable one-armed fish counter, unless I can talk them out of it.

I'm trained by the nice people at the federally funded Ick Ick project along with five other locals prepared to join fish counters already in the field. Among them is a man a full head shorter than I am; upon seeing him standing just through the doorway I assume there's a step *down* into the room, and in acting accordingly I land hard, and I stumble into him as if trying to navigate with one leg for a change.

"Sorry!" I collect myself, extending my only hand in greeting. "I'm Aaron. Here to count fish. Although I can count to five better than ten."

"Percy" is his only reply as he slips his tiny hand into mine, accompanied by a fixed stare.

It's an intense gaze everyone here seems to share. They all stare completely unabashed at anyone in their fields of vision, like babies unaware of anything but the facial recognition for which they are primally programmed as a survival lure. When I spot an average-looking woman with the exception of nose and tits in equal prominence, she too catches me staring and seems to think nothing of it, staring back, our eyes locked like a pair of horseshoe magnets.

With no further exchange forthcoming from Percy, I extricate myself and manage to approach her without colliding. As impressed as I am by her imposing breasts, I'm equally fascinated by that nose, pronounced and beakish in a way that renders the rest of her quite ordinary face extraordinary. Eventually discomforted by our optical intimacy, I'm the one who finally looks away, and therefore probably considered the socially inept oddball here.

"Do you like fish?" she asks.

"I admit, up until now I never thought of them as more than

seafood," I confess, and if that bothers her she doesn't show it. "You?"

"I'm concerned about the mass extinction of a species," she states flatly, and then, as if mimicking me, adds, "You?"

"I needed a job, and there's not a lot I can do."

Her name is Lilith and like everyone I've met at Ick Ick so far, she seems undeterred by my condition. In fact, no one seems to notice my missing arm/hand unit at all—not in the same way others choose to ignore it as a means of avoidance but by being genuinely and completely indifferent to it. I assume working in scientific research puts one in contact with a variety of oddball personalities; if they can overlook the overbites and thick glasses, poor hygiene and rumpled clothes, shrill voices and personality tics bordering on Asperger's in evidence everywhere at the orientation, what's one arm more or less?

I try to redeem my intentions somewhat to Lilith, mostly by overusing the word "fascinating" in expressing my feelings on extinction, dams, nature, conservation, and especially the fish we hope to save, although I know nothing about them yet. It's enough fake sincerity to earn me a seat alongside her in our next training session.

As our primary instruction over any kind of science or methodology is straightforward recognition, this should be easy since the species we're primarily counting, the blue paddle-snout sturgeon, is one ugly motherfucking fish. First of all and most obvious: *it has a snout shaped like a paddle.* It also has no teeth, an extendable mouth(!), and tactile "whiskers" for locating food. About a foot long, spiky cartilage runs the length of its spine, ending in a dorsal fin at the tail, and four pectoral fins actually help it mimic walking along the bottom of rivers or lakes. Described as "primitive" and "dinosaur-like," *Acipenser pseudoboscis* is in fact considered virtually unchanged from the Cretaceous period seventy million years ago, when things were genetically designed to be as ugly as possible so as not to be mistaken for food.

Blue paddle snout can also live *for a century*, but it seems unlikely any alive today will do so since 85 percent of sturgeon populations are at risk of becoming extinct, more than any other species in the world. But aside from this federally funded boondoggle on the Wabash, no one really cares because they're significantly less adorable than pandas or lemurs or baby gorillas, an observation that when shared with Lilith earns a toothy grin, revealing yet another area of prominence to her odd physicality. She's like a strange painting of a beautiful woman, or a beautiful painting of a strange one, and I find myself oddly attracted to her.

After a week in a classroom setting in preparation for the fieldwork of fish counting, I'm not sure I've learned much, distracted as I am by the effects of different strains of medical marijuana coupled with Vicodin. Yet somehow this minor accomplishment has inspired disproportionate enthusiasm from Mom and Dad, as if I'm the kid with the head injury who after many unsuccessful attempts finally managed to fit the round peg in the round hole.

Worse, with Mom joining us for Friday night dinner, this achievement of gainful, one-armed employment has prompted Steve to pontificate on his own nearly two-week vacation from "work." He holds forth on the subject as if it is the thing that dogs him, a constant gravitational pull that exerts its influence solely to prevent him from soaring as high as he could, despite a chronic lack of ambition coupled with a need for furtive afternoon naps. (Steve liked to brag that he spent most afternoons asleep in his PG&E truck behind mirrored glasses with the newspaper unfolded across his steering wheel. Why being caught reading the paper in his truck while he was supposed to be working might have been preferable to being caught sleeping on the job eluded me. I also couldn't help but think that perhaps this was why newspapers were going out of business, because the kind of people who read them, or pretend to, were guys like Steve.)

Despite a sedative cocktail of beer, Vicodin, and a fat bud of Herb Your Enthusiasm, Steve's smirking chatter makes me fidgety, and unfortunately I can still hear him when he turns his attention to Dad. "See, back in the day, you only had to compete with other white guys to get ahead. It was easier to get a job, to keep a job, to move up."

"It's also easier," I observe unnecessarily, "if you don't require a nap in the middle of the day."

"No, I'm serious," he announces with great seriousness. "It's simple math. I have to compete against women, blacks, Mexicans—if you took everyone out of the job market except white guys, that's millions of people . . . there'd be a lot less of us competing for the same number of jobs."

"So, it was better when women stayed in the kitchen," Mom wishes to clarify, "and 'Negroes' picked cotton—"

"And Mexicans were in Mexico," I add.

Jackie is silently mortified.

"I'm just saying that, like, in the sixties, when there were only white guys in the job market, you didn't have to fight off a million more guys, women, blacks, Chinese—"

"Yes, the 'Chinamen' have greatly reduced your chance for success in the modern world," I suggest.

"Aaron," Jackie snaps, two syllables that mean *shut up*.

And Steve glares at me in a way that reminds me of a mean dog I should not provoke. Then, he does something scarier. "Ask him," Steve jerks his thumb at Dad and then waits, as if he'd just punched an elevator button.

Dad weighs Steve with a long, tired stare before declaring, "He's right."

Steve leans back and beams like he's being fellated by the

world's most desirable woman. I'm so stunned by Dad's response that the dullness of pills, pot, and pilsner seems to drain through my extremities and I am suddenly sober.

"You can't be serious."

Dad shrugs simply. "Back in the late sixties and seventies, was there a smaller pool of people competing for work? Yes. When I got to be middle management, were there women, blacks . . ."—he pauses for effect—"*Chinese* in line for the same job? No. He's right. About the numbers. The pool is bigger now. Was it better then? No. And would this idiot"—Dad indicates Steve with his glass and the musical tinkling of ice cubes—"be successful in any time, in any workforce, under any circumstances? Of course not."

"Hey, fuck you, old man!"

It happens before I know it—a flash of motion, blood rushing, a gasp of breath, ears on fire, my nub of a shoulder tucking re-flexively to protect my chin, my good arm lashing out and Steve hitting the floor, his hand stanching blood from his broken nose.

THINGS YOU CAN STILL DO WITH ONE ARM
Punch your stupid fucking brother-in-law in the face

BRAWNY

I am a fucking caveman, a gloriously bestial, unthinking creature of instinct; a one-armed caveman, but nonetheless capable
of primal acts of violence to defend my bloodline and vanquish
a foe who believed himself superior to me but instead limped
back to his cave, bloody and defeated and further emasculated
by his female. He will no longer share the warmth of our fire or
the meat from our kill, nor will we suffer his chest-beating
grunts of boastful supremacy. Having beaten him in combat I
can claim his female, but she's my sister, and that might be cool
among cavemen but let's face it, that's disgusting.

And so Steve is gone, his exile extended from attic to Arca-
dia, and days later, Jackie's own plans for returning home are
vague. But I remain exhilarated by the encounter between my
good fist and Steve's surprisingly pliant nose.

(I think the hardest part for Steve—besides the ruined
cartilage—was that *no one* came to his defense or expressed the
slightest objection to his impromptu bludgeoning. I think Dad,
for all his talk of niceness, may only have felt a twinge of embarrassment to have been at the center of the conflict; and certainly
Mom's Zen cannot even fathom an act of violence, although she
never flinched except [I could swear] to stifle a tiny grin. Even
Jackie's considerable fury—eyes bulging, snot spewing, spit flying,

she looked nothing like her tattoo anymore—was directed entirely at Steve; and her shrieking hatred of him in that moment, so primal that any animals in earshot would have been incited to devour each other, made me grateful I had somehow avoided my merited share of her wrath.)

The flush of conquest lingered and I resolved to incorporate that same exhilaration of the physical into my routine, hoping to duplicate the experience without habitually punching someone senseless. I wouldn't say I've gotten fat since the accident, but "doughy" is a good word. I've also noticed a recurring heat rash in the crease of flesh under my chest grown floppy, a sweat-trapping fold where once there was only the meeting of muscle tissue, however unimpressive. To be generous, I'm about fifteen pounds overweight, and whenever I'd felt the slightest twinge of guilt I didn't have to look very far to spot the morbidly obese man on the street and rationalize, *Really, I need to lose weight?*

But now I've started running (I still had two good legs after all), doing core work (my torso still intact), pumping dumbbells with my good arm (Jackie's pink hand weights, only five pounds each but both of them lashed together with duct tape provided formidable resistance to my dormant muscles). I drew the line at one-armed push-ups—harder than they look, and when your arm gives out, the only thing between your teeth and the floor is your face. The one workout that proved completely impossible for me was skipping rope like a boxer, and what I regret most is the part where you whip the rope super fast in the final seconds just before your trainer yells, "Time!" I imagine few things feel more exhilarating than that, like being shot out of a cannon or your first full-on open-mouth kiss.

I remember the first time I ever hit someone in the face. I was thirteen years old, and it surprised me how good it felt. In goading me to fight, this kid had pushed me past the point of consciousness—I was all fury and flashing motion, completely reflexive, without thought, even as I was aware that the boy who stood across from me was poised, controlled, hands held perfectly . . . and eating my fists. They came from every angle, and he seemed incapable of avoiding them; certainly I was wide open to any reasonable counterattack but he could mount none. When someone finally intervened to stop it I was breathing heavily, but it was the boy across from me who was sweating, red faced, bearing slap and fist marks across his cheeks and a trickle of blood from his nose, embarrassed, wishing he could disappear. That moment taught me the power of fury over reason.

I'm sure Sunny Lee would be able to explain what I'd felt then and continue to feel with each pounding footfall and grunted exertion—my endorphins' natural opiates released in response to the physical activity of running, serotonin neurotransmitters firing with increased vascular traffic, the brain's frontal lobes aglow with blood-fueled activity; the dripping sweat that reminds me of sex, another activity without logic or thought, only feeling, intellect sublimated to reptilian brain.

Who says you can't get high on life? Sunny would begin. *You can, as long as your life's on fast-forward!* She'd cite hospital studies and university research, lab mice and macaque monkeys, exercise intensity and brain signals and happiness ratings . . . she'd make an *atrophy / a trophy* pun, tell us *why gray matter matters,* and sum up with *Think of it as a two-for-one pass at your gym— you do the work, and your brain gets a free workout.*

By the time I arrive at work my blood-engorged brain is primed for the task of counting fish, which actually isn't as difficult as it sounds. It's not as though you stand on the riverbank and try to spot fish from one end to the other as—simultaneously—three splash through on the far bank while two scoot in front of you and somewhere in the middle a small school passes undetected. You don't count fish from above; you go to where the fish are: underwater.

Each of us is assigned a small underground room with an underwater window. (It's like Doctor Who's TARDIS, somehow bigger on the inside.) The window overlooks a fish ladder, a series of boards that allow water to pass through but funnel fish through a single chute. The fish counter's job is to identify the upstream-migrating fish as they pass the window. (It's the difference between trying to count every car in Manhattan or waiting for rush hour and catching them as they pass through the Lincoln Tunnel, but without the horn-honking and swearing.) We enter that data into a system using a specialized keyboard and computer program. (What happens next is outside the area of my responsibility, or interest.) There are two shifts of fish counters who count real-time passage fifty minutes of every hour for sixteen hours a day, from 5:00 A.M. to 9:00 P.M. (In consideration of the absurd idea that I might be up at three in the morning to get to work by five—with or without time travel—I take the late shift.) There's also some video counting of fish passage recorded late at night, but if I wanted to watch grainy video of soggy flesh struggling against nature, I'd go back to the Loading Zone's wet T-shirt tapes.

Still, the murkiness of the water further stirred by passing fish—not all of them *Acipenser pseudoboscis*—can make spotting them a challenge. My first day I counted only eleven—which, without knowing what to anticipate other than that as "endangered" there must not be very many of them, sounded like a fine number. However, Percy, stationed at a downstream ladder from me, and Lilith upstream, both counted thirty, indicating that I missed nearly twice as many as I'd counted. The only logical thing for me to do was to engage Percy at the end of the day in casual conversation about his count before reporting mine, which worked fine at first since Percy seemed blissfully unaccustomed to being the subject of another human's interest. But I soon ran out of variations of "Pretty good day, wouldn't you say?" and "So, how'd you do?" and, when he started to catch on, "Just tell me how many fucking fish you saw!" drove him away for good. Upstream, Lilith was a clam and wouldn't reveal her counts under waterboarding.

"You're easily distracted," Lilith observes at the end of a workday, and I nearly miss the rest of what she says distracted by the grandness of her nose. "That's not necessarily a bad thing. It's just bad for counting fish."

"I have a lot on my mind."

"I could do the same thing for hours. Watch for fish. Build a birdhouse. Play the violin."

"I've never been good at that," I lament. "I'm more likely to quit in the middle of building a birdhouse for fish."

She laughs, flashing teeth that draw my attention from nose and tits, proving her point.

"Did you say you play the violin?"

"Yes. Do you like music?"

She says it exactly the way she once asked *Do you like fish?*, and having been around Lilith for more than a week now, I understand the necessity for directness.

"Yes. Yes, I do, a great deal. I'd like to hear you play."

She shrugs. "I don't have my violin here."

"Then maybe," I suggest directly, "we can go to where it is."

Back at her small, immaculate apartment, Lilith plays the violin for me, "The Lark Ascending" (and yes, over in the corner is evidence of the birdhouse she's building). It's lovely and transcendent and she loses herself in it completely, only adding to her odd allure. I find myself swept away in thoughts of seeing her naked body and tucking my nose against hers while kissing that oversized mouth. I can imagine, in the throes of passion and

OCD, Lilith counting how many times I thrust myself into her, and I hope I can manage an impressive number in the upper-double digits. This is after all why she invited me here, and my heart thrums with anticipation of having sex for the first time since my accident, especially with this strangely appealing creature. Then she's finished, her final note hanging in the air like tinnitus. She sets her violin carefully in its case and snaps it shut, turning her dark eyes on me, staring, which I take for an invitation and step forward. She parts her lips, revealing those teeth once again, and says simply:

"See you tomorrow, then."

While masturbating furiously in the attic, it strikes me that my problem focusing at work may be drug-related: I'm not taking enough. Emboldened by my caveman fitness regimen, I've cut back on pot and pills dramatically (although I haven't stopped altogether). Recalling the pinpoint focus four Vicodins has helped me achieve in the past, I'm certain that dosage coupled with a hyperalert strain of marijuana will boost my success rate considerably.

After a couple of days of experimentation I discover just the right blend of drugs and pot to set my synapses to alert-level RED: four morning Vicodins (and four more at lunch) and hourly bowls of Hocus-Focus have me zoned in. I'm capable of scanning the window like a bar code reader, registering each passing blue paddle snout, unmissable as black-light posters to my efficiently stoned self. As the days and fish pass, my counts routinely matched Lilith's and when both of ours exceeded Percy's, he looked violated. Eventually my counts became the standard for the day's final tally up and down the river. The more I counted the less ugly they looked, all flat-headed grace as they beat on, fins against the current, borne back ceaselessly into extinction.

That's when out of sheer boredom I start counting the other fish: brook lampreys, sunfish, darters, and three varieties of redhorse—silver, shorthead, and greater—each difficult at a glance to tell from the other but for me as distinct as traffic lights. Sharing this superfluous information at the end of the day is met with a mix of bemused astonishment. We sometimes gather on the riverbank before work while I call out fish species darting down the river, those struggling up too easy to spy in their slowness (although I'll occasionally announce one long past us without turning my head).

When I emerge at the end of my shift, Lilith is waiting for me.

"That was very impressive this afternoon."

"What can I say? I've gotten to love the little guys—all of them, with their thrashing tails and finny perseverance."

Her gaze is different now; instead of a dead stare, it feels alive with intent. But I've misinterpreted her motives before.

"Would you like to hear me play the violin?"

The sex is clumsy, awkward, wonderful. With the arm gone that I'd once used to prop myself upright while the other one had groped my partner, I could either prop up or grope but not both. Of course I choose "grope," but with an inability to support myself it makes for the clumsy lovemaking of a schoolboy until Lilith relieves me of command, expertly flipping me onto my back like a fish she's about to tag. She doesn't take off her top but I'm not disappointed for too long as she straddles me, sliding me inside her and grinding her hips into mine. Instinctively I begin to count but reach only five before I'm distracted by the big cartoon fish head on her T-shirt, so that instead of looking at Lilith I stare into the cartoon fish's dead eyes until both she and I come, I don't know how many thrusts later, and she falls off me as if shot by a sniper.

We lie there a long time without speaking. The pre-accident

version of me would already be listening for the steady breathing of sleep that would portend a clean getaway. The younger version of me would ponder what this meant to her, to me, to us, if we were now "us" at all—*God, I hope she's not crazy like the others.* The much younger first-time me would pray not to have impregnated her or gotten an STD, but neither of those concerns would have been enough to wipe the smirk off my face. Inexplicably, current me says this:

"What are you thinking?"

"I need more cedar for my birdhouse."

"Cedar?"

"Wood," she explains. "Cedar doesn't decay. It breathes, and insulates. It's not too thin—anything less than an inch will build up heat, not good for the birds, especially young ones. And you don't have to paint or stain it. The fumes would be harmful, and the paint is toxic if they peck at it. You shouldn't paint them anyway. Bright colors attract predators."

In the face of the least romantic postcoital glow in the history of human interaction, I say nothing. Without further prodding, Lilith also falls silent. In the quiet I wonder if this strange, wonderful encounter with this woman of many prominent features is a portent of my sexual destiny, my dating pool reduced to women whose emotional peculiarity matches my physical one. I'm pondering just how many women like Lilith I'm likely to encounter when she sits up on the edge of the bed and looks down at my stump.

"You should get that looked at," she says, and I follow her gaze to see that one of my sea serpent's eyes has gone red and puffy.

Less concerned than embarrassed, I wiggle into my T-shirt and swallow another Vicodin as she scrambles past me. She sits at her table and works intently on her birdhouse. I struggle into my pants and slip on my shoes, and then sit and watch her work for a full minute. When I get up and kiss her on the back of the neck she jumps, as if she's already forgotten I was there, and I let myself out.

Sex with Lilith is an event that never happens again, and we never speak of it. When I'd subsequently ask if she is "busy" or wants to "do something after work" (granted, not exactly irresistible seduction attempts), Lilith politely declines in a way that seems to deny any sexual encounter had ever happened and makes me wonder if I imagined it. Then one day she wears the fish T-shirt to work and I stare so unabashedly into its eyes—and her tits—that she slaps me across the face, and I'm relieved to know it did.

Most of my day is spent deep inside my submerged workstation alone with my thoughts which, owing to pot breaks at the fifty-minute mark of every hour (a routine difficult to manage in another work venue) are mostly focused on the hard-fought journey of each passing fish. Beyond all reason they struggle against technology (the dam), aided by crappier technology (the fish ladder) to do what nature tells them. It's a microcosm of our human existence, programmed to hunt and gather and live communally but instead struggling through a techno-world our cave-dwelling ancestors would find inexplicable, aided by the crappier technology of cars, cell phones, tablets, and commercials designed to sell us all those things. Yet never reaching the place nature had in mind for us. (Advantage: fish.) But here, solitary and untouchable and very stoned, I commune with nature, momentarily useful. It's a comforting, smoky womb from which I emerge each day ready to be slapped by life.

I make it a point to begin and end my workday observing the river from above lest I grow too accustomed to viewing the fish in the narrow purview of a small glass square. Here in the vast outdoors the river rushes down and the fish, somewhere below, rush up. It's the difference between a home aquarium and deep-sea fishing. The overflow weirs atop the fishing ladders catch the occasional finny passerby, and I'm struck breathless when a pair of blue paddle snout leap in tandem, passing across what appears to be my own reflection in the water—*must* be, for the simple fact that it's an armless man. The only problem is he's on the other side of the river.

I gaze across to the opposite bank to see the figure casting that reflection gazing back at me; he waves his good left arm in universal greeting, and I match him with my right as he disappears upriver like one of our fish wiggling past in an effort to preserve itself for another generation.

Jackie's been here for nearly a month, and I worry that her generously open-ended work sabbatical has begun to take on the drudgery of a prison sentence. I return from fish counting expecting to find her chalking off day 27 of her incarceration in slash marks on her cell wall; instead, she greets me in a heightened state of clinical hysteria:

"*MyhighschoolfriendCelesteishavingaCOSTUMEPARTYyouHAVE-togowithmeIwillabsolutelyfuckingDIEifImissit!*"

She's actually shaking me by the shirt, and her face, although joyful, looks like it might explode from the front of her skull, so I try to settle her down.

"How is it possible you still know these people? I'm not in touch with anyone from high school. Not that I'm complaining . . ."

"Because I was insanely popular and you were a comic book–reading dork? Come on, it'll be fun!"

"It sounds to me like less fun than staying home to scare trick-or-treaters with my nub."

Her face falls a little, and I can see how much she wants to see her old friends again and relive the former glory of her high school days, and who can blame her? Jackie looks a decade younger than her years and is in great shape, and this is her chance to leave a mark on her *old* friends dressed as a slutty fill-in-the-occupation while they struggle into plus-sized fruit. I'm about to relent anyway when she sweetens the pot:

"Who knows? Sunny Lee could be there!"

COSTUMES THAT DON'T WORK WITH ONE ARM

Juggler

Oarsman

Accordion player

Guitar god

Pool shark

Boxer

Bowman

Weight lifter

Atlas

Vitruvian Man

The Two-Gun Kid

Sword-and-shield knight

Toga guy

Suspenders

Crucified

Abe Lincoln

MASQUERADE

I'm not strong enough, like Randy Fucking Pausch, to flaunt my condition however convincingly as a character in *Saw*. Given the choice, I would choose shark over shark victim. I can however disguise my condition the same way Jackie's friends will attempt to camouflage the unkindness of years, neglect, and childbearing under an angel's flowing robes or SpongeBob's rectangles. I can disappear into robot, Transformer, astronaut, gorilla, or the ass end of a zebra.

Another option is to go as the person I used to be.

I put on a sleek, tailored suit, a navy pinstripe Hugo Boss that I wore back when I cared what I looked like. Not a costume per se, but once I pad the arm and add the fake hand, it is as transformative and misleading as any disguise. The figure in the mirror looks like I used to when I was whole, only better—because it is after all a party: I've struggled to shave and smooshed product in my hair, draping a vintage necktie from Dad's closet around my neck, still bearing a price tag (I snap it off between my teeth and my good hand). Still, when I move I appear awkward, the fake arm dangling like a hanged man. Placing it in a sling completes the costume: I look completely natural and restored to the pre-accident, pre-divorce, previously whole *me*.

When Jackie sees me, she starts to cry. Then she punches me in my good arm because now she has to go back upstairs and redraw the giant black ring around her pit bull's right eye. Dad shuffles into the room, leaning as he always does slightly to one side, a probable result of lugging a briefcase in the same hand for four decades so that even now, long after he stopped carrying it, he's used to compensating for its weight. Or it could be another toll of time travel. (There are no official studies of the possible long-term effects of piloting a Lincoln twice daily through the time barrier.)

"Nice tie," Dad notices.

"How come you never wore it?"

"I kept waiting for the right occasion. Then you run out of occasions, but still have a closetful of ties. Here, let me . . ." He reaches out and takes both ends of the tie, holding them as if about to steer a chariot. He crosses one end over the other, slowly, trying to figure this out backward. "This could take a while," he warns me.

"You should buy more clip-ons."

"Patience is undervalued."

"A virtue, I'm told."

"We race race race, always rushing to no place in particular, only occasionally stopping—"

"Long enough to blast a hole in a target."

Dad laughs. "The biathlon's a good life metaphor. Over twelve miles, you only stop five times. In between, you sprint so fast you don't even look at the countryside. Maybe to see your split times. But those quiet moments at rest—"

"Punctuated by gunshots . . ."

Dad smiles, silent. That's when the ringing in my ears kicks in, but I enjoy the moment, just being here with Dad as he squeezes the knot up into place at the collar. We stand there a long time before Jackie clomps back into the room and declares, "We should get going."

"And then, just like that," Dad releases me, "you're off again."

We glide into the house party unnoticed amid a sensory assault of frenetic movement and astonishing volume, a raucous scene that belies the expectations of a gathering of fortysomethings. This is the one-last-fling party of a dying teen, a convicted criminal about to begin a long prison term, a politician who just lost an election but has to spend his remaining campaign funds before morning. Generational denial; only instead of a sense of desperation there's a shared commitment to the suspension of reality—of age, responsibility, identity. Tomorrow they'll all feel terrible, and resume the drudgery of their lives . . . but tonight they have the music of their youth, communal sense of purpose, alcohol in abundance, and the transformation of disguise.

Squealing like a train about to leave its tracks and destroy everything in its path, Jackie's old friends suddenly surround her. I try to escape between a fat witch and what appears to be an attempt at "slutty dowager" before awkward introductions can leech all life from the room, but that's exactly what happens.

"You remember my brother, Aaron."

It's like a needle scratching across a record as all eyes lock on the arm that's not supposed to be there.

"I thought—" the witch manages, more confused than wicked, before being elbowed sharply by a Roller Derby girl, suddenly unsteady on her wheels.

"It's nice to see everyone," I lie. "I have no idea who you are, and it isn't just the costumes. My memory isn't what it used to be."

"Because of the accident?" a cowgirl wearing a papier-mâché

horse asks, and she too is elbowed by Derby girl, causing her to roll backward.

"Yes," I lie some more. "I have face blindness."

Jackie rolls her eyes.

"Prosopagnosia," the slutty proctologist clarifies the diagnosis.

"He has weird baby-brother disease," Jackie says, moving in for a group hug.

They all squeal again and I use the diversion to make good my escape. It's only later I wonder, *Could one of them (maybe the slutty rodeo clown?) have been Sunny Lee?* but quickly realize that nothing, not the happiest of occasions or the knife thrust of a serial killer, could ever make Sunny squeal like that.

I haven't been around so many people in one place since the accident. In other circumstances I'd be the most conspicuous person in the room and the subject of stares and conjecture, instead of the least remarkable—a guy in a suit too repressed to put on a costume. It allows me to observe instead of suffering the scrutiny of others, to enjoy an invisibility lost to me since the day I walked out of the hospital. Drifting from room to room I watch unwatched, and amid the colorful revelry, the gruesome decorations that mock death, and the party games that prompt shrieks of howling, drunken laughter, what I see has nothing to do with spooky traditions, pagan rituals, saints, spirits, or Celts, but a universal desire to be someone else. And if we could make it last more than just a few hours, we would.

I scan the store-bought and homemade masks and makeup, feathers and glitter, poster board and papier-mâché (and even someone dressed as a bloody head on a plate on a table), imagining who hiding behind them might be Sunny Lee. Aware that her possible attendance was only a lure dangled by Jackie, I nonetheless responded to its tantalizing flash and movement like any hungry fish would, with the hope that it might sustain me; hooked and reeled in, I can only flap around with the unlikely hope of thrashing into Sunny. It's as implausible a delusion as any here.

The bartender pours what a reasonable person would consider too much vodka into a tall glass with a splash of tonic, an inverse formula engineered to accelerate me into the mood of the others like a migrating sea turtle slipping into the East Australian Current. Peering over the glass, my eyes meet an adorable drunk. She's not adorable because she's drunk; her drunkenness and adorability are separate, nondependent things. She is innately adorable, and would be under any circumstances—working behind a desk, walking a dog, eating a giant hoagie, or drooling in a dentist's chair. And dressed as slutty Viking, she vanquishes any further thoughts of Sunny Lee.

"Boooo!" she chides me over the music, shouting, "A broken arm is no excuse for no costume!"

"I'm Aaron," I shout over the music, offering nothing to correct her.

"Ariana," she laughs.

"Aaron and Ariana, that is some sickly sweet alliteration! If we got married, we could name our kids Ari and Arial."

"We could never get married! It's too cute; people would want to vomit."

Free from any pressure to pursue couplehood, we dive into the party and alternate frozen Jell-O shots with reckless dancing to classic late-eighties music that wasn't good when it was new yet is now somehow perfect, like twenty-four-year-old scotch. For a brief moment I'm seventeen again, drunk in a neighbor's basement, grinning like a fool at a sexy, carefree spirit, ecstatic and whole.

I pull one of THC's professionally rolled joints from my jacket pocket and Ariana's face does exactly what I'd hoped, signaling approval. She grabs my free hand and leads me out to the backyard where our sweat doesn't exactly freeze on contact but hardens like the chocolate shell on soft-serve ice cream. On the street an assortment of zombies and ghosts, vampires and oversized cats ring doorbells and demand their loot. If anyone rings the doorbell here, no one answers, impossible as it is to hear over the noise. Showing the effects of our many Jell-O shots, Ariana staggers over to a side fence.

"You're pretty unsteady on your feet for a Viking."

"Sea legs," she laughs. "So tell me something about you most people don't know."

"I'm an expert at traditional Viking mating rituals," I say, passing the joint.

"Confession: I'm not an actual Viking."

"That is disappointing. What do you do?"

"I'm a physical therapist. Mostly bad backs. I also teach dance," she says, lifting a leg vertically and plunking her foot at the top of the fence effortlessly.

"You have very impressive hamstrings," I marvel.

She hoots a long, deep laugh I want to dive into and drown in. If I were still thinking about Sunny Lee I might have been pondering (in her voice) the marvel of pheromones, explosive hormones, racing hearts and flush faces, the wonder of goose bumps and the weightlessness of joy, the survival by procreation of all living things, the DNA programming of our ancestors, and the inevitable extinction of all we were or ever will be by exploding sun. But I'm not thinking about Sunny anymore—or my armlessness, until on my way out the door with Ariana when Jackie grabs me by the shoulder and whisper-shouts into my ear, *You have to tell her!*

Back at Ariana's apartment her armored chestplate hits the floor like a car crash, revealing sumptuous breasts I will recall on my deathbed. Her mouth swallows mine and our three arms collaborate in undressing me and by the time my fake arm hits the floor, Jackie is proven right: Ariana stares at my quivering serpent-faced nub, a look on her face that can only be described as adorable confusion. Then she vomits—adorably!—what appears to be blood (until I remember: Jell-O shots), and passes out in front of me.

Lifting her onto her bed is less romantic than I might have envisioned, somewhere between a graceless fireman's carry and how a hunchback might dispose of a body. Watching her stomach rise and fall, I notice her "outtie" belly button protruding like a thumb, as if some vestigial twin were seeking a fingerhold to tear itself free. Upon emerging, it too might take one look at me, vomit, and pass out.

I clean up the vomit, dress quietly, gather my fake arm in my good one and let myself out, hoping Ariana's memory of our time together is swallowed whole by alcohol blackout.

INFECTIOUS

I enter the kitchen after a late-morning jog more plodding than usual to find Jackie looking worse than she's ever looked, worse perhaps than she'll ever look, blanched white, sunken-eyed, straw-haired, hunched over, a perfect zombie in no need of makeup or costume. But grinning like an idiot.

"*God,* that was So. Much. Fun!" she croaks.

"Me too." I lean in and kiss her on the top of her head, all boozy smoke.

"Really?"

"Except for the last part."

"Ohhh . . ." she grimaces, knowing exactly what I'm talking about. "She was cute."

"Adorable," I correct her. "And I won't even tell you how she looked naked."

"Don't!"

"But then there's the problem of what *I* look like naked . . ."

"Someday, that won't matter. When the right person comes along."

"Missing her right arm?"

"Of course not!"

"Back when I still had the ability to clap, I met a 'fetal amputee'—a woman born without her lower arm."

"Please stop . . ."

"She was pretty amazing, and while I'm sure she faced her own unique challenges, they'd be completely different from mine. It's the difference between being born into a primitive desert tribe or being suddenly marooned there from Chicago to live like them. The giant lip plate alone would take getting used to."

"Are you finished?"

"Sure, but only because I'm very, very hungover. Is there coffee?"

"Hours old." She looks into her mug. "When you pour milk in it, it just turns kind of gray."

"So the trick is not to pour milk in it?" I wash back two Vicodin with truly horrible coffee.

"The trick is to make a fresh pot."

Jackie and I got through our childhood together by waiting each other out. If a dish needed washing or toilet paper needed changing or a pet needed feeding, the goal was to outlast each other. We lost turtles to starvation like the Mojave Desert. And so we sit across from each other, gunslingers staring each other down, sipping coffee that tastes like underwear.

It's warm in here and I'm sweating through my T-shirt and my arm really hurts. "I need to get stoned. Want to join me?"

"I am *not* sitting in your attic all afternoon getting stoned!" She slams her coffee mug down and gets up from the table.

"All right, take it easy . . ."

"Get dressed," she orders. "We're going out to get stoned."

I haven't been here in Crawlywood since I was fifteen, when Artie, Joel, and I used to walk the two miles just to disappear into its dark expanse, a distance that now seems a lot farther (Jackie and I drove) and a destination less vast (how could this have once seemed so endless and secret?). This is where we used to set off firecrackers, burying them up to the fuse in dirt and blasting tiny smoking craters, stacking pinecones into rickety structures before blowing them apart. I would even hold a fire-cracker in my now-missing left hand, out to the side as far as I could, letting it explode between my fingers. It stung only a little, followed by a tingling sensation, and several blasts would mean an afternoon of now-familiar ringing in my ears—small price to pay for the respect and awe of my pals.

"Did they sell part of this off?" Jackie coughs and passes the bowl back to me. "For development? It seems so much smaller."

"The whole world is smaller than it was when we were kids. Think about how big the attic seemed, even with all their crap in it."

"That's just a height thing, because we were literally shorter. This . . ." She gestures at our shrunken world.

"The distance between things was different," I slurp, pulling on the pipe. "Think about how long summer felt. Endless!"

"Until it was over."

"Everything moved so slowly, you could see it all: the grass, the bugs, the sky . . . you noticed everything. And how sluggish the grown-ups moved."

Jackie sucks at the pipe. "How did we get to be sluggish grown-ups?"

I would also come here alone, driven by the pitiful demands of my first job: paid ten dollars a week to deliver Shop Smart coupon flyers door to door; instead of knocking on doors or stuffing mailboxes I took them deep into these woods and dumped them, every week, creating a landfill of smart-shopping bargains.

"They can say all they want that the universe is expanding," I observe lazily, "but every day our world contracts like a leaky balloon."

"We never had pot this good in college," Jackie woozes.

"Science is amazing. Someday it will grow me an arm like a gecko. I mean, a real gecko arm, green and slimy with giant suction cup fingers I can cling to walls with." Her eyes fill up with tears, and I want to blow myself up with the world's biggest firecracker. "Hey, I'm sorry . . ."

"No! It's not—"

She's choking now, and before I know it my eyes are tearing and then we're both gasping for breath. Jackie sinks to her knees and just as I land next to her, uniformed men in gas masks burst from the forest. The largest of them looms over me, and even muffled by his gas mask I can make out what he says: "Oh, shit."

At the hospital, eyes are flushed and oxygen administered and explanations offered: it seems we had inadvertently wandered downwind of a training exercise by the local sheriff's department, and when the breeze shifted so did the tear gas.

"Not the first time this happened," the EMT shares. "About a year ago, this place was full of mewling Cub Scouts. Tears and snot everywhere."

"What the fuck are they training for?" Jackie spews snot and tears. "Do they think they're going to have to put down an armed insurrection?"

"You can't be too careful," I suggest. "Wait, *yes, you can.*" Idiots.

"The local Scout Council sued," the EMT leans in quietly. "And settled out of court."

I turn to Jackie with the pleased expression of a wine taster having sampled a surprisingly delightful bottle: a nod, eyebrow raised, bemused lip curl. Then the EMT brushes my nub, and it feels like she scorched it with a blowtorch.

"*Ow,* God damn it!"

"Did that hurt?"

"Like hell!"

The sweat starts pumping, triggered by contact or a fright response. The EMT presses her palm against my forehead.

"You're burning up."

"Too many layers," I groan, pulling off my jacket.

"*SHIT!*" Jackie shouts, and I follow her eyes down to my leaky nub of a shoulder and know this can't be good.

The doctor tells me my fever is 104 and the infection in my shoulder is "serious." He ignores me when I ask, *Will we have to amputate?* and proceeds to wonder aloud what kind of absolute moron would get a tattoo on such a delicate, wounded area. Mom represses any talk of dinosaur brains while Jackie, still red-eyed, grows even redder with fury, and while I think she may want to kill me, I'm certain she's going to cut Steve's balls off, and I'd rather be me with fever, infection, and balls.

They admit me overnight and jack an IV of antibiotics into my good arm while they clean and drain the pus from my bloated and bloodshot serpent head. Everyone who enters and exits reflexively pumps the hand sanitizer mounted by the doorway, rubbing hands like pensive flies. It makes me think of germs, and how hospitals are luxury accommodations for hideous, flesh-eating infections that wouldn't deign to live elsewhere; and I hope that the pick inserted into my forearm to receive twice-daily antibiotics was properly sterilized, because I'm down to my last arm.

The RNs leave me to suffer the glare of my family, seated across from me in three visitors' chairs, a tribunal of disappointment. It's quiet except for the distant hallway announcements calling a roster of doctors' names, and my hospital-mate wheezing for air on the other side of a curtain. The smells, the sounds, the sting of the IV, and the discomfort of a hospital bed are too familiar, and despite my guilt in reeling Jackie down from the rapturous joy of her party to the unpleasant depths of *this*, I'm not ready to be lectured.

"That stupid fucking tattoo," Jackie seethes.

"We don't know that's what caused this," Mom concludes. "Let's not jump to conclusions."

"Were you even taking care of it? No, because you're stoned all the time. You know, as terrible as this was for you, I was really hoping you'd grow from it . . ."

Jackie will get no further than this, ever.

"People like to say you learn from adversity," I stop her. "You know what I learned? I learned that it hurts when metal crushes your body. Is that useful? Will it help me be a better person? I also learned that anything can happen to anyone at any time, that your whole fucking life can change in an instant. I learned that people have the astonishing idea that they know what they would do if they were me, and equally strong opinions on how I should behave. I learned how selfish I am—in a good way—because I want to do what *I want to do*! I'm the one who got fucked, and I'm the only one that matters to me!"

I have to shout this last part, *matters to me*, because Jackie is up and out of the room at *fucked* and Mom is right behind her. The wheezing on the other side of the curtain grows louder, and then it stops. Dad remains seated, silently, perhaps weighing whether to linger in one undesirable situation or pursue the other. Then, inexplicably, he yelps, the loud hiccup of a tiny dog in distress, and slips two fingers between the buttons on his shirt.

"I think my defibrillator just kicked in."

JOLTED

Apparently, the way an implantable cardioverter-defibrillator works is that it's programmed to detect cardiac arrhythmia (specifically, the irregular heartbeat that can lead to cardiac arrest) and correct it with a jolt of electricity. I have my own discomforting sensations—numbness, tingling, itchiness, phantom pain—but won't even hazard a guess as to what it must feel like to experience a sudden and unexpected jolt of eight hundred volts directly into one's heart.

"How the hell do they not have ESPN on the hospital TV?"

Dad jolts the TV, repeatedly, as if trying to bring it to life via remote control. Admitted for observation but, we're assured, with no cause for alarm, Dad has taken the place of my expired former roommate, whose demise I'm almost certainly responsible for, either by distress or epiphany, as if he might have agreed with my shouted argument that *I'm the one who got fucked* and *I want to do what I want to do,* and what he wanted to do was die.

"No idea what goddamn time it is. How come the cable box doesn't have a clock?"

If casinos don't have clocks so you can lose yourself in the mind-altering trippiness of gambling, hospitals rightfully exclude them for the opposite reason, against the numbing stasis that would only be heightened by the inert hands of a clock. (Other places you might not want a clock: middle school, prison, a loveless marriage.)

"And the food. You ate this for a month?"

Except for the first week when I got most of my nutrients through a tube, seven weeks—but preoccupied with trying to feed myself one-handed, the lack of culinary excellence went largely unnoticed. I liked the pudding, though, and my nurses would often sneak me a second. The ladies love a newly one-armed man!

"Pudding's okay . . ." Dad slurps.

If I don't get out of this bed, I am going to die. It will either happen or I will make it happen, willing it like my absent former roommate. Unfettered from my most recent dose of antibiotics, I'm free to roam. Feet find slippers and I make my way to the door.

"Where are you going?"

"For a walk. Don't want to get blood clots. Or bedsores. Or more suicidal."

"I'll go with you," Dad says, without personal neediness but what sounds like genuine concern for me, and my resistance wilts.

We teeter down the hallway, with its antiseptic smell, hushed din of consultation, blank faces, and the occasional slow-moving patient teetering toward us, a nod shared among the fraternity of the walking sick. Each room we pass, left to right, is a frozen tableau of illness: bedridden figure, sometimes accompanied by silent vigil-keepers; a multipanel comic strip without punchline.

"Explosive diarrhea," I begin to imagine the maladies of patients as we pass their rooms. "Badger attack . . . Bar stool racing accident . . ."

"Stuck himself with the pins from a new shirt," Dad joins in.

"Fell trying to hang his Christmas lights."

"Serves him right; it's too damn early."

"Frostbite, from too long in a vodka freezer."

"Heatstroke from a sunlamp."

"A sunlamp? What is it, 1950? Tanning bed!"

"Fine!" Dad growls.

"This guy burned his tongue testing a battery . . ."

Rounding the corner we come face-to-face with a small boy, about eleven, plugged into his rolling IV and standing with his back pressed against the wall as if holding it up—impossible, considering his weakened appearance: wilted frame, sallow skin, hair lost to chemo. He stares at my empty sleeve.

"What happened to your arm?" he asks, wide-eyed.

"Alligator attack."

"Really?"

"We caught him. He's in my dad's bathtub. We're just waiting for him to pass the arm, and then we'll let him go."

He laughs. "You can't get your arm back after it's alligator doody!"

"I hadn't thought of that." I turn to Dad. "What's plan B?"

Dad shrugs, unable to keep up with this new subterfuge, probably mentally spent from our rousing game of Affix the Affliction.

"I'm here because my defibrillator went off," he offers instead.

"What's that?"

"It's for when you fibrillate too much," I reply. "Are you walking? Do you want to walk with us?"

He stares at the floor. "I came all the way from there," he points toward the pediatric cancer ward across the other side of the elevator bank. "But then I remembered I'm not wearing any underwear." He hugs the wall closer.

I reach behind me and pull off my underwear, stuffing it into the front pocket of my hospital gown. Dad leans on me for support and does the same.

"Let's moon some nurses," Dad says.

Cancer Boy grins and joins us, wheeling his IV, three generations of stark-white asses shining behind us. We pass a series of rooms: "This guy suffered a serious wombat attack . . . This one? Ran with the scissors . . . Caught in a gamma ray blast . . ."

"That's the Hulk!" Cancer Boy laughs.

"Necktie caught in office shredder."

"Hippo bite."

"Bee sting!" Cancer Boy shouts.

"But the weird thing?" I suggest, "It wasn't the insect, but the letter *B*."

"Bad dim sum," Dad declares of the next patient.

"Blown up by leaf blower."

"She got a wiener dog stuck in her hoo-hah!" Cancer Boy shouts gleefully, and as all heads in the hallway turn toward us, I realize there's no topping that.

Back in our hospital room Cancer Boy proves a quick study as degenerate gambler. When he hits on nineteen and pulls a deuce, I have to think he's counting cards. He's also broken the house bank of all its M&Ms.

"That's it, kid," I fold. "No bank, no blackjack."

He scoops up his winnings greedily. Dad still has four M&Ms and presses a red one between his lips, crushing it in tiny nibbles between his front teeth. Cancer Boy nudges three of his my way.

"What's this for?"

"Tip," he shrugs.

"I told you: the kid's a ringer." Dad lies back on his bed.

"We're going to check all the hospital security cameras, and if we catch you cheating, you're banned. I'll put your picture up all over the hospital, and you won't be able to get a game of pinochle in the geriatric unit."

"What's that?"

"Never mind!" I pop a single M&M. "Why are you in the hospital anyway? Wait, don't tell me: you're a big-game hunter, and you were hurt trying to shoot Monopoly."

"I have *cancer*!" he says, incredulous.

"No!"

"Yes! Why do you think I'm bald?"

"I thought maybe you had a hair-spray accident while smoking."

"I'm too little to smoke!" he laughs.

"Don't sell yourself short; you're not too little for anything. But don't smoke. It gives you cancer!" I chew my second M&M.

"Still no goddamn *SportsCenter*," Dad mumbles, flipping channels.

"I already *have* cancer, you big dummy!" he laughs harder.

"Well, I told you to give up smoking, but do you listen to me? No. Never, not once, in all the time we've known each other."

"You're stupid!" he howls. "You just met me!"

"And yet, I feel I hardly know you."

He turns to Dad. "He's stupid!"

"Dumb as a bag of doorknobs," he agrees. "But he grows on you."

"Now, we've all been through a lot: Dad has fibrillated excessively, my arm is leaking like a pus-faucet, and the boy here lost all his hair in a terrible hair-spray fire."

"Did not!" He's still laughing.

"But we've bared our derrieres, and there's no stronger bond among men." I swallow the third and final M&M whole.

"What's a derriere?"

"Our *butts!*" I shout, just as the boy's mother walks into the room.

"The nurse told me you were down here," she says, exhaling perhaps for the first time since arriving at his room to find it empty. "What are you doing?"

"Baring our *butts!*" he howls, doubled over with laughter.

"Also, gambling," I add, "in case you're not concerned enough."

She looks at me, indeed concerned for that instant before her eyes drop to my nubby shoulder and she melts. "I hope he's not bothering you." Another giant mood swing triggered by a barely perceptible eye-shift.

Introductions are made, and then the alligator in the room is acknowledged.

"He was attacked by an alligator!" Cancer Boy brags. "They have it in their bathtub!"

"Surprisingly, one of those things is true." I try to sneak one of the kid's M&Ms, but he scoops them up.

"I'm saving these for later." He drops them into the pocket of his gown.

"Don't hoard! The key to being a good gambler is to enjoy your winnings."

"I throw up less in the mornings," he explains, suddenly quiet, and whatever unfairness I've carried since the accident leaves me to perch like a parrot on this boy where it belongs.

"It's good to see him laugh," his mother says, and she wishes us well before taking him back to the pediatric ward. Dad snaps off his television, and all that's left is the quiet din of a meaningless universe.

POSSIBLE CAUSES OF ONE-ARMED AFFLICTION

Alligator attack*

Infection

Cancer

Defusing a bomb

Run over by train

Machete fight

Propeller accident

Clumsy axe murderer

Threshing-machine
mishap

Shot by your own
Confederate troops

Malfunctioning automatic
sphygmomanometer

Stupid fucking SUV
driver

*For brevity's sake "alligator" also stands in for shark, lion, angry badger, and all potential predators of arms.

REGRETS

The next couple of days pass like a kidney stone, slow and painful. My arm is still draining and Dad continues to be observed—although, thankfully, he suffers no further episodes. While I'm under the intermittent barrage of IV swaps, bandage changes, fever checks, blood taking, drug dosages (and once, just to annoy Dad, a sponge bath), Dad is left relatively unmolested. In his boredom he plays the television like a first-person shooter, never relenting in his fevered manipulation of the remote, images flashing in front of us almost too quickly to register. When he finally settles on something, he usually dozes off shortly thereafter; if I reach over to snap off the TV the abrupt silence is enough to awaken him and start the cycle all over again.

But this time instead of reactivating the TV he turns as if to make sure I'm still here. I wave with my good hand and Dad nods back, managing a smile that quickly fades. He looks a little sad, and regretful—things I'd never seen cross Dad's face before.

"Do you ever have regrets?" I ask him.

"Jesus God," he groans.

"Really," I press. "If we were to die right now, what would you regret?"

"How would *we* die at the same time right now, by meteor?"

"You know what I mean."

"Well, if *we* died, of course I'd regret that my son didn't live longer than me."

"Fine. What if it was only *you* who died?"

"Everything we do, we do for a reason. As long as it's a good reason," Dad shrugs, "what's to regret? You did the best you could with what you knew at the time."

"What about things you didn't do? Opportunities that never happened?"

"Like what?"

"For me, I regret never having sex with two women."

"What are you talking about? You've had sex with a lot more than two women."

"I mean at the same time."

"Oh," he says, thinking. "I never had sex with two women either. In my life."

This information stuns me. Dad has only been with Mom? And now, if she hadn't already, Mom has trumped Dad with her firefighter.

"That's . . . remarkable."

"Only because you believe in instant gratification—you see what you want and you have to have it. And every shiny thing around you is something new you want, and you can't imagine what it's like not to want it and not to have it."

"You say that like it's a bad thing."

"Do you think I ever even looked at two women and thought for a second *I want to have sex with those two women together*? As if that was even possible in my life?"

"I guess not . . ."

"Of course I did," Dad laughs, surprising me. "What am I, made of wood?" We're both laughing, and I find it comforting that my dull, reliable father, who had chosen the safe haven of a life modulated away from extreme emotional poles, had a hidden streak of hedonism in him. "But one of them was always your mother," he clarifies.

Just then Mom enters, with a pint of Fleischmann's and three Dixie cups she's pulled from the water cooler.

"I brought a little something for my boys."

"You're the best mom ever," I gush.

Mom pours freely and then does so again. It isn't long before Dad is draining the last of eleven drops into his cup as a nurse arrives with the news that we're being discharged. It's a good thing we live close by, although it still takes Mom twenty minutes of white-knuckled focus punctuated by occasional giggling to get there.

As we pass through the not exactly immaculate housekeeping of my father, I find myself still a little tipsy and thinking about germs again. It's estimated that the average person touches his face three thousand times a day. So perhaps one upside of one-handedness is that I touch my face half as much (I paw at my face while thinking this), or even accounting for using one's favored hand, one-third as much. That's a thousand times a day fewer chances for transmitting some contagion from a doorknob to myself. Twisting Jackie's doorknob exposes me to a different kind of danger, as I find her packing.

"Was it something I said?"

"My, what a healthy ego we have," she chides me, twisting the knife of the plural pronoun. "You're not the motivating factor in my every decision."

"No more arguing!" Dad orders from the hallway, and Mom starts giggling.

I hug Jackie, and she lets me for a beat, before pulling away to resume packing.

"The simple fact is, I have a job, a husband, a mortgage to

pay," she ticks off a joyless trifecta of responsibilities. "I've stayed longer than I thought I would. I'm sure everyone's going to be fine without me."

"We'll be fine," Dad says, drifting farther down the hallway.

"Not that we won't miss you!" Mom laughs, and Dad joins her. Jackie stares back at them, confused.

"It was nice to have you here and to spend the time with you," I agree.

"I agree," Dad agrees with my agreement, before being pulled into their bedroom by Mom and slamming the door behind them.

"Good God, I cannot figure those two out."

"They both live without regrets," I tell her. "If you can imagine such a thing."

Jackie sits down quietly. "I admit to feeling a little overwhelmed here. My life in California is pretty uncomplicated."

"That's good. You can die of complications."

"Try not to."

"You'll be back. We have some sheriffs to sue. We'll be thousandaires!"

"Sue them without me. When you win, bring your private jet to LA."

"How are things between you and Steve?"

"We're fine. The way it works is, every six months he does something incredibly stupid, he's appropriately ashamed, and behaves perfectly for another six months."

"Twice a year, I have my teeth cleaned only to have to do it again. So he's no worse than plaque."

"Marriage is work. You know that."

"Actually, I didn't. Which is probably why mine didn't . . . work."

"What happened with you two, anyway? You never told us anything."

"It's been a very long time; why spoil things now?"

She shrugs.

"Once, very early, we'd just gotten married," I remember. "We had this little apartment with a swinging door in and out of the kitchen . . ."

"I remember. Cute place."

"One time, I was coming in as she was coming out with hot coffee. It spilled on her—the way I saw it, I spilled it on her—and burned her. It wasn't a bad burn, like something you had to go to the hospital for or anything. She just ran it under cold water and seemed fine. But I remember that moment, when she gasped and tried not to drop the coffee and rushed to the sink: I hurt her. I felt such a sensation of remorse, like I never had before: I hurt her. It didn't matter that it was unintentional—I had done something that caused her pain. I actually felt light-headed, as if I might faint. I thought I was going to cry; I had to try so hard not to. She kept assuring me she was okay and even laughed that I was getting so emotional . . . but I couldn't get past the fact that I had hurt her, that she was in pain because of me. It was a completely alien concept."

"Okay," Jackie squints at me, confused.

"After a few years, I hurt her almost regularly . . . and I didn't feel like that anymore."

"God, that makes me want to cry."

"Please don't. I couldn't handle it; I'm in a very fragile emotional state. Did I mention that I haven't been stoned for like, three days?"

"Did you even hear from her after the accident?"

"No, but come on—we split up five years ago. I don't even know where she is. It's not like we wish each other dead; we just don't mean anything to each other anymore."

"I'm sorry I didn't come. Mom and Dad convinced me to wait until you came home, but I felt so guilty . . ."

"You have nothing to feel guilty about." I sit next to her on the bed. "I was pretty out of it; I wouldn't even have known you were there. If you had to miss work for a month, this was the month. Look how much fun we had! It was much less exciting in rehab."

"I could have used a little less excitement. I'm completely exhausted."

"Thanks for coming home to help. I know I'm a shitty patient."

"The shittiest."

She buries herself under my good arm and we sit like that a long time, left unspoken the fact that she gets to leave and I do not.

DRIVE

Dad has bought a new pre-owned car—a van, of all things, in what the brochure no doubt calls "sand" or "biscuit" or "cinna-mon" but more closely resembles the sickly pallor of a man on his deathbed, like the old "flesh" color of a discontinued crayon. Before I can make him feel bad about buying a flesh-colored van, he tells me:

"I thought you could take my old car. Weber knows a guy in town who can retrofit it for . . ." He trails off, not wanting to form the sounds *one-armed driving,* and I let him off the hook.

"You were just sick of driving me back and forth to work."

"It was a giant pain in the ass," he lies.

"Thank you."

"Take better care of it than the last one I gave you," he casu-ally reminds me of the used 1985 Ford Laser I drove without adding oil until its engine seized—admittedly a low bar, but I've done nothing if not set low bars for myself.

The prosthetic tricking-out is rather simple: the wheel is fitted with a steering ball or "spinner," which for practicality cannot interfere with the air bag, and should not, when swung to the bottom position, tear into the driver's groin. Another gizmo transfers hand controls from the left of the steering column (di-rectional signals, wipers) to the right. I'm reminded once more how "lucky" I am to have my right arm to shift the automatic transmission, manipulate the radio and weather controls, use the cup holder and ashtray; but never again all at once like I did in high school: drinking, shifting gears, smoking pot, blasting the Cure, and caressing a date simultaneously with the proficiency of a test pilot.

It's a thoughtful and generous gift Dad's given me, the boon of personal freedom, although neither one of us is prepared for this moment: my first time behind a wheel since the accident, that car T-boned and the world spun in a shower of shattered glass, the rending of metal, the smell of fuel and an ineffectual face full of air bag gas, blood spurting and warm piss seeping, an explosion of sound relegated to hollow ringing as I sat there, a crowd gathering, then, and now a crowd of one, Dad peering in the passenger-side window while the sweat pumps. He pulls open the door and gets inside.

"Take your time," is all he says, and we sit there until the ringing stops.

Dad actually *yelps* once or twice as I try to teach myself the very basic skill of how to drive without crashing—another low bar I'll try to clear. Soon I'm capable of driving alone, and eventually ready to fail two road tests (surprisingly, the drug cocktail that enabled me to excel at fish counting has proven less effective at the space and time management required to operate a motor vehicle). I barely pass the third and liberate myself from dependence on Dad. Equally surprising: I soon miss our mornings together at the Four Corners while I instead grab gas station coffee and a shrink-wrapped muffin on the way to work I never wanted.

I've missed a week of work while in the hospital and recovering at home, but one of the nice things about working for the government is they don't seem to care (and in fact barely seem to have noticed). I'm enough off my game that at the end of the day my count is short of both Lilith's and Percy's matching numbers. Percy is overjoyed to have his groove back while Lilith seems to be wondering, like so many others before her, why she slept with me in the first place.

The counting of fish will take a hiatus during the winter, and while I'm grateful to avoid the looming freezing temperatures I know will refrigerate my underground workstation, I have mixed feelings about returning to the attic to hibernate. (By "mixed" I mean I'm really looking forward to it but know I shouldn't.) Instead I'm offered a clerical job at the Ick Ick office, and take unkind pleasure in the fact that Percy is not. Lilith too is hired, and it's unspoken between us but understood that as responsible coworkers, we'll be fine as long as she doesn't wear her fish T-shirt to the office.

After weeks in the largely unsupervised subterranean freedom of fish counting, this first morning in the office is jarring. I imagine this is what a rescued stray cat feels like: however warm and cozy and look there's a plate of food and a bowl of water and I can't wait to scratch the covering off that couch but fuck, what's with these walls, God I'm trapped inside let me out let me out let me *OUT*! I avoid clawing at anyone on my way to my cubicle— in contrast to my underground fish counting station, alarmingly public and somehow smaller on the inside. I sit unmoving for at least twenty minutes in what must appear outwardly to be a quietly meditative state, while inside is the accelerating turmoil of a man hurtling into a future where he dies at this desk of a heart attack that took far too long to get here.

There's a knock on my cubicle wall (an odd formality for a space without a door) and leaning just outside is Will, hired like Lilith and myself to help file data and generate the necessary river of paperwork to keep our government grant afloat. It isn't until I reach to shake his hand that he steps fully into view to reveal *he's missing his right arm*. This is the man I spotted first in reflection and then across the river from me—a munitions expert and veteran, as it turns out—a mirror image of myself: left-armed instead of right, and brave where I am not.

"You serve?" he asks, nodding at my arm.

"Not unless you count Applebee's. Did a tour during college."

"Lost mine to an IED in Lebanon."

"I lost mine to three letters too: SUV."

"Well, both probably belonged to assholes."

And just like that, I've encountered the first person who knows all the things I know: the frustrations, the struggles, the shame of incompleteness. I'd met another amputee back at ITCH but like to think we shared very little because he was crazy enough to have forced the removal of his own leg. He suffered something called body integrity identity disorder—which in his case had led him to believe his own leg to be a foreign body he needed to expunge. Incapable of doing it himself, he tied a tourniquet around it in order to prevent blood from flowing, knowing that starving it of blood would ruin the leg. By the time he allowed himself to be taken to the hospital, doctors had no choice but to rid him of the offending limb. A happy ending, until he began to think of his remaining leg as another imposter. It made me realize that of all the parts of us we might lose, sanity was the one to which we should cling most tightly.

"These numbers are shitty," Will continues, and it takes me a moment to catch up to the shift of attention from our shared affliction to the tally from our weeks by the river.

We'd counted several hundred blue paddle snouts, which seems like a lot for an endangered fish. Yet the Wabash once teemed with them in numbers exceeding tens of thousands, which is what it takes to ensure their survival. Sturgeon "broadcast spawn," meaning they reproduce externally: females scatter their eggs while males release sperm, and the fertilized eggs sink to the bottom where they hatch in about a week. I imagine if the human sex act consisted of a woman expelling eggs from her body while men ejaculated all around them, we'd be extinct in a single generation (except for fetishists who might find that exciting, and those probably aren't the likeliest Darwinian genes for propagating a species). But up until and even shortly after they hatch, the next generation of *Acipenser pseudoboscis* is just fast food for river life looking for a meal on their way downstream. It takes millions of eggs to enable thousands of paddle snout to survive long enough for hundreds of them to do it all over again the next mating season, and the present numbers make that unlikely.

The problem, as Will sees it, is "the goddamn dam." Built in the sixties for irrigation, it largely blocks the sturgeon from returning to its spawning ground.

"What about the fish ladders?"

"Fish aren't built to climb ladders."

"Right," I immediately get it. "I'm remarkably fishlike that way."

"For a fish to get up those ladders, it has to engage in burst swimming: sudden, high speeds that use more oxygen and energy, and can trigger cardiac arrest."

"So if the dam doesn't kill them, the race to procreate at the top of the stairs will. It's unnatural. It's why old guys don't put their mistresses in upstairs apartments without an elevator."

"The dam's also bad for fishing and boating, fucks up the natural environment, and is a goddamn eyesore," he adds. "*They should blow that shit up,*" is Will's final assessment, and he holds my gaze long enough as if to probe what I might think of that idea, but then excuses himself before I can glean whether this professional exploder of things is joking or not.

KINDRED

Work is an enervating slog, a deathless purgatory, an endless, hopeless eternity. My day is spent filling out and filing papers, which is harder than you think one-handed so I tend to use my teeth to compensate but notice some frowning when I'm caught doing so, mostly by Lilith. (She'll find cause to frown again when she comes across those bite-marked files in the weeks to come.) Getting good and stoned is also more difficult here than in my underground hole with a view, and even though I'm legally entitled to my medical marijuana breaks, I'm pretty sure that would inspire more frowning. So I double up on Vicodin and snack liberally on marijuana goldfish, and the day seems incredibly long, an endless road to nowhere stretching out in front of me—until it's over, and then it's nearly forgotten, vanished in the rearview mirror.

But none of that matters because I have a new best friend! Where Joel was the nerdy kid I could feel superior to and Artie was the popular kid who talked me into bold adventures in firecrackers, both managed to make me feel cooler than I was. And now so does Will, completely undaunted by the singularity of his armness . . . which means *I can be too*. Will doesn't even attract the same stares that I do, possessing an incongruent swagger that lends the illusion of being able-bodied. I've been so energized by the magnitude of his presence that I've dialed back the pot and pills and resumed my morning jog. I also taught myself to shuffle cards one-handed, a trick I refined after repeated viewings of a YouTube tutorial.

"Pretty nifty," Will graciously pretends to be impressed, although I'm pretty sure he can still take apart and reassemble a rifle with one hand.

He asks if I want to grab dinner and further impresses me by ordering a *fucking steak,* holding it in place by leaning on his fork with his stump and then cutting it into pieces with his left hand.

"How's that steak?" the waitress asks.

"Hot on the outside and tender in the middle, just like some of my favorite people," he flirts, and she smiles back.

"And your ravioli?"

"Soft and cheesy. As a person, it would leave something to be desired."

I receive no smile, and she flees the table.

"How do you do that, flirt with a woman while stump-forking your food?"

"Because it is what it is, and I don't care," Will shrugs. "If you don't care, they don't care. When it bothers you so much, everyone around you is uncomfortable."

Everyone around you is uncomfortable is a dead-on description of what bothers me so much. One of us has this backward, and I can't help but think it isn't the one who's effortlessly manipulating a pepper mill with one hand.

In the days that follow we become a homoerotic music-video montage of romantic clichés, hunkered down closely over fish spreadsheets at work and sharing lunch; laughing at DVDs in my attic at night (I imagine us sharing a Snuggie), and baring our nubs (he laughs long and hard at my sea serpent tattoo!); we crash bicycles, inept as we are at hand brakes (but land, laughing), and skip stones by the river, where I suggest how much fun it would be to let firecrackers explode in our good hands.

"There's only one thing here I can see that needs exploding," his mood hardens, and his next stone careens off the dam.

It's the tiny flaw in the otherwise-perfect diamond that is Will, this occasional vague reference to the dam. He does it in a way that's incomplete, saying just enough to put the idea back on me like an undercover cop posing as a hooker attempting to trap a horny john. I resist the attempt at entrapment with a blazing five-skipped stone and the challenge, "Beat that, you one-armed fucker!" And of course he does, with seven.

It will be a while before the dam comes up again, although it will hang between us like mosquito netting through which we could no longer quite see each other.

VISITOR

"We have a visitor," Dad calls from downstairs.

The last time I heard Dad use that phrase the visitor was sixteen-year-old Pam Jaffe, who had inexplicably come over to head up to my room and press her mouth into mine but wouldn't let me feel her up. I mentally race through an unlikely list of possibilities that includes Lilith, a just-awakened Ariana, my ex-wife, grown-up Pam Jaffe, and even Sunny Lee. What I don't expect to see is our eleven-year-old cancer patient friend from the hospital on a guided tour of the family photos in our hallway as if sightseeing the dullest museum ever.

"That's my father's father," Dad pokes at an old black-and-white eight-by-ten of a man behind a desk behind a man behind a desk surrounded by men behind desks. "He worked at General Motors for forty-nine years."

"Did he make motors?"

"I don't know what the hell he did."

"How did you find us?"

"I Googled you!" he announces cheerily, oblivious to the draw-backs of growing up in a world where anyone who wants to find you can, including ex-girlfriends and Mafia henchmen.

"And here we are," Dad assesses our place in the universe. And oddly, does not leave the room. "This is Aunt Thelma," he continues the tour. "I've never seen a picture of her without a cigarette."

"Who's the guy with the big gun?"

I've passed this hallway every day for weeks now, and these photos have become wallpaper to me, beneath notice, until now. Dad is indeed the man with the big gun, in snow-covered Innsbruck.

"Some young kid I used to know," he says.

"What happened to him?"

"Nothing," Dad replies. "Hey, I know what you'd rather see than a bunch of old pictures. Aaron, take him upstairs."

"Right! I'll show him your sock drawer."

"I liked you better in the hospital," Dad mutters.

"Sure, life was easy then. Room service at the touch of a button, meals in bed, and if you didn't feel like getting up: bedpans. But the good times can't last forever."

"I want to see the alligator!" Cancer Boy laughs while Dad glares at me.

"Of course! The alligator! This way," I lead him up the stairs. "Do you have a dollar?"

"Yes?" he says tentatively.

"Well, hang on to it. Someday you may want to give it to a nice girl who dances for you."

At the top of the stairs Ali is already splashing. He seems to know when visitors are coming and sometimes gets excited, although sometimes, as with Steve, he lies in wait to surprise them. His tail is thrashing like that of a happy dog, and I expect Cancer Boy to be scared but he's not. How do you scare a kid who faces the most terrifying thing anyone could face every day of his life?

"So fucking cool!"

"He *is*!" I agree. "And don't repeat that around your mom."

"I'm not a fucking idiot! Can I pet him?"

"Here . . ." I take his little hand in mine and bring it back around the tail to stroke. Ali doesn't snap much, but why risk adding one-handedness to this already diminished boy?

"His skin is hard," he notices.

"It is. You wouldn't think you'd want to make a purse out of it—or boots. Or underpants, for that matter."

"They don't make alligator underpants!"

"Of course not. Alligators don't wear underpants."

"They don't wear any pants!"

"Exactly. It's probably why they're not more popular."

"Give him some of this," Dad tramps into the bathroom with three slices of bologna, handing them directly to the boy.

Again, I gently take his hand in mine and dangle a slice over Ali's head . . . and Ali *SNAPS* at it, and I pull the kid back, and we both tumble to the floor. He's laughing hard but that could be the shock of losing fingers, so I count to make sure all his digits remain intact. As we get to our feet Dad leaves the room in a fairly transparent attempt at "plausible deniability" should he be called to testify about the maiming of this small boy by alligator. I toss the remaining two slices at Ali and he catches them midair, and Cancer Boy thinks this is the coolest fucking thing he's ever seen, and it just might be.

When it's time to leave he stands in the doorway long enough that it becomes obvious he hasn't accomplished whatever it is he came here to do.

"You can't leave yet," I say, slamming the door behind him. "If you think feeding an alligator is exciting wait till you see Dad feed a live squirrel *with his bare hands!*"

Out in the yard the boy actually *is* fascinated as the tiny squirrel hops over to Dad, leans in, plucks the peanut like a pickpocket and races away.

"You do it!" he yelps.

"The last time I tried, it didn't go so well."

With Dad's help, Cancer Boy does the peanut trick—Dad's fingers holding his fingers holding the peanut shell holding the peanut inside, an irresistible nesting doll treat the squirrel yanks to the safety of his tree. We sit a moment and I let the boy fill the silence.

"Would you come to my school for show-and-tell?"

Dad visibly blanches and for a moment, I think he might bolt for Fleischmann's or gasoline—perhaps both, first to get drunk and then set himself on fire—presuming as I do that the kid wants me to come show off my non-arm to his classmates.

"With your alligator," the boy clarifies.

"I'm not sure I can do that," I gently explain. "Bringing a live alligator around children probably isn't the safest thing, and I'm not a trained animal expert or anything. I'd have a hard time wrangling him with one arm—did I mention I only have one arm?" I wave my nub at him.

"I know that, dummy!" he laughs. "He could help," he indicates Dad, who looks ready to bolt again.

"You're right; three arms are better than one, but not as good as two arms attached to a guy who knows what he's doing. Besides, it could be dangerous for Ali. What if someone shoots him for not wearing pants?"

I can see by his downcast face I've added another pearl to my perfect strand of recent disappointments, and I struggle for some way to make it right.

"How about instead I tell the class about my job as a fish counter?"

"What's that?"

"I count fish," I say, instantly disappointing this kid again but recovering quickly. "Here, take a look."

I Google *Acipenser pseudoboscis* on my phone and show him a picture of the blue paddle-snout sturgeon.

"It has no teeth and an extendable mouth for eating off the floor. And look at that snout! Is that one ugly motherfucking fish or what?"

"He's an ugly motherfucker!" he instantly agrees, and we have a date.

LESSONS

The school I attended as a boy is smaller than I remember it, especially inside, where I am booked, fingerprinted, and photographed like an accused pedophile and then allowed to mingle with the children. I stride into the classroom alone, nervous, despite having once commanded the dubious attention of high schoolers—10 percent of whom were stoned on something, 20 percent utterly disinterested in the forty-minute period between pokes at their cell phones, and another 20 percent as impervious to knowledge as lead is to x-rays; that's fully half of all students eliminated from a path of continued learning by the natural selection of the educational system. I write my name on the board and turn to face the undivided attention of wide-eyed wonder directed squarely at my nub.

But I'm not here to talk about me. Supplied with a pile of visual aids from Ick Ick (including the capper: a jar of perfectly preserved fertilized fish eggs meant to represent the continued future existence of a species), I'm going to tell them about the exciting world of fish counting. I rattle on about migration and spawning, rivers and dams, ecosystems and extinction. I tell them about the blue paddle-snout sturgeon, almost completely extirpated from the Wabash River, and present an enlarged rendering of one, which fails to draw their attention from my nub mostly because the clumsiness of handling it one-handed accentuates the thing they are most interested in. I can tell even the teacher is bored, smile fixed like plastic on his Mr. Potato Head face. Worse, Cancer Boy looks devastated. And he's suffered enough disappointment.

"All right, enough about fish. Let's talk about the elephant in the room."

Now I can see I've totally confused them.

"There are elephants too?"

"No. Not in the river. No elephants."

"But you have one in your room?"

"No! I don't; it's just an expression."

"He has an alligator!" Cancer Boy announces gleefully. "It tried to bite me!"

His teacher appears alarmed, and I explain that yes, we keep an alligator, but no, it didn't really try to bite him, it was really after the bologna. Another little boy wants to know if the alligator and the elephant get along, and someone else follows that with a question about who would win a fight between an alligator and an elephant, and of course the elephant would stomp the alligator to death but what if the alligator bit the elephant first and knocked him down and then bit his face and wouldn't let go, followed by the skeptic who announces that *no way* do I have an alligator and an elephant at home.

"Forget the goddamn elephant!" I shout, and the teacher stands up from the back of the room and shouts, *Hey!* before I stop him, palm outraised like a traffic cop. "I got this! Taught for twelve years—it's okay, they're just curious . . . and they might learn something."

He sinks back into his seat, and the questions come: *What happened to my arm? Did it hurt? What did they do with it after they cut if off? Could I have kept it if I wanted to, like, in a fish tank? How do I tie my shoes? Is it gross?* The teacher winces with every question and sinks lower in his chair with every answer, but Cancer Boy is beaming like he's found E.T. and brought him to show-and-tell, and by the time a boy asks, *Can we see it?* I know the capper isn't the promise of fish survival floating in formaldehyde but a real live amputated stump. The teacher tries to stop me, but he's too slow, and he rushes for help as the room erupts in shrieks of amazement mingled with horror, and one little boy throws up.

Cancer Boy and I are both in the office of the principal, who's trying his best to understand the relationship between us. It doesn't help that the kid starts his explanation with "We bared our butts!" and goes on to talk about how I took him to my bathroom to show him something in my tub.

"Just to be clear, what I showed him in my tub was an alligator," I add the clarification that will keep me out of prison orange.

"His skin is hard!" Cancer Boy adds.

"Again, we're talking about an alligator," I insist. "We met in the hospital. I was being treated for an infection. I'm not sure what's wrong with the boy. He seems perfectly fine to me; I think he may be faking something to get out of homework."

"I have cancer!" he shouts gleefully.

"And you were there for your . . ." Following the usual hesitation, the principal says, "Arm."

"Actually, it's the absence of the arm that's mostly been the problem."

"So you came here for show-and-tell," the principal tries to understand. "Which is something we don't do here. But I guess another in a series of concessions has been made for our special case."

Cancer Boy looks at the floor.

"Don't embarrass him," I snap, and Cancer Boy looks up at me, grinning again, and he turns his grin on the principal and suddenly we're tag-team wrestlers with our opponent on the ropes, and no one is tagging out.

"You swore in front of the children," the principal accuses me.

"I did no such thing."

"The teacher insists you said"—he reads—"'the goddamn elephant.'"

Cancer Boy howls his approval.

"You call that swearing? In that case, now both of us did. Whatever the punishment, let's face it together."

"There's the added serious infraction of exposing yourself in front of the children," he adds, a poorly worded and inaccurate account of events—also badly timed, as Cancer Boy's mother, called from home, enters at just that moment.

Cancer Boy rushes to hug her and when he lets go long enough to say, "Mom, you missed the coolest fucking thing *ever*," I wish I had two hands to cover my face.

Stripped of my visitor's credential I can't help but ask, "Will this go on my permanent record?" before being escorted from the building by a security lug who definitely falls into the bottom 50 percent of former students whose dismal future is now. In the parking lot, the slamming of a car door catches my attention and I turn to see Cancer Boy, still grinning, in the front seat as his mom crosses the distance between us.

"I don't know what to say," she states flatly, still somewhat cowed by my handicap.

"Understandable. This isn't a scenario one imagines or plans for." She stares at me—Oliver Twist with an empty bowl, wanting more. "If it helps, I'm sorry. Did you even know he came to my house?"

"I only found out because at a bat mitzvah yesterday, when the little thirteen-year-old girl got up to dance? He tried to give her a dollar. I found out then."

I wince. A quick, stupid joke I never thought would register. But the kid is smart.

"He's very impressionable," she says as if I'd spoken aloud. "And I might have made things worse, because then he wouldn't tell me why he went to your house. I had no idea you were coming here today."

Behind her, Cancer Boy makes the kind of goofy faces you'd expect a normal eleven-year-old boy to make behind the back of a scolding grown-up. Mom sees me looking past her but by the time she turns, he's staring blankly straight ahead and, with expert comic timing, he resumes face making when she returns her attention to me.

"You understand, he's gone through a terrible time."

"I can't begin to understand. But yes, I'm aware it must be terrible."

"The worst part, believe it or not? All the attention. It took me a very long time to grasp . . . he doesn't want the awkwardness of his friends passed down by their parents, the special treatment by teachers, the pitying stares of the neighbors. An athlete I never heard of came to the house, and people tried to raise money to send him to Disney World. He hates all of it. Little boys just want to be like other little boys." She wipes away a forming tear and quickly composes herself. "He just wants to be normal instead of goddamn special."

"That, I understand."

Prompted, she can't help but steal a glance at my arm, giving me a chance to make eye contact with her son, who's pulling his mouth wide with both hands. Something else I can't do.

"What happened in there . . . all the attention was off him for a change."

"I was definitely the main attraction, yes."

"He was even allowed to get into trouble, which hasn't happened in a long time. I was starting to worry he could burn the school to the ground and get away with it." I'm sure he can't hear us, but enough time has passed for the fleeting attention span of a boy to revert his face-making self back into another bored kid waiting in a car. "So I'm grateful that he had one afternoon where he feels normal again. But as a parent, I have to say"—she shakes her head—"he probably shouldn't be around you. I'll tell him to leave you alone."

They drive off, and the kid gives me one final pig-nose-pressed-against-the-window face, fogging the glass until he's out of sight.

DUCK

Thanksgiving seems an odd thing to celebrate without the arm that makes carving a turkey possible. A chirpy outsider would no doubt point out *at least you have your father and a roof over your head,* but even that seems more burden than boon, suffering the ignominy of a child's dependence.

They say no matter how bad you think you have it *someone always has it worse.* Of course that's true—I know a kid with cancer. And somewhere there's a man who's lost both his arms, with no one on whom to be dependent. Beyond him, there's someone with no limbs who's also blind. Taking it to its logical conclusion, who's the poor bastard at the end of this line—the person for whom *no one has it worse?* A deaf, dumb, blind, limbless leper, shipwrecked and floating atop the Great Pacific trash vortex as he's slowly nibbled to death by passing seagulls, his open wounds burning in the salt water. It isn't possible to tell that guy *someone always has it worse.*

Unless maybe it's Dad, stuck spending Thanksgiving with a mopey, mutilated son sitting across a Peking duck (who also, in its short duck life, had little to be thankful for).

"It's no turkey, but it eats pretty good," Dad says, crunching some skin.

"If it was good enough for the emperor, it's good enough for the worst Thanksgiving ever."

"That distinction belongs to the one where your sister told us she was pregnant."

I'm stunned. "When the hell did that happen?"

"Oh. I guess you didn't know. I sure wouldn't tell you. She was seventeen. She told your mother, and your mother told me. Come to think of it, I'm not even sure if Jackie knows that I knew."

He shakes soy sauce over his duck with great intent.

"She went away that summer—and then to college!" I remember. "Oh my God, you hid her and she had a baby, and I'm an uncle to some kid somewhere in the world." Maybe even that poor bastard stuck on the trash vortex.

"There's no kid; it turned out to be a false pregnancy," Dad laughs. "I can laugh about it now . . . but at the time, knowing my little Jackie was knocked up? Pretty devastating. I think all firstborns should be male . . . however terrible the shit they put you through it's never as bad as it would be with a girl, and now as a parent, you're prepared for the next terrible time. Firstborns are the calluses that toughen you for what comes next. Except for that one time, you'd have given me tougher calluses."

"That was the year no one spoke the entire meal," I recall. Dad had put his head down to say grace and never lifted it, shoveling food until it was gone and then excusing himself to the football game on TV.

"It was preferable to some of the others. I can still hear the shouting from when your mother's sister and Uncle Ed joined us."

"So it *wasn't* the worst."

"And neither is this. So stop complaining and eat. The Chinese have spent fifteen hundred years on that damn duck."

"Hopefully, not this particular one."

Dad pays the check and steals the pen. Our first armless

Thanksgiving behind us, we leave our fortune cookies untouched, neither one of us eager to know the future.

That night I get an e-mail from Steve containing two links. Steve does not send me e-mails, not since I forwarded one of his hilarious links of interspecies sex to his wife. I click on the first link and am treated to a YouTube video of Steve's narrative tattoo journey that we shot in my attic. I watch long enough to recall, *I've already seen this one,* and I'm about to delete it when I notice the URL of the second link contains the phrase *Sea Serpent.* I click and there's a super close-up of my tattooed nub, along with my narration of the tale of Bob the Sea Serpent, scourge of Vikings, and the galley hero of the *Raging Scallop.*

If, as according to Jackie, Steve's usual cycle of stupidity lasts six months, he's on an accelerated schedule. I can see *The Tale of Bob the Sea Serpent* only has six hits—half of those are no doubt Steve admiring his handiwork—and is unlikely to double that number. Still, it will take only four inspirational words of reply, *What Would Jackie Do?,* to take it offline by morning. I fire up a bowl of Herb Alpert's Tijuana Grass and watch *Steve's Tattoo Tales* again, thinking this can't be that much dumber than a reality show called *LA Ink.*

In my sleep I dream about a crew of armless Vikings lined up at the tattoo parlor to get matching Bob the Sea Serpent tattoos where their arms once were—it's an unholy pact with the sea monster that attacked their ship and bit off their arms to remake them, godlike, in his armless image. Displeased that I bear the mark of the sea serpent when I was not, like them, a true victim of Bob, the Vikings surround me, arguing about what should be done with me—although, armless, they don't pose much of a threat. That's when I notice Bob the Sea Serpent in another chair across the room having arms tattooed on his sides. He nods at me, and would give me a thumbs-up if he could.

AWKWARD

I'm jolted to walk into Broken Records and find Will and Lilith together, sifting through the classical section. (Immediately imagining their sex together, I surmise that Lilith doesn't have to flip Will onto his back to perform but may in their lovemaking be the flippee.) Lilith is showing Will a copy of "The Lark Ascending," the torturous equivalent of pouring salt on my nub. I imagine what kind of scene I might make if I were prone to scene making, and what kind of duel might ensue between two one-armed men—I'm supposed to slap him with my gloves, but does one glove constitute a halfhearted challenge? More disturbing is that I can't figure out who I'm actually jealous of, Will for having Lilith or the other way around.

"Hey, look who's back," Mr. Madnick cheers from behind the register.

"Don't get too excited, Mr. Madnick. I forgot my homework again."

I walk over to fist-bump Will, our usual greeting, and then I hug Lilith, something I've never done before but am curious if, in pressing against her tits, I might get a rise out of Will. But his face reveals nothing except genuine happiness to see me, while hers bears the usual blank stare of a catatonic.

"Lilith is trying to get me into classical, and I'm trying to turn her on to System of a Down."

"This is lovely," I say, plucking the album from her fingers, adding coyly and with my own piercing stare, "I've heard it before."

"Of course you have. I played it for you in my bedroom."

So much for coy. Will grins and resists the urge to high-five me.

"It was voted to the top spot of Classic FM's Hall of Fame last year," she says as she takes it back and examines it.

Mr. Madnick joins us. "How's the arm?"

"Still missing. I was thinking of putting up flyers."

"Neal Madnick," he introduces himself, reaching to shake Will's missing hand.

He never noticed. The Will effect.

Will offers his inverted left hand and, startled at how he could miss such a thing, Mr. Madnick clumsily shakes it. Lilith steps in to hug him, as if having just learned what a hug was and deciding to try it out for herself. Mr. Madnick takes the LP from Lilith and looks it over.

"Nice piece. Influential. Did you know it inspired some of the strings on King Crimson's *Larks' Tongues in Aspic*?"

"I think I'd like to hear that," Lilith thinks aloud, and she and Mr. Madnick head over to the listening station.

"So, are you two a thing now?" I query Will. "You know that means we'll have to call you 'Wilith.'"

"Nah! Both just killing time."

"Did you get the full treatment—violin solo and sexy birdhouse talk?"

"She played for you? Now I'm jealous."

I know he's playing but I'll bank this implausible idea that *Will is jealous of me* to call up and savor in my darker moments.

"We probably shouldn't be talking about her," I suggest, cowed by the presence of my former teacher. "She'll get a bad reputation and her name in the boys' bathroom, and the bullies will go after her."

"God help the bullies; she'd eat them alive."

I'm enjoying hanging with Will at the record store like a love-struck teenage boy when a single furtive sentence starts to un-ravel everything. "So, I've been thinking about the dam . . ."

God damn it.

"We're in a position to do something. Doing nothing is the same as doing the wrong thing where I come from."

And just like that, I take the bait. "Isn't there a happy place in the middle between something and nothing that's less dra-matic than blowing up the dam?" I search his face for some sign of agreement to this obvious point. "You know we can't do that, right? And by 'can't' I don't mean 'not capable of' but 'it would be unwise to do so.'"

"What's unwise is building impediments to the natural order of things. Fish got to swim; birds got to fly."

Tell me I'm crazy, the rest of the lyrics go. But I'm not the crazy one.

"Ah, ignore me; I'm just talkin'," Will waves me off as Lilith returns from listening to King Crimson.

"Wow," she says without exclamation. "That was terrible."

BRAIN

In the morning I don't see Dad in his usual morning place hunkered down over a bowl of cereal in front of *SportsCenter*. Peering outside I'm surprised to see him sitting in his van in the driveway. I head outside and pull open the passenger-side door and before I can say anything, I'm pleased to hear Sunny Lee's voice. I sit next to Dad and we listen together as she talks about brains:

We've all heard about left-brained people and right-brained people, the division of labor of separate but exactly equal hemispheres . . . but the truth, like your brain, is more complicated than that. First of all, on a microscopic level, the architecture, types of cells, neurotransmitters, and receptors of the human brain are markedly asymmetrical between the two sides. Symmetry is SO overrated!

Then there's the myth that right-brained people are creative dreamers and artists, while left-brainers tend to be calculated thinkers and wordsmiths. In reality, aspects of language and calculation occur on both sides of the brain, communicated to each other . . . and it comes out HERE. The job of all this cross-communication belongs to the corpus callosum, the band of white matter connecting the hemispheres. Without it, you might

function like "Rain Man": great at counting cards, but not so
great on social occasions.

"Isn't she great?" I ask rhetorically. "Wait for the blow . . ."

With so much going on, it's no surprise the human brain is
the most overworked organ this side of a hockey game: Da da da
DA da DA! Cha-arge! I'm Sunny Lee, with The Sunny Side.

"Well, they can't all be gems."
Dad continues to stare straight ahead.
"Are you coming or going?"
He sits there unmoving, and it's only when I feel how cold his
hands are and he still does not budge, that I realize something
is very wrong.
"Dad!" I shout, holding his freezing cold hand—he must have
been sitting here like this since late last night—and when he
still doesn't respond I run inside to get a blanket to throw over
him. He remains motionless as I swaddle him like a shipwreck
victim. Panicking, I attempt to shove him over to the passenger
seat and, failing that, tip him onto his side so I can drive, dangerously one-handed, to the hospital.

At the hospital I'm told Dad has definitely suffered a "neuro-
logical incident," the eight-syllable way doctors say "stroke."
He's admitted and it's a very long time before I'm able to see
him, and I'm not sure he can see me. Lying in bed he stares straight
up at the ceiling and makes no acknowledgment of my presence.
I take his hand in mine, and it's like holding something inert.
"Dad, can you hear me?"
No answer.
"If you can hear me, squeeze my hand."
Nothing.

"Blink once for yes, twice for no."

No response.

"If you're there, pick up."

I wonder if I'll ever hear his voice again, the one that challenges me with kindness masked as gruffness and shouts at *SportsCenter*. Or if he'll ever look at me and recognize who I am. Or walk—or piss—by himself. I pray that he's not "locked in," frozen in place but completely aware of the world around him as he's poked and prodded and stabbed with IVs and inserted with catheters and spoken of in the past tense as if he's already gone, or worse, still here but useless as old meat. Just then, he closes his eyes, and I hope he hasn't died and wish in the same moment that he might have.

I'd give anything for him to start punching channels on the remote and complain about his inability to find ESPN. Mom shows up only long enough to make it clear that this is beyond her, that her early exit from their marriage absolves her from this unhappy turn of events the same way walking out of a movie in the middle spares you from suffering its crappy ending.

"The reason I left your father," she explains right in front of him, defenseless, "is because he refused to take care of himself. The cigars, the bad food. Do you know the last time he went for a walk? Only as far as the backyard, to feed peanuts to the squirrels. Even then it was one for them, one for him."

I look to Dad for rebuttal, but there's none coming.

"So you just walk away from this."

"I already walked away. My occasional friendly interaction with your father is not the same thing as bearing the burden of responsibility for him. I left because I knew this was coming."

"You can see the future," I say, unkindly.

"Some futures are apparent. If you lie down on railroad tracks and refuse to move, your future is clear. I had the sense to get out of the way. I shouldn't have to be hit by the train regardless."

"So tell me my future."

"Your future is mutable. It can still go any one of several possible ways. But your immediate future no doubt will be taking care of your father, whether you do it yourself or delegate it to some capable outside agency."

"And you'd be okay with that?"

"It's impossible to know what to do here. And your recent decision making has been remarkably poor. You've probably managed to do the wrong thing about half the time . . . which means you've been right the other half," she surprises me, patting me on the head, gently sliding her hand to cup my face. "Even odds are the best most of us can hope for in a crisis."

And Jackie, for all her tears and long-distance anguish, has a career and a family and a life two thousand miles away. She thinks she'll lose her job—the precious thing that gives her purpose and validation—if she takes any more time away from work, and I reassure her that another trip at this time won't be useful anyway. She asks me to hold the phone to Dad's ear, and I do, and as she sobs her love for him, I half hope that my cell battery explodes, killing him instantly and taking my remaining hand so I can bleed out next to his headless body here in the hospital, and all our problems will be over. When she hangs up, head and hand are still intact and both Dad and I stare off into a future that may be "mutable" but looks pretty shitty from here.

After a long day at the hospital I finally come home to crash—a poor choice of words since that's also something I almost do twice in Dad's van from a near-lethal mix of fatigue and one-handedness. The front door to the house is wide open—if a couple of meth addicts are waiting inside to kill me, they'll find me surprisingly cooperative. While I don't quite welcome death's sweet embrace, I'd be happy to dodge the awfulness of my looming circumstances.

I'm actually disappointed to realize that I probably left the front door open when I raced in and out for a blanket. I'm peeing a long time before I notice that the bathtub is empty, that in our long absence Ali must have gone roaming in search of food. A quick room-to-room search leads me to conclude that the insufficient nourishment provided by our empty house has led him, hungrily, out the open front door.

Mom would no doubt consider the future outcome of this particular situation immutably bad—Ali either winds up feasting on neighborhood pets or hunted down by law enforcement, possibly both. What she possibly could not foresee is that *I don't give a shit.* The universe has hurled one too many trials at me, and my response is to ascend to the attic and *thunk* the world behind me and disappear in an ill-advised combination of med mar and an odd-numbered dose of Vicodin washed down with the remaining Fleischmann's I plucked from under the kitchen sink that I plan on draining to its final eleven drops. Fuck me, Universe? Fuck. You.

THINGS THE UNIVERSE DOESN'T GIVE A SHIT ABOUT

Rogue alligators
The neighbors' pets
A good man's brain
A small boy's cancer
Being told, "Fuck you"
Fairness
Irony
Genocide
Fish

CLARITY

I awaken more than fourteen hours later knowing two things with absolute certainty: (1) The trajectory of things already in motion will not stop just because I lock myself in the attic and get stoned beyond all reason, and (2) I guess I already knew that.

After a breakfast of instant coffee and toaster waffles poorly and laboriously managed under the twin hardships of handicap and hangover, I get to work on a LOST flyer for Ali, settling on the following language:

> LOST: *90-pound alligator, Muhammad Ali Gator, answers (sort of) to "Ali." Sweet disposition!* WARNING: *May be hungry. Capable of running quite fast in a straight line. Zigzagging recommended if he appears uncooperative.*

I add contact information and paste a photo of Ali with his mouth closed that looks as if he's smiling, although I wish it looked more like the funny cartoon smile of a Disney gator than the menacing grin of Killer Croc. I'll stuff a few nearby mailboxes with these and hope I don't attract too many cranks and/or law enforcement. (In the balance between the survival of our neighborhood's small pet population or losing Dad's alligator to Animal Control, Dad, having lost so much already, wins.)

Next I jump over to Craigslist, the perfect place to find qualified home care if you're resigned as I am to accomplishment via the least possible effort. I craft an ad asking for experience, references, and a recent photo, the last of which may strike some as odd but that just helps me cull applicants with an aversion to odd. While I'm there, I also put my car up for sale, which will help pay to convert Dad's van into a handicapped vehicle for both driver and passenger, leading to the next call I make to come pick up the van. After inhaling a goodly amount of Herbtastic, I call Ick Ick and request time off from my job, choking on a bong hit, which they mistake for crying and assure me I am welcome to return any time I'm ready and to please take care of myself, both of which seem unlikely.

At the hospital, Dad is just how I left him, with the exception of his position, propped sitting up to stare forward into space instead of up at the ceiling—a tiny improvement in his situation if not his condition. According to the doctors, of whom I've had quite enough, the brain is a funny thing, although by "funny" they seem to mean its exact opposite. Dad's condition may over time "change" (which is not to imply "improve"), or it may not; despite the prognostications of Mom, it appears his future is "mutable" in that he might regain his speech (or not), movement (or not), memory and awareness (or neither), the ability to walk (or not) and completely care for himself (unlikely), and/or complete cognizance. (Or none of the above.) He may with physical therapy regain much of his former strength and ability, but not his mental faculties; or he might remain physically disabled while his brain slowly rewires itself, bypassing the damaged areas and compensating with other parts of the brain until he emerges, at some indeterminate time, some modified version of the self he used to be. Or someone markedly different. Impossible to say.

It's all very similar, I cannot help but think, to my own condition: I may learn to do things differently, like shuffle cards one-handed or drive a car with a spinner or allow myself to be flipped on my back for intercourse; but none of those are the same thing as my arm growing back. Nor will the damaged parts of Dad's brain recover so much as his brain will learn to do things differently. (Or not.)

If he understands any of this, Dad gives no indication. Perhaps he's just playing possum. After a lifetime of caring for ungrateful children and a wife who left him to seek selfish fulfillment in a yurt, maybe it's his turn to be taken care of; after an appropriate period of time, he'll leap from his wheelchair like a cartoon stripper from a cake and shout, "April Fool!" and we'll laugh . . .

But for now I'll play along.

HOME

It turns out my car is worth more than I'd expected and while that extra money could prove useful in any number of ways, I like the symmetry of devoting the entire sum to the refurbishing of Dad's flesh-colored van; as I see it, the best way to do that is to transform it into a van that is not flesh-colored. I have it painted a stunning metallic purple, a color best suited for a Plymouth Prowler or a prostitute's fingernails, and turn things up a notch by hiring an airbrush artist to paint a side panel mural of a Viking battling a giant, angry ferret. All that's missing is a bumper sticker reading, "IF THIS VAN'S ROCKIN' PLEASE KNOCK, BECAUSE DAD COULD BE HAVING A SEIZURE IN HERE." (I'm dismayed to learn that the vanity license plate "VAN GO" is already taken.)

I hire Consuela based on her references (which in summary paint her as an adequate caregiver who, to quote her most recent employer, "never stole nothing"), and her photo of a vaguely pretty but unsmiling plump, Guatemalan woman (it would distress me to hire a smiling applicant for a job that will offer little to smile about). It's disconcerting to discover on her arrival that she doesn't speak a word of English, but that little speed bump actually seems inconsequential when measured against the enormity of everything else I'm facing. I point and gesture and grin stupidly like a man inordinately happy to be landing small aircraft, and somehow it works.

Dad never spoke in the hospital and still has not after returning home. His difficulty with speech seems not to be the result of the brain no longer knowing how to direct mouth, tongue, and teeth to shape sounds into words, but a deeper disconnect. Although he seems almost completely unaware of his surroundings, I pretend to detect a glimmer of recognition when *SportsCenter* is on. He's also able to respond to cues to eat (he'll open his mouth to accept food, chew it and swallow, only occasionally choking in a manner where I'm pretty sure he's about to expire), and he'll actually stand as Consuela—astonishingly strong for this compact woman—helps him into bed, doubtlessly grateful to put another day behind him. I manage to avoid the more debasing moments when his diaper is changed, praying on my own behalf that if some blood-clot complication races from my stump to my own brain that it explodes upon contact, leaving nothing intact in the white flash that kills me.

Sunday morning I think Dad could use a treat, so Consuela and I load him into the rockin' van to head to the Four Corners. As we begin to accelerate Dad yelps, the high-pitched squeal of a small dog, the first sound I've heard him make since his stroke. I pull over to the side and his body visibly relaxes, but when we start to move, he yelps again.

In his afflicted state there is clearly something about swift movement he cannot abide; this man who had once traveled effortlessly back and forth through time now finds a trip to the diner equivalent to hurtling through space at light speed. Pulling over again, it strikes me that if we can shut out the world instead of seeing it fly past, Dad might be okay. Pantomiming this idea with Consuela elicits an affirmative nod, pretty much the only response I've been able to muster since her arrival and one I take as agreement, although in her native culture it could mean anything, including *I think this is a terrible idea.* Pulling a reusable canvas grocery bag over Dad's head not only calms him but has the same effect as placing a cover on a birdcage: he thinks it's night and goes to sleep.

If the arrival at the Four Corners in our pimped-out eighties van leads anyone to expect a hair metal band to leap from its confines, they must be disappointed to see instead a weary one-armed man, a Guatemalan caregiver, and the incontinent elder lowered mechanically to the ground in his wheelchair with a bag over his head. I anticipate our entry to be greeted with swiveled heads and stopped conversation, frozen stares and coffee suspended midair; instead I'm surprised by the overall warm greeting, and then Fred Weber, arms open, stoops to hug Dad like he might a bundled-up toddler. This is the first time Mr. Weber has seen him out of the hospital, and he doesn't let go for a long while. Dad seems not to respond, but at least he doesn't yelp.

They slip the Lumberjack Special in front of this man for whom the jacking of lumber remains forever out of reach. (Michelle ignores that we've missed the 11:00 A.M. cutoff, and silences any customer complaints of unfairness with a deadly glare and the implied threat of hot coffee.) Consuela expertly slices and dices Dad's breakfast and feeds manageable forkfuls to him, alternating between his and her own meal.

"About time you turned up," Mr. Weber admonishes me.

"Been a little busy."

"I understand," he doesn't. "I also understand you stopped working?"

"Well, I need to take care of Dad."

"Look, you've got a full-time caregiver now," Mr. Weber grins at Consuela, who does not smile back. "You need to get back to your own recovery."

"Thanks for helping me get the job, really. But I might not go back. I actually liked counting fish, but I'm not good in an office."

"Who's good in an office? You think I liked going to an office every day after years in the Merchant Marine? Or your father, coming off the slopes half a world away—at the Olympics, for Chrissake!—to find himself behind a desk? My contacts at the center told me you were doing good work there."

"I left teeth marks in the file folders and had sex with a co-worker. I don't think the Employee-of-the-Month parking spot was in my near future."

"You were getting out, meeting people, doing work that matters, engaging in the world again."

"I did make a good friend. He also had one arm. I was thinking we might form a club of similarly stump-limbed members, but then I was afraid we'd get sued for discriminating against the able-bodied."

"I'm sure your father would agree with me."

"That's not really fair," I protest. "He's dormant. And shouldn't be used to back up an opinion he clearly can't express."

Dad chokes a little on a forkful. "See? I'm sure he'd agree."

"For a guy with one arm, you're remarkably good at pushing people away."

Mr. Weber gets up from the table and once again stoops to hug what remains of his oldest friend, holding him a long time while Dad chews, unaware.

SMOKED

That night while I'm igniting a rich yellow bud of On Golden Bong, the attic door creaks and descends, snapping into place. There's a long beat while I wonder if the head I see breaking the surface will be Dad's, improbably better or, having expired, Zombie Dad's, here to eat my brains. (He can have them.)

Instead Consuela's round face comes into view and without a word, she sits next to me and plucks the bong from my hands and expertly inhales a plume of sweet smoke while its source glows red and then expires, spent. She hands it back with a long, expectant look, and before I know it I've refilled and emptied it three more times. Since Jackie's departure this is the first time I've gotten stoned with anyone, and it infuses me with a feeling of well-being. Despite our inability to communicate (and the continued absence from Consuela's face of anything resembling a smile), smoking together feels socially responsible, or at least less like the furtive solitary episodes of a strung-out dope fiend.

Over the next week Consuela continues to join me in the hours after she puts Dad to bed. We smoke and vape and I talk and gesture and she listens and nods, again indicating understanding, assent, or possibly *What an idiot*. But this new intimacy as we orally intoxicate ourselves, each taking turns puckering a thin nozzle or a fat joint, is seductive. I find myself attracted to her although any reciprocal desire isn't forthcoming, her unsmiling face impossible to read. And when she's had enough (her already impressive threshold increasing nightly) she returns to her room just above the downstairs den we converted for Dad, to whom she is caring and attentive during his waking hours. Then we smoke and vape into the night all over again. I should be less surprised than I am to discover that we've powered through a month's supply of pot in about a week.

I'm viewed with what I perceive as unwarranted suspicion when I show up too soon to refill my prescriptions at The Hemp Collective. Following their worried looks out the window, I'm forced to see things from their perspective: outside in the van, my nervous Guatemalan drug mule watches over the informant bound for execution with a bag over his head. Which renders me the desperate pot dealer under the criminal thumb of drug lords.

"How I've run out is completely innocent," I explain with the whiny high pitch of a completely guilty party. "I was baking the pot into brownies when it caught fire, and that took care of my whole stash. Excuse me, my much-needed prescriptive remedy."

"This is a controlled substance, regulated by the federal government," I'm told with the kind of cautious handling reserved for deranged felons and nitroglycerine. "Without exception, your prescription cannot be refilled prematurely. But I see you can refill it in just a week," he notes, consulting my file as he sneaks another nervous glance out the window to see my dad, head-bagged, still hasn't moved while Consuela, perhaps sensing how things are going, has taken on an even grimmer demeanor.

"It's just a week," I concur as I get up to leave. "Of course I can wait. It's not like I'm some kind of addict."

"I think Dad could benefit from some medical marijuana," I tell Dad's doctor with an unfamiliar sobriety made necessary by circumstance.

"I see," he says, not seeing at all. "And what makes you say that?"

"He has trouble sleeping."

"I could prescribe some Ambien," he muses, shining a tiny light into Dad's eyes that fails to illuminate any understanding behind them.

"I'd worry about him becoming dependent on a sleeping pill. Or sleepwalking to the supermarket and buying all their Cool Whip."

"Ha! The stories of sleeping pill–induced shenanigans are greatly exaggerated."

"Good to know. I'd hate to find out he slipped out late one night and married a horse."

"I'd be very concerned about the psychotropic effects of marijuana on him. The brain is a funny thing . . ."

"Hilarious! But aren't there strains that are so precisely engineered as to avoid those kinds of potent effects?" The doctor looks up from Dad at me. "Or so I understand," I waffle.

Back at the house Consuela and I break routine, agreeing (she with a nod) not to wait until later to dig into our renewed stash. We wheel Dad inside his darkened bedroom and adjourn to the couch to sample Tickle the Dragon, the desired engineered effect of which I've forgotten but infer from its name is some combination of mirth and danger. The seeds I failed to clean in my haste pop like tiny fireworks as I inhale and pass to Consuela. It takes me by surprise when she makes a tiny circle of her lips an inch from mine and blows her smoke into my lungs; then she is full-on mouth to mouth, resuscitating my high with the recycled smoke of her lungs until finally, her tongue finds mine.

I kiss her back with the full force of my prolonged abstinence. I imagine the days and weeks of this that might follow, Dad parked in front of the television where the sensory assault will hold him while I thrust myself into his caregiver; stoned midday sponge baths; and maybe someday little bronze children who speak both our languages and can translate.

Consuela pulls open her blouse for me and presses her stiff brown nipple into my mouth. She moans, and I moan louder, and then she moans even louder and before I can top her again, my cell phone rings. I have no intention of answering it—until I notice over her bosom Dad's face on my caller ID. I reach for the phone and both of us fall to the floor.

"What the hell do you think you're doing?" Dad growls from the bedroom phone, clear as a bell.

WIRED

While not entirely lucid on the phone, Dad has managed to communicate effectively enough to extract me from Consuela and rush into his room. Lights on, I can see Dad still has the phone pressed to his ear.

"Dad?"

Just as suddenly, his face grows slack and he returns to that familiar blank state. Clicking off the lights seems to reactivate him, and he hangs up the phone.

"What the hell is going on?"

Consuela crosses herself and leaves the room.

"What were you doing to that woman? Why are you here? What's that smell?"

It becomes clear that Dad doesn't completely understand what has happened to him or why I am once again living under his roof, smoking pot, and having sex on his couch, three things he couldn't abide back when I was a teenager and apparently still make him pretty cranky. I sit with Dad in the dark and try to explain what's happened.

"You had a stroke."

"A stroke," he repeats. "How long?"

"A couple of weeks."

"I was fine yesterday." It's good to hear his voice . . . although eventually it grows weaker and less sure, as if he's adjusting to the darkness, and it too soon overwhelms him. "Car van doctor breakfast Weber phone."

Soon he's gone again, and we sit quietly together in the darkness.

According to his doctor's interpretation of things, it turns out Dad's silence was not wholly a loss of the speech-functioning part of his brain but a combination of factors that apparently made it impossible for him to manage his surroundings or person-to-person conversation. His brain's circuitry gone haywire, Dad appears to have been overwhelmed by sensory input and, further, could no longer interpret faces—his ability to understand their complexity and nuance was completely lost, and the added distraction of visual overload (which at high speeds proved much worse, causing him to yelp) had resulted in his profoundly confused state. Besieged by this rush of indecipherable external stimuli, he'd simply shut down. But as his recovery progressed, Dad slowly discovered that a completely darkened room posed no distraction. Unlike here, back in the blazing lights of the ER where his mind is once again still as he's reduced to a squirrel-like state, accepting tiny pretzel nuggets from Consuela's hand without expression.

Back home Consuela puts Dad to bed and declines our evening attic ritual. Whatever spurred her earlier sexual aggression also seems to have dissipated, and I suspect there will be no opportunities forthcoming for stoned sponge baths or little bronze babies.

Alone in the attic, my heart leaps to see an e-mail from Will, who I feared had forgotten me, with the subject head, *Is This You?* The message says only *Hope you're doing well,* and there's a link, which I click on, taking me to a YouTube video of my "Bob the Sea Serpent" clip that Steve was supposed to take down. Apparently before he did, someone downloaded it and reposted their own version, inserting human lips and rhythmic jump cuts so that my tattooed nub appears to be dancing and singing, in the auto-tuned-within-an-inch-of-its-life voice of Rod Stewart, "The First Cut Is the Deepest." Even worse, the video has somehow wracked up millions of views. It's only a matter of time before it catches up with Randy Fucking Pausch.

WORK

They say work takes your mind off your troubles—and by "they" I mean Fred Weber, repeatedly, in calls, e-mails, and in person at the Four Corners and even once at Broken Records where I ran into him looking for a collection of sea shanties. I feel a little guilty leaving Dad, but I know he's in Consuela's good care and will spend the day largely dormant, and upon my return home I can awaken his senses by shoving him into a closet.

Although I haven't missed the drudgery of my tiny cubicle at Ick Ick or the taste of file folders clenched between my teeth, I'm forced to admit it feels good to be around Will again, and Lilith—no longer "Wilith" judging by her circuitous avoidance of Will on her way to greet me. Once again she presses up against me in an uneasy hug; this seems to be her preferred manner of greeting now, even for minor encounters like running into the mailman or refueling at a gas station.

This isn't the place for ambition. You don't come in early and leave late or send e-mails on the weekend to demonstrate your dedication; there is no success to dress for or meetings at which to impress, no competition to get ahead or backstabbing revenge on those who made you look bad in front of the boss. (There's no actual "boss"—things run as they are remotely from D.C.) We bear none of the trappings of business: no boardroom, no conference table, no charts showing dramatic growth or plum-meting sales; no staff meetings or pep talks, no performance review threats or the incentive of a set of steak knives. In a man-ufacturing company, there would be a need to sell the things we manufacture and plan their obsolescence; in the service indus-try, there would be an equal urgency to provide those services at a high enough level to encourage repeat business.

But we count fish.

Not an end in and of itself, of course. The purpose of our fish tallying is to determine how few or how many fish are returning to spawn as nature intended. But if there's a threshold—what might constitute "too few" or "enough"—we haven't been told. So for weeks and months and then years, those counts are passed up the ladder in the manner of our struggling sturgeon to the upper echelons of the government agency to enable them to . . . do what, exactly? Prove that the fish population is doing just well enough to avoid tearing down the dam. If there are promo-tions and bonuses and coveted seniority, fat pensions and gold watches at the end of an illustrious career, it happens far upstream from here, where bureaucrats and politicians fertilize each others' eggs.

But everyone here at Ick Ick does the work because they care and believe it matters, and it would be cruel of me to disabuse them of that notion so I pretend it matters too.

"It's good to be back," I lie. "I missed my dead-eyed friends. I'm talking about the fish."

Only Will laughs, the others standing in place like Children of the Damned before dispersing wordlessly. He follows me to my cubicle, somehow grown smaller.

"You're a YouTube sensation," Will reminds me, dispelling any idea that it had all been a bad dream.

"In the most embarrassing music video since 'Ice Ice Baby.'"

"How's your father?"

"I think he's recovering. He's starting to speak. But only from a dark room, like a closet."

"That's pretty weird."

I consider the irony that Dad is revealed by darkness the same way a blackout exposes who we really are—selfless rescuer, fearful victim, opportunistic looter.

"I'm sure science and medicine have seen stranger things, like *The Man Who Mistook His Wife for a Hat* or something. Which would be hard on any marriage. So, what did I miss?"

"We're on video night counts, just for a week to see if there's any pattern difference. Not that it matters. Because next up is the data dump."

"If that requires manual labor, I picked the wrong week to come back to work."

"We collate six months' worth of records, make assessments, and file reports."

"They received our counts daily," I remind him. "Can't they just add all the counts up, put it in a nice flowchart, or maybe a pie chart with a big piece missing to represent certain extinction?"

"Ha!" Will barks in appreciation. "But the assessment is kind of the point. We're supposed to bundle it all together and include our judgment that things are okay—or at least going in the right direction. Ensure the continued survival of the dam, and secure funding for next year."

"One hand washes the other."

"Then why do I feel so unclean?"

"What if our reports said the numbers are *not* okay, and not going in the right direction? Use words like 'extinction.' Also, 'shitty' and 'sucks.'"

"They'd just fire us and hire new guys," Will sighs. "Wouldn't change a thing."

Is he kidding me? It could change *everything*. Freed of our commitment to Ick Ick, Will and I could go into business together, open a cupcake bakery, or a make-your-own-sausage restaurant. We could be pet sitters specializing in fish or open a day-care center, sell handcrafts on Etsy, operate a food truck. Kickstart a thing, build an app, microfund small businesses at usurious rates. We could be wedding photographers, amputee bloggers, start a driving school, rescue baby pandas, invent a gun that shoots bacon. E-commerce Internet meme fluff-and-fold web thing energy drink surf shop pumpkin something—

"Freaking *dam*," Will disrupts my mental wet dream and heads back to his desk.

Over the rest of the week we collate and compile and eventually bundle it all under an assessment of lies with words like "improving" and "reversal" and imply a future where the Wabash is once again teeming with sturgeon, a scenario as much science fiction as *Zardoz*. When it's finished Will drops it on my desk and mouths a silent *ka-boom*, effectively gesturing a small, slow-motion explosion with his good hand.

THINGS YOU CAN GESTURE WITH ONE HAND

OK

Beckon

Stop!

Benediction

Blah-blah-blah

Check, please

Black power salute

Cross your fingers

Finger gun

Fist bump

Fist pump

High five

Hitchhiking

Metal horns

Thumbs-up

Scout's honor

Nazi salute

Hat tip

Wave

Peace sign

Mahalo

Live Long and Prosper

Finger wag

Talk to the hand

Loser

Fuck you

GUNPLAY

Saturday morning when I ask Consuela where Dad is, she nods at the closet. Before I can reach the door my phone rings.

"I'm bored out of my skull," Dad complains on his cell phone.

"You've been through a lot. You need rest."

"I'm unconscious all goddamn day."

"What's it like?" I ask into the phone and through the closet door. "Are you aware of what's going on around you?"

"It's like watching TV three rooms away. You can't quite make anything out. And someone keeps switching channels. And it smells like toast."

"But you're getting better every day. This . . . being able to talk to you. I never thought I'd hear your voice again."

"I think I'd like to try some of that medical marijuana."

"I'm not sure that's a good idea. The doctor was concerned—"

"What the hell difference could it possibly make?"

Dad and I share vaporized hits of Rastafazool in the closet. I wonder if it will affect Dad's scarred brain the same as mine.

"Not exactly the same as Fleischmann's, is it?" is all he says.

He giggles a little in the dark but is otherwise quiet, so I take him out into the light where I watch for any indication of its effect but see none. There's no way to tell if Dad is entirely unaffected or if his brain is snowed under by psychedelia. Consuela wheels Dad out to the backyard, where she gently coaxes a squirrel to take a nut from his fingers. I imagine Dad enjoys the touch of her hand against his, her hair grazing his face, her voice in his ear, despite not being able to understand. (Or maybe his amazing scrambled-and-rewired brain can decipher every word.) As I'm feeling guilty about having left him to return to fish counting (making a mental note to investigate whether there might be a marijuana strain that mollifies remorse), the doorbell rings, reminding me why I really returned to work after all: it's Will!

"Nice ride," Will gestures to the heavy-metal van and enters, and instead of fist-bumping, we reach to embrace in a modified bro-hug backslap and handshake, sans handshake, backslaps made awkward by arms on the same side. "I thought I'd drop by; hope it's okay."

It's awesome.

"How's your father doing?"

"A little better every day."

"Really!" Will sounds pleased but incredulous. Spotting Dad through the backyard sliding doors, hunched and staring, I can't blame him.

Will roams the hallway, looking at the pictures on the wall of Dad, rifle in hand, ready to shatter the snow-blanketed quiet at the foot of the Wetterstein mountains.

"Must be tough for a guy who used to be so active," Will remarks.

"Dad's spent most of the past thirty years sitting on a couch in front of *SportsCenter*. I'm surprised the blood didn't stop moving to his brain years ago."

"Still, this guy"—Will points to the photo of my snow-skiing, gun-toting father—"must be in there someplace."

Whether fueled by Will's presence or an especially perky strain of marijuana, I experience a eureka moment and set a plan into motion.

"Consuela!" I shout outside. "Can you pack a picnic lunch for five?" I gesture the universal symbols for five, lunch, and picnic basket that she's somehow able to interpret.

We load the picnic lunch, a twelve-pack of beer, and Dad into the van where I pull a bag over his head, earning a look of stunned disbelief on Will's face, the first I've ever seen. Lest it dissipate too quickly I don't bother explaining, and we're off to pick up the only other person my pot-stoked brain can imagine needs an adventure as much as Dad.

About a block away from school I spy a weary-looking Cancer Boy, further diminished, stooped under the weight of his back-pack like prey caught in the moment of pouncing. Walking home with a small group of kids, he turns when I honk my horn, both happy and astonished to see me.

"Cool van!"

"I know, right?"

"You're on YouTube!" he shrieks, and then to his friends: "This is that guy!"

"I don't believe you," a skeptic challenges.

"Show them!" he begs me.

I do, and this time no one screams or throws up, although they collectively coo and wow and coo some more, and Cancer Boy beams like the kid who just introduced his schoolmates to his rock-star friend. As even Will looks at me with admiration, they may be right.

"Hop in," I tell the boy, knowing this could be considered child abduction but refusing to be deterred by technicalities.

Arriving in Crawlywood, Consuela takes a staple gun and a stack of color targets pulled from the inkjet printer and disappears into the trees. I remove Dad's hood and he awakens instantly. He and Cancer Boy stare as if each is seeing the other for the first time. Then Cancer Boy smiles and Dad attempts a grin, which merely stretches his face into a scary grimace and Cancer Boy instantly stops smiling, and so does Dad. Left alone with each other I'm certain they'd repeat this in an endless loop, so I move us along.

Will and I help Dad from the lift over the wobbly terrain into the woods. If he's aware of his surroundings, it isn't clear. I produce Dad's bolt-action .22 caliber rifle from the van and I can tell Cancer Boy thinks this is even cooler than the alligator that no longer resides in our bathtub. I place it in Dad's hands and point it out in front of him—which happens to be directly at Consuela as she emerges from the trees. We all quickly gather in the only completely safe place around a rifle-wielding stroke victim—directly behind him. Using our good arms, Will and I each grip a handle on Dad's wheelchair and race down the trail while Dad yelps.

It takes about a minute to get deep into the woods where we stop, about fifty yards away from the first target stapled to a tree. (I'm pleasantly surprised to see Consuela has mistakenly downloaded and printed not just any target but the Who's "mod" logo, a perfect red dot at the center of concentric white and blue circles.) I lean forward and whisper in Dad's ear, "You know what to do."

Dad takes aim and blows a small hole in the tree, missing the target. The thunderclap makes Cancer Boy jump and laugh simultaneously. Three quick shots follow in the vicinity of the target, including one that straddles the outer blue ring and the white that surrounds it. Will and I pull beer cans from the cup holders on each of Dad's armrests and clink them. Dad rests the butt of the rifle on his thigh, pointed straight up, and closes his eyes, and we take off deeper into the woods, Dad yelping, Cancer Boy cheering, and Consuela grunting to keep up.

Eyes shut, Dad is able to feel the exhilaration of wind on his face and the bumpy rush of the ground beneath him. He blasts another target, his marksmanship better this time, scoring in the white between the red bull's-eye and the blue outside ring. Pressing on, Dad blows the hell out of three more targets and Cancer Boy pulls the last one from the tree, rushing it back to show Dad, who again bares his teeth at him.

We move on to the next target, which holds twin surprises: Consuela has inadvertently stumbled across the pit of Shop Smart coupon flyers I used to dump here (the summer job I failed with great intention), rotted and pulped together by decades of exposure to the elements; the second surprise is Ali, spread out over the mulchy, nearly unrecognizable mash, basking in the sun.

"*Is that a fucking gator?*" Will takes only a single step back but drops several notches on the cool scale.

"Yay!" Cancer Boy shouts. "You brought Ali!"

Suddenly a shot scatters confetti as the coupon flyers are blasted apart by Consuela, having seized Dad's rifle in panic. I shout, "No!" and leap between her and Ali, my brain telling both hands to dart out and up in the universal sign for "Don't shoot!" and falling short by a hand. Grateful that she's missed her first shot, I gently take the rifle from her as a hostage negotiator might after talking a disturbed gunman into tearful surrender. She crosses herself and makes a dash for the van as I lean the rifle against Dad's wheelchair.

Ali stares back at us, and if there's recognition in his eyes, I can't see it—unless it's the fact of knowing a small boy for food. For the second time I place myself in harm's way, only this time the alligator is not the one that needs protecting. I quickly toss Ali a tuna sandwich from the cooler.

"I take it you know this animal?"

"It's a reptile," Cancer Boy remembers. "Can I feed him?"

"Maybe later!" I invoke the parental magic phrase to ward off a child's bad idea. "Will, how many sandwiches do we have left?"

"Four," he counts.

"That should be enough to lead him back to the van."

"Fuck that; I'm eating mine." Will takes a huge bite out of one in an attempt to recapture his cool. It mostly works.

"Let me do it!" Cancer Boy plucks a sandwich and waves it hypnotically.

I stay close and we back-walk Ali with the three remaining sandwiches through the woods and to the van. Pulling open the rear doors, I toss the last sandwich inside and Ali scrambles after it as Consuela crosses herself once more and leaps from her seat. I slam the rear door and pop a can of beer for Cancer Boy, and we clink cans in unison with the sound of a rifle shot.

The four of us race back and every jarring step of the way, I can't help thinking how stupid it was to leave Dad alone with his rifle. What if he tried to get up and fell? Or am I really afraid that he might have deliberately turned the gun on himself?

Ahead of the others, I burst through the clearing and there's Dad sitting, pleased, his face stretched in an approximation of a happy grin. And why shouldn't he be happy? In our absence, he's scored a clean bull's-eye on the last target. We're all impressed, even the sheriff who appears suddenly to arrest us, at gunpoint, for discharging a firearm in public and destroying park property.

DEFENSE

Cancer Boy sits swinging his feet, clearly impressed by his step up in class from the principal's office to the sheriff's, one more way in which his friendship with me has paid an exciting dividend (although I doubt his mother will see it that way). Will and Consuela have been separated from us in the method, I imagine, that dangerous gangs are divided and interrogated and tricked into betraying one another by being told they've already been betrayed by the others. Clearly, I've been determined the leader; what this has to say about the roles assigned to my brain-challenged father and the little boy riddled with cancer is unclear, although I like to think "henchmen with nothing to lose."

It's only when the sheriff declares, "You do recognize me without my gas mask, right?" that I realize this is the man who tear-gassed me, and who I'm suing so as to never have to toil in the arena of fish conservation or any other meaningful work again.

"No hard feelings?"

"Oh, nothing but," he assures me, before neatly summing up the facts of the case: "So, in a nutshell, you took a stroke victim out to fire a rifle in a heavily wooded public area, and brought along a small boy to whom you have no relation as part of some recreational exercise."

"Things haven't been so great. I thought they both deserved a treat."

"It was fucking awesome!" Cancer Boy shouts his endorsement, and any trepidation I had scatters like nervous townsfolk as I face down the sheriff.

"And your other accomplices . . . ?"

"A friend from work and Dad's nurse. Not their fault, really. I take full responsibility."

"You boys *with the arms*," he says, really meaning *without* them, "belong to some kind of club?"

"That *would* be fun. And the amputee-company picnic could have a true three-legged race! But no. We worked together over at fish conservation."

"Goddamn fish counters," he mutters, as if the Illinois Center for Ichthyological Conservation were some kind of notorious outlaw motorcycle gang renowned for their mayhem.

With no satisfactory reply forthcoming, the sheriff turns his attention to Dad. When I try to explain his condition I'm cut short by a perfectly executed lawman's glare. (Even Cancer Boy stops swinging his feet.) Dad sits staring and unresponsive to questioning, but at least he doesn't bare his teeth. I recommend moving Dad into the closet, from which I promise he'll answer all the sheriff's questions via cell phone. The sheriff fixes me with another long, murderous stare before relenting.

Suddenly verbal on my speakerphone, Dad, in clear but rambling discourse, gives his view of what had happened in the woods . . . and leading up to the woods . . . and events as he recalls them in the weeks and months preceding the woods— more than the sheriff or I had wished, including our shared use of Dad's marijuana and my truncated sexual fling with his nurse—tying it all back to his time as an Olympic biathlete, and Tommy Baker serial-fucking his way through the Innsbruck Games. Several times, the sheriff attempts to interrupt and steer

Dad's testimony back on some reasonable track, but there is no easy silencing of Dad behind the closed door as he grows more agitated and soon shouts *Shut the fuck up and let me finish!*, a perfect entry line for Cancer Boy's mother as he himself doubles over in hysterics.

While she listens to the sheriff's explanation of events as he shakily understands them, I remove Dad from the closet.

"I admit, I didn't think this through," I interrupt. "I just wanted both of them to have a good time. Fun is a rare commodity when you're sick."

"Not as lacking as common sense, apparently. A stroke victim with a rifle?"

"The kid was as safe as I could make him under those admittedly treacherous circumstances."

"Am I to understand he did not have permission to take the boy?" The sheriff is barely able to repress a smile. "That's a more serious charge—"

"I don't want to charge anybody with anything! I just want to take my son home!"

"Of course, he's free to go."

Cancer Boy's mood contrasts sharply with what would be expected of someone just released from police custody. He shuffles sadly past Dad, who again shows all his teeth, forcing a reluctant smile in return.

"Hey," I demand his attention. "How cool was today?"

"*So* fucking cool!" He smiles wider, and high-fives me just before his mother yanks him from the room.

With the boy gone, the sheriff's language and face take colorful turns as he challenges me to provide one single goddamn piece of evidence supporting the absurd claims of my brain-scrambled father's speakerphone testimony. When I again produce my cell phone, I swear he seems poised to shoot me and am convinced the only reason he does not is because then he'd also have to shoot Dad to eliminate any witnesses. Ultimately I am able to tap my way to Dad's Wikipedia entry as a member of the 1964 U.S. Olympic Biathlon team, which also notes the official record of Tommy Baker without mention of his note-worthy indoor triumphs. When a deputy enters with a folder, the sheriff thrusts my phone back at me and settles in his chair, riffling the pages.

"So that's an Olympic event, skiing and shooting?"

"Before you say anything that would understandably dispar-age the sport, so is curling."

"What do you know about your friend Will?"

"Great guy. Bad at patty-cake. Why?"

"He's on probation."

If I had two hands, I'd hold my head in them. "And that makes this"—I gesture aimlessly—"worse."

"That it does," he agrees, still looking down. "Also, your nurse, Consuelo—"

"Consuel-*a*," I let escape without thinking. His eyes dart up at me like a weapon locking on target.

"She's illegal."

That's just perfect.

"Also flunked her drug test. And so did you."

"I have a prescription for that."

"I'm sure you have pre-scrip-*shuns*," he accentuates the plural, "for all the shit we found. Doesn't make it legal to operate a mo-tor vehicle or discharge a firearm."

"I didn't fire anything," I offer weakly.

"Here's how it's gonna go," he explains, elaborating on the unnecessary attention garnered by the Boy Scouts litigation, and the further embarrassment of facing an upcoming sheriff's election with yet another incident. Even Dad can see I'm about to be extorted into dropping my lawsuit and in no time at all, promises are made and weak handshakes exchanged, and only one of us grins.

"What about them?" I ask, powerless.

"Can't help. She's federal; ICE wants her. Your friend Will?" He shrugs. "Depends. Maybe just a slap on the wrist."

"Yeah, well, it hurts more when you only have one wrist," I grouse. "If there's bail, I'll pay it. But he doesn't have to know."

"That's between you and your club," he pokes needlessly.

"The guy's a war hero. He doesn't deserve to be punished just because I talked him into doing something stupid."

The sheriff appears bemused for the first time, perhaps ever. He waves the folder with the expertise of a game-show host. "There's nothing here about any military service."

"That's impossible."

"Not really. Lots of assholes pretend to be heroes. There's even a law makes it illegal, 'Stolen Valor' or some such."

The ringing in my ears grows louder. "Can I ask what he's on probation for?"

"Sure. Blowing off his arm with a homemade bomb."

Having purchased our freedom by way of extortion, Dad and I are released to the custody of the Wheels on Wheels ("WOW") wheelchair taxi service. With my undiscovered van back on the outskirts of Crawlywood it's our only option, a lonely one, with Will, Consuela, and Cancer Boy gone—the Will I thought I knew gone for good. Dad yelps a couple of times but placing his head in a bag seems like the kind of thing that might initiate an elder-abuse investigation, so instead I put my baseball cap on Dad and pull the brim down low over his eyes. It seems to help.

Our driver is surprised to find his destination is an abandoned van on a quiet dirt road, but in helping to move Dad, he's more surprised to see the large alligator inside. Thanks to the motionless torpor induced in Ali by the semi-refrigeration of hours inside a metal van, I'm able to convince the driver that this is a dead, taxidermied specimen—which, had the sheriff found him, might have been his actual fate. Driving home, I'm glad I don't have to call Dad in his closet to tell him of Ali's tragic and violent end, another lost link to his better past.

CONNECTED

We all know cell phones can be annoying, but can they also make you happy? Yes, according to scientists in Germany's Technical University of Darmstadt, where they tested happiness in subjects newly in love only to discover, quite by accident, something unexpected: the mere ringing of a call from their better halves triggered a pleasurable, anticipatory response in both males and females.

Is that a cell phone in your pocket, or are you just happy to see me on your caller ID?

One notable gender difference was that when an attractive member of the opposite sex was introduced immediately after such a call, males remained on . . . ahem, high alert, while women returned to a normal brain-wave state. Go figure!

Sadly, as relationships progressed—"for better or worse," as the saying goes—this effect wanes over time, even in happy liaisons, in much the same way a cell phone battery eventually dies. At least Pavlov's dog always wanted that drink of water.

This is Sunny Lee, with The Sunny Side.

Perhaps emboldened by his exchange with the sheriff who could not silence him, Dad becomes as obsessed as a teenager with a new iPhone, dialing everyone for lengthy, sometimes lucid chats. The first time he called Jackie they spoke for nearly fifteen minutes, although her side of the conversation consisted mostly of wailing sobs and eventually even Dad got bored and hung up. He also phones Fred Weber, Tommy Baker, Mom, and Mom's fireman at the firehouse. He calls Michelle at the Four Corners to make unnecessary reservations, and Dim Sum & Then Some to gloat, "I have your pens." He calls his former place of employment where he hasn't worked in years, old schoolmates and girlfriends he had not spoken to in decades, and wrong numbers with whom he chats anyway. All from the dark sanctuary of the hall closet, where I'd cleared a path so he could enter and turn around, and I'd even added a little end table with a bud vase for ambience he could not see in the blackness.

Dad and I also continue to chat, inches from one another, separated by a hollow-core door and a billion misfiring synapses. Although his mental stamina has increased enough for lengthier conversations, he still eventually trails off into fugue: *dark phone hungry doctors baseball Fleischmann's* . . . the line gone dead or, more accurately, slowly dying. Then he plugs in his earbuds and listens to music in shuffle mode—a nonlinear playlist matching the workings of his own brain—until our new burly, fifty-five-year-old Hungarian male nurse, Béla, comes to bring him back to the light, where Dad shrivels along with his pupils. (Even here he seems better: watching the Olympic trials together, when a U.S. biathlete missed his target I could tell by Dad's muted *grunt* that he knew it.)

My own transition back to solitary pot smoking has felt a little lonely so I turn for solace to Internet porn, where the sheer number and diversity of aberrant behavior only depresses me further. That I have no desire to relieve myself on someone's chest or have objects inserted inside me or dress up like one of the Banana Splits while chained spread-eagle to a sawhorse makes me feel repressed in a normalcy that seems, judging by the Internet, to belong to a tiny minority, rendering me that much more the outsider.

It's while clicking through and past these flash-frames of limitlessly imaginative sexual ignominy that I stumble across the latest meme—an offshoot of voyeuristic amputee sex, arguably the basement of debasement—hilarious amputee homages to the original "The First Cut Is the Deepest" video featuring a variety of other artists, including Sheryl Crow, Drake, a surprising number of reggae singers, a rap version by I-Roy, and of course Cat Stevens's original. Dozens of them, with tens of thousands of views apiece, of singing and dancing arm and leg stumps, with hand-drawn Señor Wences faces, lipstick smears, Sharpie scribbles, and yes, the occasional tattoo (mine included). Any sexual urge I might have had vanishes faster than if Béla had suddenly appeared in all his beefy, hairy nakedness to hose me with ice water.

(If it's possible to feel worse, I even stumble across a podcast where a disgruntled Steve unconvincingly makes his case as the originator of the meme, going so far as to show it in its original form on his phone, which of course is me telling the tale of Bob the Sea Serpent. I forward several links to Jackie and pass out knowing that by morning my current displeasure will be multiplied, like a true virus.)

What I did not count on was my e-mail spurring Jackie back on a plane here, unannounced, grim-faced, sadder than I've ever seen her.

"You shouldn't be here," I argue against the logic of my eyes. "You were very clear that you had a life in California—a job, a husband, a mortgage to pay."

"At the moment, all I have is the mortgage," she says, dragging her wheelie past me. "I left Steve. Or more accurately, I told him to leave. That was a *horrible* thing he did with your video!"

"Technically, all he did was post it and then try to take credit for the work of more ambitious morons with advanced editing skills and too much time on their hands."

"That was just the last straw. There's so much more I won't get into. Did you know he's addicted to Internet porn?"

And too dumb to clear history, I'm guessing. "So this isn't my fault."

"Not really. You're the catalyst, though."

I hug her. "You can't be mad at a catalyst. That would be anti-science. What about your job? You haven't been out of work since you were a type-A teen."

"I needed time to deal with all of this, and of course Dad. They said they'd fire me if I took any more time off, so I quit."

"You showed them!"

"Don't worry, I'll find something challenging and less soul sucking."

"Not here, I hope. You're not cut out for the glamorous field of fish counting."

"I'm exhausted." She flops on the couch. "Where's Dad?"

If Jackie is surprised to find Dad inside when I swing the closet door open, she doesn't show it. But Dad's face, after a glimpse of recognition and joy to see his only daughter, grows slack again. I nudge Jackie inside and gently shut the door behind her.

"Hi, baby," Dad says in the dark, and I can tell by rustling clothes and muffled sobs that Jackie has leaned in to smother him in a hug.

After three days spent mostly in the closet yakking away like sports talk radio, Dad stops speaking completely. Understandably concerned, Jackie calls me to join them in the closet where she sits, holding Dad's hand. I try to jump-start Dad with a stream of conversational prods but get no reply in the darkness. We take him out to daylight and then back into the darkness, rocking him back and forth like a car caught in a snowdrift, but he remains stuck. I put a bag over his head for a minute and then pull it off, but he neither dozes under it nor does he leap back to life with its removal.

At the hospital Dad's doctor is equally stymied, although he's always been skeptical about the restorative properties of a dark closet. He leaves us and I turn out the overhead light, hoping to jolt Dad from dormancy, and Jackie and I sit with him in silence. Suddenly, Dad lets out a short yelp and taps his chest with his fingers, and I know his defibrillator just went off for the second time. His face, no longer blank, turns first to Jackie and then toward me. His eyes meet mine with great clarity, and I see in them the quiet defeat of a vanquished boxer tired of fighting.

"This is no way to live," he says.

And despite the hospital's best efforts, Dad is true to his word.

GONE

Dad has hurtled into the future one final time, having crossed middle age and then suddenly retirement and now even more sudden, vanished, along with all the versions of himself that came before: small boy, eager teen, college roommate, Olympian, newlywed, worker, father, abandoned husband, reluctant caretaker, stroke victim, crippled closet talker. It's our job to mourn him and sum up his life, to send him off and plan life in a world without him. But first, we have to dress him.

Deep inside Dad's walk-in closet are suits I recall from his days commuting to Terre Haute, where this Olympian had found himself brought down to earth and shackled to a desk, although he never once complained. There's nothing here that looks current or would probably fit . . . although I suspect "fitting" is a problem the undertaker solves by cutting apart the back of jacket and pants with the same benign effort with which he harvests organs for autopsy. I decide to stop thinking about the work of an undertaker and lift a simple, slimming pinstripe suit on its hanger. Jackie approves. It's her idea to add the vintage necktie I wore to the masquerade, the one Dad had saved for a special occasion, although probably not this one.

We've been told he doesn't need shoes—a shame, really, because of the abundance to choose from here, shoes of every variety from loafers to Hush Puppies, black oxfords to white patent leather(!), sandals to snow boots, wing tips and running shoes. I expect to find his baby shoes here, not bronzed but ready to wear as if Dad might try dipping his toes in before giving up and moving on to the next available pair he also kept forever.

Jackie insists we stay with the task at hand and avoid the memory land mines planted all around us, but I can't help but notice a box overhead that I haven't seen before.

"*No.* Do not! I won't. You can't," Jackie stammers as I lift the top off the box to reveal tiny boxes of old thirty-five-millimeter slides, a hobby of Dad's I never knew he had.

Now hopelessly transfixed, Jackie snatches them from me and doesn't even bother leaving the mustiness of the closet; she just sits on the floor and holds them one at a time up to the light and then passes each along to me, a stretch of Dad's life in tiny colorful rectangles: campus shots, scenics from Innsbruck, his wedding, tiny babies growing to small children—and then they simply stop, skidding to a sudden halt, interrupted by the arrival of his future.

"We should do something with these," she says sadly.

"We will: we'll fight over them," I know. "But in the meantime, why don't we blow this one up for the . . . thing," I say instead of *funeral.*

As the man behind the camera he's in so few of these, but Mom must have taken over for this one, shot on their wedding day in wonderfully archaic Kodachrome color, an image of Dad, resplendent in tuxedo, white tie, and shiny black shoes I have no doubt are somewhere here in the closet with us.

"It's perfect for the thing," Jackie agrees, and then we cry for a very long time.

Dad is fortunate to have among his mourners those who knew him when it mattered, from his shared boyhood with Fred Weber to a once-devoted wife and, in between, Tommy Baker, who brought a much younger date. Also in attendance is Will—with a prosthetic arm!—who pulls me in for our modified/awkward bro-hug, slapping my back. Then Lilith presses herself against me and retreats to a chair in the back. Also attending is Consuela, who informs me in the perfect English she'd hidden from me that she was not deported after all but instead hired by ICE as a translator. (Apparently what Consuela had been speaking while caring for Dad wasn't Spanish at all but Q'anjob'al, one of about a dozen Mayan languages still spoken across Guatemala, making her of extreme value to protecting our borders from undocumented Q'anjob'al-speaking aliens.)

Further packing the house is the breakfast crowd at the Four Corners and a squad of off-duty firefighters, a kindness courtesy of Mr. February. All sit with respectful passivity alongside forgotten cousins and their unfamiliar spouses, and a dozen or more of Jackie's classmates, once again demonstrating the supremacy of her popularity as I can boast only three unrecognizable high school friends gone fat. I struggle to identify them as each acknowledges my loss with a handshake—an oddly congratulatory gesture given the circumstances—before taking seats far from Mr. Madnick. Jackie sits stroking Dad's hair until Mom coaxes her away to dissolve in quiet tears in a corner, where I join them.

"I'm glad you were home," I mumble to Jackie, a little too stoned, earning un-Zen-like disapproval from Mom.

"Me too," she whimpers, and pulls me into their embrace. "We had some nice talks. He was so . . . just Dad again."

"I wish I'd seen him too," Mom regrets.

I shrug, which she reads quite correctly as *Whose fault is that?*

"But I'm so happy we spoke on the phone. I remember the last thing he said to me," Mom muses . . .

"Was it 'Sheriff lunch *SportsCenter* fireman divorce'?"

"He told me he was sorry, and that I was right to leave him."

"That must have been very gratifying."

"Nothing in my entire life has ever made me feel worse."

During the service before they take Dad to blast him with flames that will reduce him to ash, Tommy Baker sits between Mom and his date holding both their hands as if they were stage actors before a curtain call. Or swingers about to depart for a three-way at his motel. Tommy remains fit and vigorous and can probably still ski and shoot, and whether aided or not by Cialis still no doubt willing to service a gold-medal winner or a noncompetitive date and/or widow. As the minister does the rote droning required of him, the buzz of four Vicodins does its job of reducing him to a pinhole. But Dad too is farther away than I'd like, and when I'm able to bring him into focus, I lose him again in tears.

By the time the minister starts speaking of Lazarus and the Resurrection and the right hand of God (forcing me to ponder, *What if He's a southpaw?*), sirens blare from the street, getting closer and louder as he tries to shout the word of God over them. The sound suddenly winds down, directly out front, as the minister yells, "For wherever you go, I will go!" and all the firefighters rush from the service, outside, and climb aboard, sirens screaming again as the firetruck roars away. Before the minister can resume his tale of God's magnificent house, I take advantage of the diversion and wobble from the room. Will follows me.

"Haven't seen you since—"

"Busy."

"Sorry about your father."

I don't know if I've been mad at Will because he's a liar or because he's a criminal, and now I have a new reason: because he's betrayed our one-armed solidarity with his prosthetic.

"Thanks. You look different," I observe without looking at him. "Shave your mustache? Put on weight?"

"Just this couple of pounds," he raises his arm with a *whirr.* "Affects my balance, actually makes it harder to walk after all these years."

We pass a room packed with mourners and another empty except for the sole occupant reclining at its center. Despite the utter sadness of both, I begin to mentally muse as to the cause of death for each tableau we pass: Murphy-bed accident. Fatal gelato brain freeze. Died laughing.

"You ever wonder how these people died?" Will asks.

"I was just thinking that!" I blurt out, giddy, before I can stop myself.

"This one," he points, *whirrrr* . . . "Slipped on a banana peel."

"Basketball player, stood up into a ceiling fan."

"Half-price sushi."

"Texting while bullfighting."

"Shopping-cart pileup."

"Drowned bobbing for apples."

We both stop at the last room, filled with children facing a coffin small enough to convey enormous tragedy, too profoundly sad for comic speculation. I read the name, *Jimmy Ferris,* in white plastic letters on a black grid board. Poor little Jimmy. Then I recognize one of the little girls, and the boy who threw up when I'd showed my nub, the principal who banished me . . . and then I spot Cancer Boy's mother.

Somehow she sees me through grief-soaked eyes and makes her way over to me. Without a word she grips me, sinks into my chest and weeps, and nothing since the accident has made me wish harder for two arms, so that I might hold her the way she deserves to be held.

AFTERMATH

I'd have bet a fistful of M&Ms that Cancer Boy would have lived into adulthood to wonder someday about the strange one-armed man who once spent an inordinate amount of time with the small cancer-riddled boy he used to be. Instead he is buried, or cremated, underground or gone to the sky along with everything he might have been. Extinct. On the plus side he'll never again suffer the pain of surgery, the sickness of chemo and radiation, the ignominy of bare-assed hospital gowns. It's a weak plus side, scales as out of balance as the newly limbless.

That it never occurred to me he might die demonstrates my inability to consider possible outcomes. If Mom can know the future, looking forward I can only see what is certain: which now is a world where Cancer Boy will never grow up to have an ex-girlfriend or Mafia henchman search him on Google, or to feel the tingly goose-bumpy goodness when he locks eyes with the pole dancer to whom he hands his first dollar.

The other certain future I can see is Fat Jackie.

Having remained here at the house after the funeral, she's taken to late-night snacks of Caramel Swirl Crunch in unseemly proportions. It's easy to imagine her, like Alice after heeding the cookie's command, "Eat Me," filling the house so her legs pop out the side doors and her arms through the upstairs windows, her head squeezed through our chimney. It's equally effortless to imagine her as one thousand pounds of bedridden flesh calling out for more Caramel Swirl Crunch, which I bring her by the shovelful until her heart stops, and Mom's firemen come to take out some walls and remove her to be buried in a piano case.

Perhaps that's unfair, as it's only been three days since the funeral.

My own future doesn't seem much brighter as evidenced by the fact that I've barely left the attic. Jackie's grown tired of waiting on me, carrying up the many Tupperware meals dropped off by friends and neighbors, sympathy food to sustain the bereaved until they decide they are strong enough again to hunt and gather for themselves. If she's thought about it at all, I'm sure Jackie believes I'm at least making the short trip to the upstairs bathroom when necessary. Although I do venture down to relieve my bowels alongside a cooing Ali, I hold urinating to a lower standard, peeing out the south side window (if anyone looks closely, they might wonder as to the cause of a squiggly patch of bleached grass).

Because right now, I'm simply too busy to leave my work.

I've been toiling nonstop to create a *Dad Is Dead* video mixtape, pulling all our photo albums, home movies, videos, clippings, Dad's thirty-five-millimeter slides, and even the pictures that lined our downstairs walls up here to the attic to scan, digitize, collate, label, log. There are thousands of images and a hundred hours of tape, and it would take me years to do this even if I wasn't doing it with great deliberation, dallying over each photo and reading and rereading every clipping and scrutinizing videos so as not to miss some activity in the background at their wedding, or Dad waiting his turn at the Olympics.

Then, there's the careful selection of just the right music, and I listen to all I can think of, from classical (Barber's "Adagio for Strings") to opera ("Nessun Dorma," "Musetta's Waltz"), film

scores (*Requiem for a Dream,* Kenneth Branagh's *Hamlet*), jazz
("Moon Dreams," " 'Round Midnight") and blues ("Death Don't
Have No Mercy"); artists as diverse as Milt Jackson, Jerry Jeff
Walker, and Esquivel; "Asleep" by the Smiths, "This Bitter Earth"
by Dinah Washington, "100 Years" by Five for Fighting, and an
endless stream of musical musings on death: "Knockin' on Heav-
en's Door," "Everybody Hurts," "Time to Say Goodbye," "Bela
Lugosi's Dead," "(Don't Fear) the Reaper," "Always Look on the
Bright Side of Life," "Danny Boy." Of course I have to lay down
each one under some video, which will then have to be reedited
for time and to fit the rhythm and punctuated beats of that particular song. This could take a very, very long time. It's a good
thing I have nothing else to do, having finally quit Ick Ick.

A week into the project I am impossibly stoned on Ganja Din
and "Forever Young" is blaring, and there's Dad on my laptop,
alive again and scoring a point at the Olympics and marrying
Mom and posing in front of his Lincoln Mark IV and goddamn, I have to piss and I do, out the window, long and hard
and in agreement with Steve that *Damn, this does feel fucking
good,* then slamming the window shut behind me and I turn to
see Jackie and Mr. Weber, their entrance smothered by Dylan's
wailing exhortation to "Have a strong foundation when the
winds of changes shift." And I stand there, unaware of how much
time has passed but completely aware of myself—unshaven, ill
fed, stinking, bereft, lost, and with my pants down.

"This is no way to live," I mumble, and Jackie crosses the attic
to slap me, knocking me backward and my laptop crashes to
the floor, music and images ceasing, Dad suddenly gone all over
again.

"Don't you say that!" she shrieks. "Don't you ever goddamn
say that again!"

And with that she's gone, and I'm alone with Mr. Weber and
the ringing in my ears.

TESTAMENT

We meet in Mr. Weber's home office for the reading of Dad's will. Jackie still has not spoken to me since shrieking at me in the attic, a shrill echo that I can still mentally conjure to allow me to recall her voice if I want to. Invoking Dad's last words in a threat to vanish was her breaking point; she's completely given up on me and I have neither the energy nor the inclination to dissuade her from doing so.

I assume that what Mr. Weber sees across his attorney's desk is a familiar tableau of broken families: sister not talking to brother, mother swallowing grief and regret, son completely lost as evidenced by their pantsless attic encounter. I worry about Mr. Weber, a decade retired and in no condition to muster the guile necessary to orchestrate the emotions he's about to trigger. He should at least stretch first so he doesn't pull something.

Instead he reads the will; a will never changed since before Dad's split from Mom, and certainly one that never considered the twin possibilities of armless son and divorced daughter; a will that leaves the house and its accumulated, valueless contents—somehow described as "worldly goods"—to his beloved wife who, at the conclusion of the reading turns to us and says, without a mean intent in her body, "Now, you both need to go."

"Wait a minute; you're not even 'wife' anymore, never mind 'beloved.'"

"Actually, she is," Mr. Weber informs us. "Your parents never divorced. And I can say personally, from conversations with your father, she remained very much 'beloved.'"

"You never divorced?"

"I asked. He wouldn't. I thought we'd get around to it." She redirects her attention. "Fred, can you help with the sale?"

"I can bring in the Bowmans. Brother and sister realtors, very well regarded." Mr. Weber folds up the will and returns it to his file. "They'll be in touch."

Mom rises and we do the same in succession, a joyless, three-person wave.

"Where are we supposed to go?" Jackie wails.

"Back to your lives. Whatever that means to each of you. Jackie, you have a husband. Yes, he's a lunkhead, impulsive and childlike—and not in an oh-he's-adorable-childlike way—but he was all those things when you married him. Yes, people change and grow. Look at me and your father—"

"One of those things is not like the other," I point out. "Dad didn't leave to live in a yurt with a fireman."

"If you've decided you don't want those things anymore"—she ignores me the way a hippo ignores flies—"then you leave. But you move forward, not back. The house you grew up in is no longer an option."

"What about Aaron?"

"I don't need you to stick up for me."

"You shut the fuck up," she says without looking, but at least she's spoken to me.

"I thought this would be temporary, but you've demonstrated that it's not."

"You thought I was a salamander?"

"We all thought you'd been dealt a terrible blow," Mr. Weber joins in. "And that you'd come out stronger for it."

"Sometimes, those things that don't kill you just ruin you instead. You know that, right? We're not all Randy Fucking Pausch."

"Who's Randy Fucking Pausch?" Jackie wants to know.

"I'm glad you're talking to me again."

"I'm not. Fuck you. And fuck you too," Jackie snaps at Mom, and she leaves, and if there's a flicker of hurt Mom manages to bury it beneath the surface, an iceberg where nine-tenths of her disappointment swims.

Mom approaches me from my defenseless left side, where she smooths my hair and pats my head. "This is what needs to be done. I know this to be true."

And then she too is out the door, leaving me once more alone with Mr. Weber and the ringing in my ears. At least this time, my pants are up.

"How about lunch? We should talk about what to do with that damn alligator."

He punctuates his invitation with a slam of the file drawer, as Dad's final wishes return to mingle in the darkness among the wishes of other long-dead clients who no longer wish for anything.

HOMELESS

The house has been emptied of its contents, first picked over in a two-day estate sale (where strangers haggled over the evidence of our lives), then whatever remained hauled away by an estate liquidator (presumably to be rendered liquid). Jackie and I were first allowed a wordless, brief excavation of the house's pointless artifacts, an archeological dig through long-dead electronics, stacks of out-of-print magazines, and bundles of pens from restaurants whose kitchens have long since gone cold. Separately—as Jackie refused my proximity—we also unearthed some minor treasures: the owner's manual to the Lincoln Mark IV, Jackie's baby clothes, my old report cards reflecting mostly decent grades (except for the D from Mr. Madnick) alongside a serial run of *Unsatisfactory*s for behavior, self-control, and attitude, giving me the upper hand in any argument that I've changed since the accident.

Priced by our determined mother well below market with a thirty-day escrow, the house has sold quickly to a family with a sullen teenage son who would continue a tradition of attic sulking; so in the time it takes to receive a set of nonstick pans ordered from a late-night cable commercial ("allow four to six weeks for delivery"), I'm rendered homeless.

Jackie is already gone, forced back to California by Mom's

inarguable mandate and her own unwillingness to watch her childhood home reduced to bones as if by African army ants. (Of the house's former occupants, only Ali is better off, having been taken in by Mr. Weber.) I'm fairly certain Jackie still isn't speaking to me, but I'm forced to try when I receive from Mr. Weber Mom's check for half the sum of the sale of the house and assume Jackie got the other half. She doesn't answer but texts back, FUCK YOU.

Off that fruitless effort I turn to Mom, seeking fruit. "You kicked us out of the house, sold it, and then gave us the money?"

"Why are you calling to tell me something I already know?"

"So basically, Jackie and I could just pool the money and go buy the house back."

"I doubt that. No one moves into a house just to sell it back to the people they bought it from. That's the definition of pointless."

"As pointless as kicking us out of a house and then giving us the money?"

"Now you both have a little something to help you move forward. If you decide to move backward instead," she muses, "yes, you could both chip in some more on top of the purchase price and offer a profit incentive."

"I understand how commerce works."

"That would be up to you," she continues. "I can't help what you do now. I can only help what I can help. The rest is out of my hands."

I take with me as much of the attic as I can fit in the van, a wardrobe box of Dad's old suits and shoes, the basement painting of the racehorse, and a cluster of Mom's zinnias, pulled from the earth and stuffed into a pot sitting next to me on the passenger seat, silent as Dad under his grocery bag. I also have

Dad's ashes, grateful to have not gotten around to scattering them around the yard for the squirrels to romp in. It would have felt bad leaving him behind like that.

Pulling away from the house a final time, just ahead of the moving van pulling in, I head to the Sunset Elks Motor Inn, a foolish gambit to get back at Mom by squandering her generosity at $79 a night ($89 on weekends). Clutching Mom's zinnias, I ask for a smoking room and am informed that all their rooms are smoke-free.

"That's okay," I reply, only to be greeted with the kind of skeptical look once conferred upon me by Dad when I told him I had no homework. I'm given a key card anyway, and make my way to my room, bleak as a prison cell.

Soon I'm sucking up spirals of Moe Larry Hemp, engineered for the wakefulness presumably required of a Stooge. Waking up here in a lonely motor inn on my first day away from my lost home is going to feel crappy, and the only way to avoid that is if I don't fall asleep. I have no illusions that I can keep this up indefinitely but if I can stay awake for one or even two nights, then I'll either have accepted my situation or be too exhausted to care.

Nothing keeps me awake like bad television and I find myself compelled by a law-enforcement reality show where moronic car thieves are entrapped by luxury cars left unattended, keys inside, along with several hidden cameras. Despite being unlocked, this particular vehicle has its window smashed anyway, by an overeager perpetrator who then fumbles through the arm console for loose change before driving away, laughing to himself, only to have the engine cut off (the cops staking out the vehicle have a kill switch). Arrested and placed in handcuffs, the perp seems to enjoy being on television, and while I ponder the special type of criminal mind that delights in this kind of notoriety,

I again hear glass smashing and wonder how they jumped to a second storyline so quickly. Then I realize the sound came from outside where my van is parked.

I race outside with the only weapon I can grab, and two mulleted youths flee at the sight of me, either because my remote control looks like it may be a gun or, more likely, they're terrified of the shirtless, one-armed, nub-tattooed madman who leaps without thinking, wild-eyed, from the safety of his crack den. When I awaken the desk clerk to report the attempted robbery, he sniffs the air in my room and is instantly unhappy.

"I said this was a smoke-free motel."

"Hey, I have a prescription for this."

"You also have a driver's license. That doesn't mean you can drive your car into your room and spin doughnuts. 'Smoke-free' means smoke-free."

I resist the urge to argue that if we're going to be so literal, "motor inn" might imply that I could in fact drive in here and spin said doughnuts.

"They tried to rob my van!" I shout. "And now the window's broken. I can't leave it unattended."

"Right, because you're leaving."

"Fuck you," I tell him, slamming the door in his face, suddenly understanding how good that makes Jackie feel.

The next knock at my door isn't the desk clerk but the now-familiar face of the sheriff, without gas mask, visibly sagging upon seeing me and declaring, "Oh, for fuck's sake."

We argue over my rights as a prescription-drug user and my entitlement as a paying motel customer to a safe environment; losing both arguments, I attempt a new one over the full refund due me if I do decide to leave—which I haven't yet said I'd do— only to lose that one too. Winless, I relent and head for the van when the sheriff stops me, gently prying the van's keys from my fingers as he reminds me that prescription or no, it remains illegal for me to drive under the influence.

That's when I discover that "Fuck you" doesn't universally lead to feeling better, although its current usage solves my temporary homeless dilemma. Instead of waking up on my first day away from home in a lonely motor inn, I wake up in the sheriff's holding cell where Will, armless once more due to the early morning hour, stares down at me through the bars, having come to pay my bail.

"I called your friend," the sheriff explains. "Figured he owed you the bail."

On the way back to the Sunset Elks parking lot, Will asks, "So why didn't you tell me you paid my bail? I thought they just let us go."

"We were only in trouble because of me. That shouldn't cost you money."

"I did think it was a little weird, just releasing us like that."

"Aren't you used to being so pitiable, you get away with anything?"

"Not with cops," he mutters as we roll into the lot to see my van, nearly completely ransacked overnight. Gone is anything of value, and worse, those things with no monetary worth I care most about, as evidenced by the handful of Dad's thirty-five-millimeter slides dotting the parking lot like oversized confetti. Dad's suits, too unfashionable to steal, are left untouched, his ashes spilled but salvageable. Mom's zinnias remain in the passenger seat where I dropped them before being relieved of my keys. But the mother lode most deliciously struck by the thieves is a month's worth of weed, Vicodin, and Valium. Instead of a reality show celebrating the dumbness of car thieves, the returning thugs found themselves winning contestants on a game show, probably weeping with joy and clutching each other as they jumped up and down, balloons and audience applause raining over them as their families rushed the stage under closing credits.

"You okay?"

"Fine," I lie, so pitiably that Will offers to let me crash at his place "for as long as it takes," and regardless of how ill defined "it" is, we both know that no guest's stay can reasonably be that long.

I thank him and tell him I'll follow to his place, climbing into the van and crunching a million tiny nodules of car window under my ass. I reach to turn on the CD player but it too is gone, and with it my *Dad Is Dead* mixtape, which I hope the thieves find more perplexing than enjoyable.

Screeching into reverse, I cut the wheel hard and take out a row of bushes, slam the car into drive and plow unlooking into traffic—who cares?—speeding forward, closing the distance on Will's rear bumper. He throws his one good arm up in the air, an asymmetrical shrug, and I can see him mouth the words *What the fuck?* in his rearview mirror, but I don't give a shit anymore, and there's nothing left to sedate me or placate me or otherwise-ate me. I want to shut out the roar of the blood in my ears and the world rushing in my broken window, so I plug in my earbuds and hit shuffle and the Judybats remind me that "Pain Makes You Beautiful." So knowing what an absolutely breathtaking motherfucker I must be, I slow down.

THINGS I COULDN'T HOLD ON TO WITH ONE HAND

Black-light poster

Black light

Painting of a
   racehorse

Laptop

External hard drive with
   Dad's scans

My CDs and Dad's LPs

Dad's Olympic
   memorabilia

A life in thirty-five-
   millimeter slides

Buttonless shirts

Zipperless sweatpants

Laceless footwear

One fancy Hugo Boss
   suit

One box of ridiculous
   self-improvement
   books

One box of armless sports
   trophies

Bottle of Fleischmann's

Vicodin (30×500 mg)

Pot (half ounce, give or
   take)

ROCKETS

Will tries to encourage me to return to work at Ick Ick, but that seems as ill advised as a retired boxer's comeback. Without the zoning-in qualities of Hocus-Focus and even-numbered multiples of Vicodin, I'd be a shadow of my former fish-target-locked self. But I agree to meet him there for lunch, arriving all dappered up in one of Dad's old suits and his white patent leather shoes. I'm surprised by how happy everyone seems to see me, even Percy. Lilith hugs me tightly, pressing her tits up against me, and I can feel her nipples harden. When I move in for a second clinch I see that look in her face that would precede a hard face slap, and I abort my approach like a seasoned pilot, changing my heading for lunch with Will on the dam.

"You were pretty mad yesterday."

"Everything I owned was in a van. Then it wasn't."

"I get it. Your father, the house you grew up in, your stuff. All gone in a hurry."

"Don't forget the broken window I used to enjoy rolling up and down."

"I'm mad too."

"But look at the bright side: you have a window."

As we walk I find myself scanning the fish ladders to test if I can still spot *Acipenser pseudoboscis* without the aid of performance-enhancing drugs. But here in the off-season the sturgeon are content to flap around downstream until their genetically programmed hormones tell them it's Amok Time at the top of the river.

"These things kill fish," Will berates the dam. "Not just live fish either, but all the fish that would have been born here, at the top of the river, but won't be. Generations that were supposed to happen. And they won't, because they'll never make it to spawn."

"It's like a generational cock blocker, this dam."

"All so the power company can generate electricity at a penny a kilowatt."

Will marvels at the dam's engineering the way a medical school teacher extols the virtues of anatomy right before dismantling a cadaver. "It's designed to curve upstream so that the force of the water presses against the arch, actually making it stronger as it pushes into its foundation. Up here"—he indicates the rim under our feet—"is where it's strongest . . . but the deeper you go, the greater the stress."

"And the more you talk about this stuff, the more my stress levels go up."

We walk quietly for a bit. I believe I see a pair of fish struggling through a fishing weir, but that's probably a drug-deprived hallucination.

"So, when you bailed me out," Will finally exhales, "what did the sheriff tell you about me?"

"That you never served. That you blew off your arm making a bomb."

"So you think I'm a liar."

"I'm not one to judge. I told a little boy with cancer that an alligator ate my arm."

Will explains, telling me about growing up in his hometown, considered the geographic center of the United States: Lebanon,

Kansas. That's also where he worked for the family business, making fireworks. I guess any handmade explosive device takes a certain amount of improvising, so I'll give him IED too.

"That is one sweet misdirect," I gush.

"Well, you get treated better if you have a good story."

"Hence the alligator that ate my arm."

Will knows more than just how to blow things up. Depending on how it's packed, he elucidates, gunpowder can serve as both propellant and explosive, launching a sphere packed with explosives into the sky and then detonating. How you distribute the powder inside determines what pattern the explosion takes— lay it out in the shape of a star, you'll get an exploding star; ditto a map of America, an American flag, and presumably anything else uniquely American, like jazz hands. The colors come from burning metal salts—different salts make different colored flames—and powders have different burn rates, trailing a slow burn or gone in a flash. Most importantly, everything is made of wood or paper or any nonsparking material, lest an unintentional clattering together of, say, metal containers result in a stray spark that leads to an unplanned detonation. It's all a far cry from my own experience, letting firecrackers explode between my fingers.

And I wish we were talking about those "pretty" kind of fireworks, instead of the kind I know we're talking about.

I finally confront him. "Will, I don't want to help you blow up the dam."

"I never said anything about blowing up the dam," he states flatly. "*You* keep bringing that up. Are you sure *you* don't want to blow it up?"

"Wouldn't that kill all the fish in the immediate vicinity?" I argue. "And won't they just rebuild it?"

"The government programs that went dam-crazy fifty years ago don't have those kinds of resources anymore. If this dam were to vanish overnight—"

"Or as the case may be, explode . . ."

"They'd never build another one. And in just a few generations, the fish would be restored to something much closer to their natural population."

"I can see how, on paper, I look like a good partner for this: between us we have two hands, and that's a plus. I'm also angry and you want to tap into that. But let me point out, if you got a partner with both arms then you'd have three. Also, I'm not consistently that angry. To get the best out of me you'd have to keep making me angry, like the Hulk."

"Sometimes I'm so sick of the way things are, I just want to disappear," he muses. "Let's forget it," he says, and I do.

But I'm aware that I'm angrier now than when Will and I went shooting with Dad, and was angrier then than when we'd first met. The trajectory of my anger leads up, like a rocket—and rockets don't come down; they explode spectacularly.

There's no further talk of dam demolition as Will and I spend the next week living at his place like newlyweds, cooking together, our two hands in concert preparing meals—I hold and he chops, and together our hands cup meat into meatballs—and then washing and drying, until we plop in front of the television and argue over the remote. When Will goes to work I do the laundry, even taking the time to carefully fold—a degree of difficulty that makes it an act of love. I even dress up in Dad's suits to look nice for him when he comes home. Will won't take rent money so I pay for everything I can: groceries, movies, gas, towels for the guest bathroom, and dinner out at Dim Sum & Then Some, where I steal their pen. I'm Will's sugar daddy without the sex in return.

With pot and pills lost to van-ransacking junkies, I resume jogging to burn off the excess energy, good arm churning, nub a stubby metronome ticking back and forth. The Vicodin withdrawal renders me occasionally irritable, which I tamp down with Fleischmann's and lemonade. I can tell Will interprets these hot flashes as rocketing anger that will burst spectacularly in the destruction of his dam. Because that's what anger does. The angry man rationalizes his bad behavior; he steals from work and cheats on his wife, is rude to people who try to help and yells at someone who doesn't deserve it. Sulks mightily, throws things with his good arm, says "Fuck you" to a sheriff. And pours Fleischmann's down to its final eleven drops. But no amount of anger could make me blow up a dam. That would be crazy.

"We're out of Fleischmann's," I hear my father's voice emit from my face, as I grab my coat and head for the door.

Grief is something entirely different from anger. It too might be cause for rationalization but is strengthened by desperation as the losses pile up until there's nothing left to lose. I've lost nearly everything: my father, twice—first to the stroke and then frustratingly brought back a little at a time only to be taken all at once; rejected by my mother, banished from the home where she raised me; lost to my sister who, two thousand miles distant and silent, might as well be dead. And of course my arm, and with it whatever small dignity I'd managed to cling to stolen by a viral YouTube sensation.

The last remnants of my old life are Mom's zinnias. Somehow those are enough, those tiny blooms a living generational link to my lost home and a past from which the trajectory of my future had not yet been set to lead here.

Until I return from the liquor store and find them gone, eaten by Will's cat, shreds of stems in dirt all that remain.

I wake Will and tell him, without a trace of anger, "Let's blow that fucking dam."

His response—"Whatever"—makes me wonder if this was actually my idea all along.

DAMOLITION

If you can turn explosives into fireworks, it stands to reason you can reverse engineer fireworks into explosives, just as you can pull apart a half-eaten BLT to rescue the bacon. Hitting more than a dozen fireworks outlets we load up on enough rockets, mortars, and shells to arm a third-world power—skyrockets and repeaters, fountains and spinners, and even "Exploding Rifle Targets"—which, if I'd known about them before our mock biathlon in Crawlywood, would have made it even more fun and dangerous for a small boy.

The same way Will and I collaborated to prepare meals in the kitchen, we put our good arms together and unpack, unroll, and otherwise dismember these legal fireworks until what we have left is a discarded pile of paper, plastic, sticks, cones, and fuses on one side, and a ten- or twelve-pound pile of illegal gunpowder on the other. I'd like to think we can create something flashy and spectacular to elicit *oohs* and *aahs* from an appreciative crowd; but since the explosion will happen at the dam's weakest point—underwater—any fancy starbursts or roundels, willows or palms, would be as pointless as a fireworks display in blazing daylight.

With enough explosive powder gathered, we start packing our first "chube," brightly colored chew tubes for hamsters that

Will found at a pet store. Once filled, each end is carefully sealed with perfectly fitting plugs—black acrylic ear gauges, whose unfathomable purpose by design is the stretching of one's ear lobes, here put to good use. When we begin packing the second explosive chube the first one rolls to the floor and is pounced on by Will's cat, who proceeds to knock it from one side of the apartment to the other and back again while Will tries to stop him and I mostly scream *Holy shit holy shit holy shit fuck* before Will is finally able to snatch it away, the cat eyeing it like a prize he knows he'll catch later before trotting away.

"I'm not complaining, but does this mean we built a dud?" I ask.

"It's not nitroglycerine. It's not necessarily that volatile or combustible," Will explains. "I wouldn't want to make a habit out of that, but if we do this right, it shouldn't explode by contact."

I'm heartened that not blowing Will's cat through the floor of his apartment indicates we might actually be doing this properly, but I suggest a true test. Which is how we find ourselves early the next morning in Crawlywood, where I once exploded much tinier powder-filled tubes between my fingertips, and where both of us were arrested for doing something incredibly stupid but somehow far less stupid than this.

When Will lights the fuse it occurs to me to ask, "Hey, how is this going to light underwater?"

"I'll come up with something. Probably airtight plastic. You should throw that."

"But won't the burning fuse melt the plastic?"

"There are ways to do it," Will seems agitated. "We'll figure it out. Throw that fucking thing."

"M80 fuses burn underwater," I recall, and I throw it as far as I can into the trees. It doesn't even have time to land, exploding about a foot off the ground, the shock tearing the leaves from a nearby bush with the efficiency of an atomic-powered leaf blower. Pleased to know we don't have a dud on our hands, we leave before the sheriff can arrive to teargas us.

Back at Will's we make dozens more just like it, packing powder into chubes that we then bind together. At one point Will ties the first assembly of ten around him like a bomb vest and laughs . . . which makes me uneasy for the first time. Up until now I've put complete faith in Will, ignoring the fact that he once blew off an arm doing something much like this under undoubtedly safer and more controlled conditions. Certainly I knew before now that this was both dangerous and stupid; but like drunken sex with a stranger, focusing on the stupid part allowed me to mitigate any sense of danger, of blowing myself up or catching an STD. Now that it's hot on my radar, I find my performance suffering, my rhythm off, my will to continue gone limp. When Will asks if everything is okay, I blame a headache.

By morning we have thirty brightly colored chubes of river-liberating explosives. It seems insufficient for such a large task but I assume Will knows what he's doing and defer to his expertise. Maybe all we need to do is blow a small hole where the pressure is greatest, and then the onrushing torrent of water will tear the rest of the dam apart as it surges through. But I don't know that; as all this became more real I stopped asking questions. Giving myself over completely to Will in the absence of medical marijuana and Vicodin seemed the best way to replicate the same mindless focus that once allowed me to count fish expertly.

When we're done Will pops open two cans of beer, hands me one, and clinks them together.

"Tomorrow," he says. "Let's do this thing tomorrow."

Will's plan calls for him to take possession of the explosives and for me to meet him at the dam at six, early enough to still have some daylight, but late enough that any possible innocent bystanders won't be standing by.

I dream that night of explosions and rushing water, of a river long held in check blasting forward, a million concussed fish in its wake, floating, bloated, each one transforming into a dismembered arm, rafts of limbs drifting downriver like logs.

BOOKED

Back in the early days of rough-hewn men settling America, one of our solutions to taming the wilderness was to DAM IT! *No, I'm not swearing . . . I mean, literally, the damming of rivers and lakes, either to retain water, divert it for irrigation, or even harness its thundering power to generate electricity. But those dams also threw a serious obstacle in the migratory path of certain fish species, especially those engineered by nature to return to the place they were born to spawn. Imagine that! It would be like you racing back to the hospital delivery room where you drew your first breath, now to mate with your spouse—not the most romantic weekend!*

But if that's a fish's idea of a good time, who are we to judge? In many parts of the country, this treacherous birthing ritual has gotten easier: since the late 1990s, scores of dam-removal projects have been under way across America, allowing migratory fish to complete their upriver journey unimpeded, an event that in some cases hasn't occurred naturally for more than a century. So break out the bubbly, lady fish—you're about to have all the suitors a gilled girl can dream of . . . and this time, they won't be so tired from the commute that they fall asleep in front of the TV.

This is Sunny Lee for The Sunny Side. *Don't forget, I'll be signing my new book,* Sunny Side Up, *at Books-A-Million in Terre Haute on Highway 41 tonight at five o'clock.*

I nearly drive off the road at this announcement that two of the momentous events of my life are destined to happen on the same day barely an hour apart.

Growing up I was never good at priorities, believing instead in both cake-having and -eating. It was evident in the behavior of the adults in my orbit that maturity meant routinely forgoing the thing you wanted for the thing you promised, and I was in no hurry to do so. (The moment those priorities flipped for Dad could possibly be traced to the last slide he took, as the growing demands of his family obliterated further pursuit of his picture taking.) Accordingly, I always resisted trading the thing I wanted for the thing I promised, opting wherever possible to pursue both, although not always without guilt: I still recall when Mom's birthday barbecue fell on the same day Artie scored a fresh mat of firecrackers; I'd slipped away under the pretense of sharing homework to meet in Crawlywood and returned, late for Mom's party, redolent of gunpowder and scorched fingertips and the stink of disappointment.

This particular conundrum will at least occur in the right order: Sunny first and then the dam. Were the order inverted, rushing the necessary process of dam-blasting so as not to miss the signing seemed perhaps fatally unwise; and of course there's the risk of arrest or accidentally blowing myself up and therefore missing the signing. Regardless, I try calling Will to convince him to push even half an hour to be on the safe side (if there is a "safe side" to blowing up a dam). There's no answer on his cell, and psycho-dialing him repeatedly yields the same result.

Whether to fortify myself for the industrious task ahead or as rationalization of a possible last meal, I drive to the Four Corners where I lard myself full of chicken-fat-fried meat,

mashed potatoes, biscuits, gravy, and just for good measure, order a side of bacon and melted cheese. This would be more enjoyable if Dad were here, and if Mr. Weber wasn't so angry
when I run into him in the parking lot on my way out.

"Where the hell have you been? Your mother is worried sick!
If you're not going to answer your phone, you can at least return
the calls!"

"If she wanted to know where I was all the time, she shouldn't
have sold the house."

"Stop being such a goddamn baby!"

"I'm staying with my friend Will. Remember Will? You
would if you saw him. Guy I used to work with."

"What about work?" he's still shouting. "Are you going back?"

"The dam might not be the future employer it used to be. Besides," I navigate from confession to blame, "with all this money
Mom gave me, who needs to work? She ruined my initiative
with a trust fund of thousands."

"Good God, is that your father's leisure suit?" he suddenly
notices.

"It is!" I strike the dashing pose of a supermodel reaching the
end of the catwalk to give him a good look.

What follows is an incredulous silence and with nothing
much to fill it, I assure Mr. Weber I'm fine and excuse myself.
Climbing into the van, I slam the door hard enough to dispel the
lie but have to quickly throw it open again when my stomach re-
jects its contents, burning on its way up before obliterating the
blue handicapped parking stripes in the lot. As I drive off past
Mr. Weber I can't help feeling sorry for him, forced to keep stum-
bling across his dead friend's son expelling fluids from his body.

Traffic on Highway 41 whizzes past Books-A-Million as if
there were some better place to be than here with Sunny Lee,
even an agreed-upon rendezvous to liberate a river in a criminal

act. There's a poster in the window showing her book jacket, and her face—*Lovely!*—inviting passersby inside, alongside lesser works by Russo, Lethem, Helprin, Chabon, Franzen.

Checking myself in the rearview mirror for traces of vomit, I see my chin stubble is clean but dammit, I spotted the lapel of Dad's leisure suit. As it's on the right side, I can't reach across myself but struggle, vertically, for several minutes to disperse it with spit on a handkerchief. Now I'm sweating profusely—it's not the heat but another nagging symptom of the drug withdrawal I've suffered since my van was looted. I wipe my brow with my good hand but now my hair is matted, and this isn't how I want to meet Sunny Lee so I settle down, turn on the air-conditioning, and wait out the wilt. I scroll through my phone log of missed calls from Mom and Mr. Weber but see nothing from Will.

Heading inside, I expect to encounter a long line of smart sophisticates who appreciate intelligence and humor and the universe around them, leading to Sunny Lee, behind a table, smiling warmly under thick black hair pulled back, dark almond eyes sparkling with intelligence. Instead, the store is quiet and the table empty.

"Am I early for the signing?"

"Late," the woman behind the counter says. "Decent crowd, a few dozen readers. She stayed about an hour, signed, chatted, and left."

"But it's still a few minutes before five," I protest.

"Not here it isn't," she declares in a way that says it's happened a thousand times to her before, here on Highway 41 just across the meridian into eastern standard time. An understandable mistake for anyone, but not the son of a man who once time traveled twice daily for his living.

I could have been here, in the future, an hour ago, met Sunny and then headed back to the dam before I even left. Instead she's already gone, and I don't even realize how openly bereft I am until the woman behind the counter offers me a 20 percent discount on Sunny's book if I'll stop crying.

Book in hand, and with a time zone hour to kill before my criminal rendezvous, I limp to the bar across the street and order a beer. Thumbing through the book, I find some of it familiar, about grasshoppers and attraction and brain hemispheres, but much of it waiting to be discovered. I wish I could read it all tonight, cover to cover, peacefully in bed, but know I cannot.

"Thanks for coming," I hear in her familiar radio voice, and I turn to see Sunny Lee at the other end of the bar from me, sitting behind a glass of wine, smiling warmly under thick black hair pulled back, dark almond eyes sparkling with intelligence.

I want to say something clever, with the combined wit of every member of the Algonquin Round Table, or brilliantly observed, like Stephen Hawking gazing into a distant black hole. Instead I gape at her and start to sweat again.

"I didn't see you at the signing," she says, eyes dropping to my arm. "I'd have remembered."

"Late," I grunt. "Forgot about the time difference."

"Oh, I grew up around here and still mess it up."

"Blame the European railroads," I recall some useless bit of information I once passed on to my students. "We used to add four minutes for every degree of longitude. So when it was noon in Bristol, it was ten after noon in London. It made it hard to catch a train."

"Can I steal that from you?" she laughs, typing into her smartphone.

"Is this how it works—chatting up strangers to steal their otherwise useless trivia?"

"Only when it's this good! Usually I find it in the stuff around me in the moment. I'm already planning one on bookstore germs."

My phone rings and it could be Will, or Jackie, or a super-model, the president, or sweet Jesus. Without looking, I shut it off.

"Would you like me to sign?" Sunny nods at my book, and I nudge it toward her.

"That's why I'm here, an hour in the future."

"Should I make it to anyone special?"

"Me," I reply. "Not that I'm special."

"Okay, *me*," she teases.

"Sorry! Aaron."

"Aaron . . ." She starts to scribble and then looks up at me. "You went to Paris High?"

"I did. Not often. Cut a lot of classes. The world outside," I gesture, "the one you're always talking about on the radio, was a lot more interesting to me than whatever useless information my poor teachers were attempting to force into my head."

"I was ahead of you. In your sister's class."

"I didn't know that until recently."

"I had a little crush on you," she resumes scribbling. "I remember you were really funny. And that long hair, so cute."

"Less hair is easier to take care of. Although somehow, less of me is harder. On the plus side, I know all kinds of useless stuff about nerve endings, pain management, blood infections, and lizard regeneration. Do you know that's mostly a myth? Of course you do."

"Sounds like you could write for me." She hands the book back, and I clasp it to my chest like a pastor embracing the Bible.

"I've learned a lot about minutiae, and a little about things that are huge. I know more about the human brain than I thought I could store in my tiny human brain. Wow, that sounded remarkably stupid," I lament.

She laughs. "You sound like two things I like: interesting and interested."

YES, I'M BOTH OF THOSE THINGS! I manage not to shout.

"Seriously, I use freelancers from time to time," she turns the subject away from me loving her to why I love her. "It's not easy coming up with three-hundred-some-odd segments a year."

"I would be the best generator of weird, obscure ideas you ever had," I wheeze.

"Not too weird! But humor helps. E-mail me a sample or two." She produces a business card, scrawling her cell phone number on the back. "And here's my personal cell. Call me," she smiles beatifically, and I can feel the sweat pumping. "I have to go. Say hi to Jackie."

With just enough time to meet Will at the dam, I start the engine and restart my phone to see two voice mails: one from Mom and one from Jackie. If Dad were still alive, this would be a sure sign he was dead and both had called to tell me. Or else maybe Mom called to tell me Jackie's dead and so did Steve calling from Jackie's phone. I should call Mom back first but if my sister is dead, I don't want to make Mom say it, so I punch Jackie's number instead and am surprised and relieved to hear Jackie on the speaker.

"You have no idea how nice it is to hear your voice. Even if you just called to say 'Fuck you,'" I tell her, imagining an angry Stevie Wonder song.

"Did you talk to Mom?"

"No, but she left a message. What's wrong?"

"Nothing, unless you count Mom marrying the fireman."

"Oh God, no!" I almost swerve off the road again.

"It gets worse: I'm her maid of honor, and she wants you to give her away."

"This already sounds worse than a *Game of Thrones* wedding," I whimper, resolving never to listen to Mom's message.

We groan about Mom and the firefighter, tag-team-bash

Jackie's soon to be ex-husband, laugh about my being kicked out of the Sunset Elks motel by the sheriff, and commiserate over losing nearly everything to car thieves, and the loss of the zinnias. (I make an especially big deal about the zinnias until Jackie tells me to just go back to the house and ask if I can take another bunch of goddamn zinnias—a ridiculously simple solution to my paralyzing bereavement that I somehow never thought of.) Sharing the news that I just met Sunny Lee at her book signing earns Jackie's accusation of "stalking," which only sounds worse when I mention that Sunny might have offered me a job writing for her. Absentmindedly, I flip open her book to read:

Still so cute! Symmetry is overrated. Love, Sunny, a radiant sun sketched next to her name.

I'm not sure I've ever felt better than this moment, even with two arms. And then I remember what I'm about to do.

"Look, this is great that we're talking. If something bad happened to one of us when we weren't speaking, I think it would be very bad for the other one."

"Why? What bad thing is going to happen to you?"

"Why is it necessarily *me* something bad might happen to? It could be either of us—you could be crushed by a block of frozen urine falling from a passing airplane, or your appendix could burst before I finish this sentence."

"For God's sake, what's wrong with you?"

"Or even just the lesson of Dad: aren't you glad you spent that last time with Dad, so there are no regrets? Besides having to sit in a dark closet for three days, I mean."

She's silent a long time. "I didn't tell you a lot of what we talked about. Because I was a little pissed."

"Why were you pissed?"

"Because he spent a lot of that time talking about you!" She sounds supremely annoyed. "About what good care you were taking of him!"

"He must have left out a few things."

"I can only imagine. It was weird. He said you were 'nice' like a hundred times, like it meant something incredibly wonderful."

I'm stunned.

"He also talked about that poor, sick little boy—how come you never told me that?"

"Let's just say Make-A-Wish isn't rushing to recruit me."

"Dad said you'd stopped thinking about yourself and were more concerned about him. Ugh," she says, with obvious love, "he was really proud of you."

It's a velvet-gloved gut punch, a moment both wonderful and sickening as I imagine what my proud dad would think now about his son, the dam bomber. I've had a series of good intentions with bad outcomes, and maybe I need to flip that equation. Reexamining this particular good intention, I'm forced to conclude:

Fuck those stupid fucking fish.

I have Mom's wedding to go to and a sister who, against all logic, loves me and, equally unfathomably, Sunny Lee thinks I'm "still so cute" and might let me write things for her to tell the world in her lovely radio voice. These are the things I want, weighed against the foolish promise I made to Will. I push my foot farther down on the accelerator, convincing myself that if I can talk Will out of it, I can have the thing I want without breaking a promise—a bit of wisdom that never occurred to my thirteen-year-old or adult self when forced to choose between what I wanted and promises made.

"Jackie, I need to call you back . . ."

Crossing the intersection, I see the other driver's face before we crash, and I wonder if the SUV driver who crashed into me saw mine, head turned, wide-eyed in terror, broadsided, glass and metal everywhere, face disappearing behind an explosion of air bags. The last thing I remember before blacking out is the voice of my sister, who had spent more than a month refusing to speak to me, now shouting into the phone, "What happened? Talk to me! SAY SOMETHING!" and feeling pretty good about that.

EMERGENCY

Waking up in the hospital is different this time, starting with the observation that my good arm is handcuffed to a gurney.

So, I've been arrested for criminal terrorism, the dam blown and Will in custody (or worse), and I wasn't even there. What a stupid plan, anyway . . . we killed thousands of fish and endangered everyone in the area, and now I'm going to jail where a one-armed man is easy prey, unless I join a gang for protection and wonder if my nub tattoo will earn me any prison cred. But I don't care about any of it.

"*Is she dead? Did I kill her?* What about her arm? HOW IS HER ARM?" I shout the questions over the curtain until it's slid aside by Mom and Mr. Weber.

"Settle down," Mr. Weber urges.

"She's fine, honey," Mom assures me. "See?"

They stand aside and I see the woman whose face was swallowed by air bags sitting across her emergency room gurney, legs dangling, dazed, a few cuts, attended by her recently arrived husband and, happily, limbs intact.

"I'm so sorry," I cry, my own dam blown and a river of tears rushing, unstoppable, carrying with them a torrent of emotional debris.

"Ohhh . . ." Mom leans in to hold me.

"Easy does it," Mr. Weber tries again to settle things down. "You didn't do anything wrong. According to the police, she ran a red light."

"I'm sorry . . ." she whimpers. "Are you okay?"

"They had to amputate my arm!" I shout back, suddenly laughing.

"He's hysterical," Mom tosses over her shoulder.

"Hilarious," I correct her.

"Then why is he handcuffed?" Mom asks Mr. Weber, and I start crying again.

"DUI. Sheriff says he expects his blood to test positive for all kinds of things."

I start laughing again.

"Did anyone check his head? They should check his head."

Of course, after more than a week's worth of painful withdrawal, my drug test will come back negative and the sheriff will have to release me. Except any minute now, I expect this emergency room will be crowded with victims of the dam bombing, possibly including the late shift in their underground counting stations, windows blown out and drowned—collateral damage I hadn't even thought about in my addled, drug-withdrawn state until now. I deserve everything that's coming to me and am about to confess my role in these terrible events when I see on the overhead television shaky cell phone footage of a masked suspect rushing from a bank with a sack of money and a bomb vest of thirty colorful chubes strapped to his torso.

Thinking back, Will never actually *said* he wanted to blow up the dam.

DECISIONS

I can only imagine the confusion of a teller receiving Will's bank robber's note if that teller also owned hamsters. A vest adorned with colorful hamster-chewable tubes would appear more fanciful than menacing unless, like some comic book villain, each chube were to produce a ravenous razor-toothed mutant hamster. But Will's note, published in the newspaper, would have dispelled any doubt as to the seriousness of his purpose:

I am wired to explode. Give me all the cash in all the drawers. I
will check the bag when you hand it back to me, and if you include
any booby-trapped dye packs, I assure you the force will be enough
to blow us both up. I have nothing to lose.

What also proved effective was Will's prosthetic arm cloaked in sleeve and glove and on which the loot swung freely as he made his escape. Not a single witness took note of his arm, so no one was looking for a one-armed bank robber.

Doing the necessary research I should have done then, I discover it would take several hundred pounds of explosives to blow a hole in a dam, far more than the meager amount we were able to wring from rockets and roman candles. Will never had any intention of anything so noble as dam destruction, seeing instead an opportunity to enlist my witless complicity in his plot to commit a different kind of felony; ergo, I no longer feel any inclination to reveal my role in the actual felony I thought I was committing. And recalling how deliberate he was in shielding me from complicity (Will had purchased the fireworks without me, and by directing me to meet him at the dam he deliberately diverted me far from the crime scene), I feel confident that he will not give me up if apprehended.

Especially as his capture seems unlikely.

An hour after the robbery a stolen vehicle matching the description of the getaway car exploded while crossing a bridge over the upper tributary, hurtling into the river below where it presumably killed many fish. Despite the fact that no body or money were recovered at the scene, the conventional wisdom holds that the unknown bank robber died like he lived: recklessly, money and self blown to tiny smithereens. My own feeling is that Will wasn't stupid enough to be still wearing a bomb vest more than an hour after the robbery; he also seemed quite capable of timing an explosion even in a moving car he no longer occupied. Despite his humiliating deception, I prefer to think of Will as a one-armed D. B. Cooper still at large.

Conscience, concussion, and drug test clear, I'm released from the hospital and Fred Weber offers to let me move in with him—temporarily—if I'll promise to get a job and stop wearing Dad's old suits. It's a kind offer and better than the only other option I can think of, which might be to join Mom in her yurt with the firefighter (although she hasn't suggested any such thing).

Dad's suits earn enough at the vintage store to buy everyone at the Four Corners breakfast, and I encourage them to order the Lumberjack Special. Having contributed an unhealthy rise in local cholesterol levels, I walk mine off just far enough to spot the Help Wanted sign in the window of Broken Records.

"I'm just the man you're looking for," I announce to Mr. Madnick, pulling the sign from inside the window.

"Actually, I wasn't looking for a man at all," he counters. "More of an after-school gig for a student."

"Some bored teenager in here staring at his phone all day? That'll just make you lose hope for the future of humanity," I argue, his silence telling me I'm right.

I up the ante by telling him I can compensate for his area of weakness—any post-1980s music, especially from my own formative nineties. Before he can object, I download everything I know from A3 to Z-Ro, and then I L-M-N-O-P him with Lemonheads, Meat Puppets, Nas, Outkast, Portishead. I impress him by ticking off all the samples from Digable Planets' *Reachin'* and knowing what happened to each of the founding members of Fine Young Cannibals.

He reminds me that *none* of that music is on vinyl and then hires me anyway. Good for him; now I don't have to play the discrimination-against-the-handicapped card, which I had planted next in my deck ready to produce with a magician's flourish.

As if to prove how nondiscriminating he could be, Mr. Madnick gives me most of the work requiring two hands, like moving boxes of albums and working his antiquated credit card carbon copy imprinter, while he uses the smooth one-handed pricing gun to rub it in. Revenge on a former student is a dish best served with two hands.

After school, one of those hapless teens jacked into his iPod comes in and spends about an hour alternating swipes at our record stacks with pokes at his phone. But he redeems himself with his purchases: Bob Marley, Frank Zappa, the Ramones, and George Harrison (whom he remembers nostalgically as a Wilbury, not a Beatle). It isn't until well after I've wrestled his credit card through the imprinter (and handed him a carbon to stare at incredulously) that it strikes me: all these people died of cancer.

But at least they weren't eleven years old.

Arriving at the school building from which I've earned a life-time ban, I would likely be immediately hustled away and/or Tasered by the wide-eyed security lug who previously escorted me from the premises, but he also recognizes Cancer Boy's mom.

"I'm sorry, miss, but I can't let him into the building."

"He's with me."

"I'm not allowed—"

Cancer Boy's mom begins to weep, and the security guard steps aside and bows as if welcoming a foreign dignitary. Once inside the building, she immediately composes herself . . . until we're turned away at the principal's office, and her eyes well again and his assistant tells us to *wait right here* and rushes inside.

"You're good at this," I say.

"I've had lots of practice. The harder part is turning it off."

The principal escorts us personally to Cancer Boy's class, where his teacher winces upon seeing me. But we're allowed to address his students, and soon consent forms are distributed and a field trip is arranged for the next day.

A morning out of the classroom is the greatest gift you can give a bunch of kids and these happy young students are no exception. A couple of boys have to be stopped from running and jumping into the shredded mulch of the Shop Smart coupon flyers, and it takes a while to gather them all in place to focus their attention deficits. We're here to remember their fallen classmate, friend, and the boy they will only occasionally recall as adults, usually to prop themselves up in the face of a much more minor setback with the rationalization, *I could have died of cancer at eleven like that poor kid in fifth grade.* After fidgeting through opening remarks by their teacher, all eyes turn laser-like to me, no doubt in part due to the possibility I might flash my nubby sea serpent. (The little boy who threw up last time appears especially distressed.)

"Jimmy . . ." I struggle not to call him Cancer Boy in front of his mother, "only came here once, but it's a place where he was happy just to be a normal kid. Not the boy sick with cancer. He ran and laughed . . . felt the sun on his face, and touched the trees. Just like a normal kid. He wasn't tired, or sick . . . or tired of being sick."

His mom smiles approvingly, but only for a moment.

"He helped a sick, old man remember what it was like to feel vital again. He helped us rescue an alligator, and he gave that alligator his sandwich, and three more to lure him to safety." His mom's stare reminds me, *Shit, she didn't know about the alligator,* and I change the subject. "And he had his first beer here, just like I did."

She covers her mouth and shakes her head, and his teacher lets out a long whistle.

"Whatever," I try to regroup. "I don't want to get off track. But let me tell you about the boy I knew. He showed his ass to a hallway full of nurses and played blackjack like a riverboat gambler. Who hits on nineteen and wins? His favorite word was . . ."— the intent curiosity on the little girl's face stops me from saying *fuck*—"started with *F*, and no one in history said it with more joy. Now, drinking beer and swearing like a sailor, ducking bullets and being chased by an alligator just prior to arrest may not be what most people think of as 'just a normal kid.' But you know what he *wasn't*? He wasn't sad. He wasn't pathetic. He wasn't sick. Not the way I knew him."

His mom sobs a giant snot bubble, and just when I think I may have gone too far, she manages, "Thank you."

"Should I continue?"

She wipes her face and nods, and if the teacher has any objection he keeps it to himself. "I had this plaque made and affixed to a tree here." I step back to the small patch on the tree draped in a length of fabric. "These trees were here long before Jimmy, and they'll be here long after we're all gone—"

"Where are we going?" A little girl asks, sad.

"Extinction," I comfort her. "And this plaque will be a simple reminder of that ordinary day for a boy who never wanted to be special."

I pull the fabric to reveal the small bronze plaque embedded in the tree just below Dad's bullet hole:

JIMMY FERRIS
HE WAS AN ORDINARY BOY

His mother tears up all over again, and the kids manage tiny, uncertain applause.

"I also want to take a moment to remember my father here, in this special place where they both felt alive and vital."

I take out Dad's ashes and start to shake them out at the base of the tree. It feels right, and natural—Dad literally returning to the earth, and in the final place that mattered to him. Then a sudden shift of the wind blows a great gust of ashes at the kids, and some of them are blinded and begin to cry while others choke on Dad. They're still coughing when their teacher hustles them back onto the bus.

Now I know how the sheriff felt with all those Boy Scouts.

LOVE

As I walk Mom down the aisle, her hand resting on my only arm, and present her to her fireman, I consider for the first time the queasy notion that this union might technically make the former Mr. February my stepfather. He says "I will" and she says "I do" and somewhere, Dad looks down on all this while my lost arm hugs him in a creepy but well-intentioned effort to console and assure him that we all still love him.

I'm forced to think about love, about who might someday love me and what kind of woman I can love in return. If I could assemble the perfect female from the best parts of the women I've known, she might have sixteen-year-old Pam Jaffe's innocent allure, Ariana's adorability, Lilith's . . . prominence, Consuela's boldness, the tolerance of Cancer Boy's mom, Jackie's tenacity, Mom's Zen, and my ex-wife's willingness to marry me. Even with all those attributes, would this Frankensteinian ideal be the equal of Sunny Lee?

I'm about to find out because Jackie's "date," I discovered upon arrival, is Sunny. Having reached out to reconnect, Jackie invited her to the wedding in a most generous act of date swapping, especially since I brought no date to swap.

"You seem surprised to see me," Sunny laughs musically.

"I admit, you have me off balance. Even more than usual."

"Remember what I said about symmetry being overrated?"

"I actually did some research, and you're right. Turns out most of the universe is actually asymmetrical." I tell her about spiral galaxies and the DNA helix and seashells that only coil in one direction, and a universe that is more matter than antimatter. "I think it's called *chirality*," I say, enough to spur anyone else to excuse themselves to the bar and spend the rest of the evening dodging any further attention.

Instead, Sunny pokes an abbreviated version of all this into her phone and tells me, "Don't think I'm not stealing this."

The reception is a modest affair emboldened by the presence of the men of the firehouse who, when not battling blazes or posing for calendars, apparently eat and drink like pirates. The theme is "firefighter," everything dressed in fire-engine red, beer flowing through a fire hose, and the wedding cake, shaped like a firefighter's helmet, is cut with an axe. Mom's classy touch is the frozen bottle service of Fleischmann's on every table, alongside tiny potted zinnias Jackie and I were forced to steal from our old backyard. (I couldn't believe the assholes who bought our house said *no*.)

Over a meal of five-alarm chili I gush to Sunny over her book, which I had insisted be recovered from the wreckage—*No, you can't buy me a new one, I need that one!*—and consumed in the hospital. I'm able to cite specific instances of lunar cycles and cicada invasions and tide pool tadpoles until she makes me stop, impressed and embarrassed. So I shift our focus to the new material around us, and Sunny starts Googling while I dash off notes on our paper tablecloth.

On marriage: "Theories concerning the origins of marriage are many, including a man's need to assure the paternity of his children; he might therefore be willing to pay a bride in exchange for exclusive sexual access."

"Do you take this woman," I scribble, "to carry your seed to full term?"

"Romantic!" she observes.

On drinking: "The first clear evidence of distillation comes from Greek alchemists working in Alexandria in the first century A.D."

"Thank goodness for the Greeks, who gave us . . ."—I scratch out a list—"philosophy, democracy, hangovers, and awkward mornings-after in strange beds."

"You're good at this!"

On weddings: "The wedding ring possibly originated in the Roman belief in the vena amoris, which was believed to be a blood vessel running from the fourth finger directly to the heart . . ."

"That still doesn't explain nose rings. Or toe rings. Or—"

"*Cock* rings," Sunny announces, snatching my pen and writing it down in big bold letters. "I'm not sure we can use it, but I'm not letting it get away."

She said *we*. My face is on fire, and I hope it's not another infection.

On dancing: "Dance is a type of art involving body movements set to music, also sometimes used to tell a story, or as a prelude to mating."

"I think the story being told by those two," I say, gesturing to a clutching, wiggling couple on the dance floor, "is that there will be mating later."

On love: "Interpersonal love refers to a more potent sentiment than a simple *liking* of another. Biological models view love as a mammalian drive much like hunger or thirst."

"I don't know about a radio segment, but that's a great title for a song, "Mammalian Love." 'Baby baby baby, I hunger for your thirst.'"

"'You make me wanna burst,'" she joins in.

"Catchy! What rhymes with 'mammalian'?"

"Italian!"

"I smell a hit."

"If we're gonna be rock stars, we should drink like rock stars," Sunny pronounces, grabbing the slowly melting Fleischmann's bottle.

"That's pure rock-star vodka, the best $5.98 can buy."

When the Fleischmann's is seemingly gone, I demonstrate Dad's eleven drops hypothesis to Sunny's appropriate astonishment. Having depleted those drops and then those from our neighboring tables, we head to the bar to drink flaming shots and then move to the dance floor, where we create art with our body movements set to music. When a slow song comes on, without hesitation Sunny steps up to me, takes my hand in hers and places her other hand squarely on my shoulder nub, as intimate an act as one is likely to commit in front of a roomful of people outside of an orgy.

I make it a point to dance with Mom and congratulate her new husband before stealing their limousine to ensure Sunny gets home safely, earning a peck on the cheek and a smile before watching her recede into the darkness. Before sending the limo back, I drop myself at Fred Weber's. He's still at the wedding of course, so I let myself in the back door—which, in a stupor of alcohol and infatuation, I leave open, allowing Ali to escape once more. He'll turn up nearly a year from now, startling an underwater munitions diver after the dam, having been deemed an "insurmountable hazard to endangered fish species," is decommissioned and scheduled for removal. The resulting explosion is quite spectacular.

THINGS I NEVER DID WITH TWO ARMS

Jog
Wear handcuffs
Count fish
Rescue an alligator (twice)
Show-and-tell
Show a dying kid a good time
Pick up a slutty Viking on Halloween
Hire an undocumented nurse (later hired by Homeland
    Security)
Star in a YouTube viral sensation
Pimp a van
Build a bomb
Steal zinnias
Aid and abet a bank robbery
Manipulate a credit card whacker
Take care of my father
Eliminate my brother-in-law
Realize my sister loved me
Dance at my mother's wedding
Assemble a perfect 1970s configuration of stereo
    components
Cowrite radio segments, and a terrible song
Sell my children's book about a river of magic fish and a
    dam-busting sea serpent named Bob

ACKNOWLEDGMENTS

First and foremost, thank you, Mitchell Waters, who I first met in high school and then decades later blind-queried without recognizing his name. I remain astonished to have found you again and grateful for your representation, your tolerance, and your thoughtful notes on *Amp'd*. Thanks are also due to Steven Salpeter for responding to my sample and knowing it would likely appeal to Mitchell. Thank you, April Osborn; I was thrilled by your enthusiasm for *Amp'd* and grateful for your promise to be our champion—I hope for many years to come.

It is with deep gratitude and admiration that I acknowledge authors Bruce Cameron and Joseph Monninger for taking the time to read an early draft of this work and offering praise beyond my wildest dreams tempered with well-considered suggestions for improvement. Similarly, I thank those who graciously accepted the presumptuous imposition to read a debut author and offer blurbs—the kindest of acts in the face of the most thankless of writerly tasks.

I gratefully acknowledge Sandra Loh, voice of *The Loh Down on Science,* who inspired the character of Sunny Lee, and with whom, like Aaron, I perhaps fell a little bit in love upon first hearing her disembodied radio voice on my arrival in Los Angeles. I must also acknowledge that when stuck for a name for a character both warmhearted and rock solid, I looked no further than former seaman Fred Weber, who, to my knowledge, has had no firsthand experience with lawyering or medical marijuana.

With so much "real" science and medicine at work here, certainly there should be sources to acknowledge (beyond a sweeping nod to Wikipedia), but I have only these: a June 2008 *60 Minutes* segment on endangered salmon, "Fish Fuss," as reported by Lesley Stahl and produced by Karen Sughrue; a pair of e-mails from the U.S. Army Corps of Engineers, Portland District, dashing my fantasy above-water fish counting scenario and forcing me to, quite literally, dig deeper; and multiple visits to the U.S. Fish & Wildlife Service Web site. But although I visited many sites on fish and dams, amputations and medical marijuana, this is after all a work of fiction, and I confess to fabricating nearly everything: from the aggressively ugly blue paddle-snout sturgeon, which does not exist in reality, to the many strains of medical marijuana I had great fun in naming. (I confess only a passing acquaintance with the effects of Vicodin and medical marijuana, and in far lower doses than those consumed herein.) As for any credible-sounding passages of one-armed experience, I can only admit hours spent attempting the simple tasks of an ordinary day using a single arm, grossly insufficient to the reality of such an injury but enough to inspire awe and admiration for the daily courage of anyone so afflicted.

On the subject of fictional liberties in a work populated by oddball family members, it seems appropriate to acknowledge that no character here is based on my actual family. My mother was a devoted, engaged parent at a time when such a thing was considered unfashionable, and wildly supportive into adulthood; my father is far from a withholding stoic; rather he's vigorous and engaged, interested and interesting, and always a friend. My younger sister is ebullient and giving where the fictional Jackie is all manic calculation.

Finally, I must acknowledge and thank, too inadequately, the efforts of my extraordinary wife for her meticulous editing of *Amp'd* beginning with its earliest drafts, from proofreading to her good sense to encourage some flight-of-fancy deletions, much to the betterment of this book. And, as during the writing of this book, we worked almost daily in a shared home office, back-to-back, I am forever aware of, and grateful for, her quiet omnipresence in my writing and living.